D1306369

When the Spotlight Fades

When the Spotlight Fades

SUSAN MARIE

Doubleday

NEW YORK

1987

All of the characters in this book
are fictitious, and any resemblance
to actual persons, living or dead,
is purely coincidental.

Library of Congress Cataloging-in-Publication Data

Marie, Susan.
When the spotlight fades.

"A Starlight romance"—
I. Title.
PS3563.A6545W5   1987   813'.54   87–9014
ISBN 0-385-24335-9
Copyright © 1987 by Susan Marie Manzke
All Rights Reserved
Printed in the United States of America
First Edition

*For two very important people, who allowed and encouraged
daydreams—my parents, Chuck and Isabelle,
and for my sister, Karen,
with whom those dreams were shared*

When the Spotlight Fades

CHAPTER 1

"I have no idea why I'm here for tryouts tonight. I'm too busy to be thinking about acting in a play," Gwenn said in a semiwhisper. "I mean, I could be using my spare time constructively, doing something fun like washing out my garbage can."

"Gwenn, you've probably had that can for three years and never touched a brush to it. Don't tell me tonight it's drawing you home like a magnet." Shirley's voice didn't lower in awe of the dark theater surrounding them. She loudly spoke her mind, as usual. "You're just chicken."

"Don't call me chicken. Adults don't call each other chicken."

"Well, that's what you are," Shirley said firmly. "You're chicken. You don't have what it takes to act any more. You're not the same person who acted in college. You and my baby sister were quite a team then. They had to drag you out of the spotlight, you were such a big ham."

"First it was chicken, now ham. Let's forget the menu and get these tryouts over so I can get home to my garbage can."

Shirley looked into Gwenn's dark brown eyes. "You better try your best. I can tell if you're not. And if you flub up on purpose I won't help you refinish that antique desk of yours."

"Insults. Threats. Shirley, you're such a good friend. What would I do without you?"

"You'd sit home alone, reading. That's what you'd do. Gwenn, just think of me as your guardian angel in charge of nightlife."

Gwenn slowly rose from the theater seat and brushed at imagined wrinkles in her grey suit. "If you're my guardian angel I'd hate to think what heaven's like," she said.

Shirley's hands went to her mouth covering a mock gasp. "You'd better go home and change, Gwenn. You're embarrassing me. There's a piece of lint on your shoulder. But never fear, Shirley's here to save you." She picked the lint off her friend, then gasped again. "Gwenn has dandruff! Hang your head in shame, girl!"

"Would you like a real knife to stab in my back, Shirl? Or is it more fun killing me with words?"

"Why didn't you wear jeans like I told you to? No one dresses up for tryouts." As Shirley finished speaking a tall blonde came in the door, slithered down the aisle and up to the stage. She was wearing a dazzling hot pink jumpsuit and spiked heels. The theater was no longer dark. The dim stage lights sparkled with the color of the material.

"What were you saying about me being overdressed?" Gwenn laughed lightly. "I should have worn heels. Next to JoJo Adams, that goddess in pink, I'll look like a munchkin."

Shirley tucked her maroon sweatshirt into her jeans and ran her hand over her short, curly, not-blond-not-brown hair. "I've decided," she said. "I've decided that I'll let you try for the lead in this play all by yourself. I don't want to give you any unfair competition."

Gwenn laughed, "Oh no, you don't. We made a pact. Remember? We were going to do this together or not at all. Unless you go up, I go home."

"You promise you'll really try for the part?"

"Cross my heart I will. But you have to remember I haven't acted since college. Don't blame me if I'm terrible."

"Gwenn Nichols, grade A number one ham, not good? Ridiculous. Let's go." Shirley took Gwenn's hand and dragged her down the aisle toward the stage.

"Wait. My coat." Gwenn tried to pull back.

"Leave it," commanded Shirley.

A small group of nervous-looking people milled about the wings of the stage. They spoke . . . but in hushed tones.

Suddenly a young man laughed out loud. His voice crossed the theater as if he were using a microphone. Immediately he swallowed the remainder of his laugh. "This place is eerie at night," he said softly.

"Where's the director?" Shirley asked in her normal voice. "Couldn't he have been on time, at least for tryouts?"

"He's on time," came a deep male voice from behind a black curtain. "If it matters, I'm trying to find someone who knows how to work the light board. I like to be able to see the actors on the stage."

Snap, went a switch. The bare stage was filled with a golden glow. "No special effects, please. Just white light," said the director. Off went the gold and everything else. For a moment there was total darkness. "I think you'd better try again." Then without a sound the lights went on and grew brighter until the stage was near daylight. "That's fine."

A man stepped into the light holding a clipboard in one hand and a handful of loose papers in the other. Gwenn realized that his dress slacks were the same shade of grey as her suit; but without a jacket, and with his shirt sleeves rolled up, he looked very casual.

"I'm Randal Cochran. I'm going to direct this play," he said. "Now that we can see, would those trying out please fill in this stat sheet for me? Give me as many details of your past experiences in theater as possible, but do it fast so we can get on with tryouts." He gave the stack of papers to Shirley.

When Shirley handed Gwenn her sheet she quickly whispered, "Who the heck is he?"

Randal didn't look directly at Shirley as he continued speaking. "Most of you don't know me. I'm fairly new to this theater group. And I have to admit I acquired this job rather dishonestly." He smoothed back his dark hair as he spoke, his fingers brushing quickly past a sprinkling of grey at the temples.

"After Lil Terran, the last director, was promoted and transferred to New York, I mistakenly opened my mouth at Bennie's one night. Some wonderful civic-minded woman heard me admit to directing back East when I was still teaching. . . . That'll teach me to open my big mouth after drinking on an empty stomach."

"I'll take him over Lil any day," Shirley whispered and rolled her eyes skyward. "What do you think, Gwenn?"

"He hasn't directed anything yet, Shirl. Remember, good looks don't make the director, common sense does."

"Anyway," Randal continued. "I quit teaching and directing about the same time, when I realized I could make more money out in the business world than in a classroom."

After seeing to the handouts Randal Cochran sat back on the stool on the stage and surveyed the group before him. "It's been a long time since I directed or taught. So we'll all see if I can still handle this clipboard.

"Okay, now you know me. I'd like to know why you happened into this theater tonight. You first." Randal pointed to the young man with the loud laugh.

"Well," the young man started in a squeaky adolescent voice. "I don't know," he said.

"Of course you do." Randal's voice took on a dramatic air. "You want to be an actor, don't you? Become a star? Have all those starry-eyed girls swooning after you?"

The young man shuffled his feet and crumpled the paper in his sweaty hands. "No, I came because if I stayed home I'd end up helping Mom paint the kitchen."

The laugh that followed echoed off the back wall of the theater and bounced back, quieting the crowd.

"Honesty! I like that," said Randal. "Next? How about you?" This time he pointed to Shirley.

"I want to be a star," Shirley said. Melodramatically she held her arm to her forehead and winced as if in great pain.

Everyone laughed, except Randal.

"A comedienne. Just what this drama needs. Okay, next?" Randal's finger pointed to Gwenn.

"Since honesty seems to impress you," Gwenn said, "I came because my friend, the comedienne, blackmailed me."

"This really is going to be challenging." Randal made a note on his clipboard before continuing to the vision in fluorescent pink.

JoJo Adams took a deep breath that expanded her already overemphasized bustline and straightened her posture before speaking. "I came to offer my services to help bring creative theater to our quaint little community."

"You have no aspirations at all about stardom then?"

"None," JoJo said firmly. "If I wanted to be a star I would have stayed in California."

Randal made another note and mumbled something about a big fish, then said, "I think that's enough honesty for the time being. The rest of you just scribble your reasons on the back of your stat sheet, please."

He stood and looked about the stage. "Oh, there they are," he said as he spotted a box barely peeking out from behind a black drape. "If you'll all take a play book," he said as he brought a shoebox of play books out into the light, "we can get started."

Gwenn waited until last to pick up a book. As she stood back from the others she thought, "I've outgrown all this nonsense. I shouldn't be here."

"I know most of you read for Lil before her sudden departure." Randal moved the stool offstage. As he walked he continued speaking. "I called everyone here tonight so I could choose my own cast. This play isn't one I would have selected and I'm sure there are some that'll say Lil would have done a better job, but one thing I guarantee. I'll do my best.

"For those who aren't familiar with this play, there are five characters, three male, two female. The play revolves around the two women, mother and daughter. The young woman, Natalie, is caught between her husband and her lover. She's come back home to her mother, Edna, after a ten-year absence, seeking answers to her questions."

"Read fast, Gwenn." Shirley poked her friend in the ribs with her bony elbow. "Tell me if Natalie finds any answers. I could use a few."

"Shirl, you don't have a husband to worry about anymore. And I doubt if you'll find any answers here," said Gwenn as she looked at the play book. "A man wrote this play."

Randal cleared his throat. "I know you probably have a particular part in mind. But I'm going to be shuffling everyone around tonight so I can get an idea how well you act. I'll take the papers back now and let's have you, you, and you up first."

He chose three hopefuls and assigned each a part starting on page twenty-one.

Gwenn and Shirley took seats in the front row, to watch and to wait for their turn onstage. Randal soon was in the audience too, about seven rows back.

"Lets start with the line, 'Who do you think you're talking to?' " commanded Randal.

Gwenn had to listen closely as the three on the stage read their lines.

After two pages of dialogue the director broke in. "We're waiting. Is there a problem?" Randal called loudly up to the stage.

"We already . . ." began one red-faced reader.

"You already what? You'll have to speak up." Randal held his play book up behind his ear. "Start again, please. And if you would, speak up a bit. I'm sure those in the front row would appreciate it."

This time Gwenn was at least able to understand the words the three read to each other. She kept waiting for them to begin to demonstrate their acting abilities. They never did.

"Doesn't watching them make you want to jump right up on stage and show those kids what acting's all about?" Shirley whispered in Gwenn's ear.

"No, it doesn't," Gwenn hissed back.

Shirley watched the actors a few minutes longer, then moaned. "This is making me ill. I knew I should have remembered to bring some antacid tablets."

"Shirley! Shhh! I'm trying to read." Gwenn leaned as far away from Shirley as the theater seat would permit and continued reading the play.

Randal finally interrupted the three on stage. "Thank you. Now I would like to see . . ."

As he named three others to read the same scene, Shirley whispered, "Hand that man a cigar. He just saved my life. . . . Maybe I'll just offer to be the new director's assistant. . . . What do you think of that idea, Gwenn? Could be we'd make a winning team."

Shirley's sultry voice told Gwenn her friend had more than the play on her mind.

Gwenn hissed, "Why did you come tonight? To try out or to pick up the director?"

"Oh, come on, Gwenn. Admit it. Randal Cochran is a handsome man."

"I'll admit that his looks are pleasant, if you'll be quiet and pay attention."

Shirley sighed heavily. "I wonder how he is in bed."

"If you don't keep your mouth under control I'm moving to another seat," threatened Gwenn.

"Excuse me, ladies." Randal's deep voice made the hair on the back of Gwenn's neck stand on end. Gwenn knew he was addressing her. "I need quiet if I'm to judge all the actors fairly. I'm sure everyone would appreciate it if you could wait your turn quietly."

Shirley giggled.

Gwenn stood up and walked ten seats to the left and sat down again. There she studied the play until her name was called.

To Gwenn's dismay the other woman called for the same scene was JoJo Adams. Gwenn had to concentrate just to swallow as they faced each other on the empty stage.

Randal directed Gwenn to read the daughter's lines first. This little fact made her smile and Ms. Adams's lower lip stick out.

NATALIE: "Mother, you haven't changed a thing in this old house since I left."

EDNA: "And why should I? I like it this way."

NATALIE: "I'd think you'd be bored to death with that ancient oil painting. I was sick of it the day after you put it up."

EDNA: "Your Aunt Willa painted that the year before she died."

NATALIE: "I know that, Mother. But she'd never know if you just happen to move it to the spare room, where no one can see it."

EDNA: "It stays."

As Gwenn read the lines her feelings for the daughter and mother began to grow. Gwenn felt a tingling sensation in her stomach like she used to experience when she acted in college.

JoJo didn't seem to be having fun with the mother part.

After another page of dialogue between mother and daughter, the parts were reversed. JoJo looked radiant as she assumed her rightful place as the daughter.

NATALIE: "Mom, I've met a man."

EDNA: "You already have a man. His name's Will. Or have you forgotten?"

NATALIE: "I haven't forgotten Will. He's there, like always."

EDNA: "You treat him like your pet, a dog."

NATALIE: "I do not. I care about Will. He's comfortable to be with. But . . ."

Randal directed them to move to the last scene in the play.

EDNA: "I don't have to explain my actions to you!"

(Gwenn read to JoJo, building up the steam that the scene called for.)

"Who asked you to stick your perfect nose in here again, anyway? I sure as hell didn't!"

NATALIE: "Don't act like an ass, Mother. You're getting old. You're going to need me some day."

EDNA: "The day I need you is the day I roll over and die. I've got Henry, now. He's all I'll ever want."

NATALIE: "What? Your lover? You'll soon wish for more than that dirty old man!"

EDNA: "Look who's talking about being dirty. Maybe I should get a husband and a lover like my big-shot daughter. Maybe I should get myself two or three lovers."

Randal interrupted. "Ms. Nichols, could you tone that down just a bit. I believe you're overacting a touch."

Gwenn's emotions were still in the argument. "What? Overacting?" she flared.

"And you, Ms. Adams," Randal continued directing. "We already saw your beautiful face in Act One. Here you have to emit more feeling. Be bitter. Try spitting out your lines. But not too close to Ms. Nichols, please. Especially emphasize the line about the dirty old man."

Gwenn stewed as Randal spoke to JoJo. How could he accuse her of overacting? He obviously didn't know what he was talking about. "A man shouldn't be directing this play," she thought. "It's about women and their feelings. He probably only directed children's theater back East."

The tryouts lasted over two hours. Randal was true to his word. He shuffled and reshuffled everyone. Some people, Gwenn was sure, had more than enough time to show that they knew nothing about acting, or living, for that matter.

Finally, Shirley and Gwenn were paired together for one short scene. All either could do was laugh. Gwenn ended up being upset with herself for behaving unprofessionally. But it was more than she could bear, imagining Shirley as her mother.

"I think I've got a pretty good idea what you people can do," Randal said, bringing the group around him again on the stage. "I want to thank you all for coming. I'll get in touch with each of you later this week, when I make my final decision. If there was more time we'd have another call-back but I'm confident after tonight's tryouts, and with the help of Lil's notes, I'll be able to make a fair judgment.

"I hope those of you who don't get a part will be able to help on the crew. There's always a shortage of competent people backstage, but you can bet this production or any production couldn't go on without a good crew."

"Done," Shirley said, ending Randal's speech. "Now who's for Bennie's?"

A muffled cheer of approval circled the stage and the group started breaking up.

Gwenn's fall coat felt almost too heavy to pick up from the theater seat. "Shirl," she said. "I'm going home. I'm too tired for Bennie's."

"What? Don't you want to corner Mr. Cochran and tell him why you're the best person for the lead?"

"I'm sure he can make up his own mind. He's a grown man."

"No kidding. Even JoJo figured that out. She's going to Bennie's. JoJo's sure to burn Cochran's ears the rest of the evening. Don't let her get to him, Gwenn. You deserve to be Natalie."

"I'm going home, Shirl. See you tomorrow afternoon."

"Tomorrow afternoon?"

"Remember, it's my late morning at the office. You have to open bright and early, partner."

"It'll be early, but I'll not guarantee the bright part."

"I don't care, just as long as you can unlock the door. We'll never make any money in the real estate business if the office isn't open. Now, good night."

Gwenn winced at the exterior of her old dingy-white house as she pulled into the driveway. The dark windows begged for help, for caulking and paint. The whole exterior needed paint, gallons and gallons of it, and enough repairs to keep her broke for years.

"Don't look so pitiful," she said to the house as she passed the sagging front porch and its weather-worn gingerbread trim, circling to the rear of the building. "You'll get all the paint you can soak up in the spring. I promise. I'll get to everything, in time."

From the garage, a onetime carriage barn, Gwenn raced across the yard and up the back stairs. "If I had known the night air was going to wake me up so, I'd have gone to Bennie's," Gwenn said aloud with a shiver, but she knew better. She wasn't in the mood to talk about politics, or the weather, or the play, at least not tonight.

Gwenn kicked into a large tin garbage can as she crossed the unlit back porch. She laughed and kicked it again before she entered the kitchen and switched on a light.

The few steps from outside to inside brought Gwenn backward in time. Black utensils hung on the stark white walls. At first glance, the ceiling appeared fifteen feet high; in reality it was ten. A wood bowl, filled with fruit, graced the heavy five-legged oak table. The wall lamps were electric, but the fixtures looked suitable for oil.

A glass library lamp hanging over the table still burned oil, as it had when Gwenn's grandmother had purchased it in 1902 from the Sears, Roebuck Catalogue for the outrageous sum of $6.85.

The room was warmer than outside but not quite warm enough. She quickly crossed the large room to the thermostat and turned it up. Deep below her the furnace came alive. She was glad to hear it. There were times when she touched the thermostat and nothing happened.

"It's too cold for autumn," Gwenn expressed her complaint aloud. "I'm not ready for winter, yet."

Gwenn waited until warm air was blowing from the vents before removing her coat. By that time she had a hot cup of tea steeping before her on the table.

A muffled thud came toward her from the other end of the house. Gwenn looked up from her steaming cup as her eighteen-pound grey angora cat approached.

"Hello, Westminster. I'm honored you decided to get out of your warm bed to greet me."

The cat took his time crossing the room. After allowing Gwenn to stroke him once, Westminster went to his bowl by the sink for a snack.

"You haven't asked about tryouts, Westminster. Aren't you interested?" The cat continued eating, tail in the air, as he directed his backside toward Gwenn. "I was wonderful. Or at least I thought so. I'd make a great Natalie, don't you know. That's if I really wanted the part in the first place, which I don't."

Westminster left his bowl and walked out of the kitchen.

"I wonder what that Mr. Cochran's going to do. He seems such a know-it-all. . . ." Gwenn shook her head as she spoke. "Oh, it doesn't matter if I don't get that part. I'm too busy, anyway."

It occurred to Gwenn to phone her mother in Florida. She knew her mother would be excited about the play.

No, it was late. Her mother would already be asleep. A phone call at that late hour would only get her excited, she'd be sure to assume something was wrong. The doctor said any undue excitement would tax the older woman's heart. The call would wait until there was news about the part. That way Gwenn would save herself a second long-distance phone call.

Gwenn finished her tea and headed to her bedroom. As she left the kitchen's neat nineteenth-century atmosphere she was assaulted by a stepladder and mass confusion in the living room.

The few pieces of furniture in the room were collected in the center and covered by a paint-splattered dropcloth. The walls were stripped bare. Even the wood molding was in a pile near the front door.

"One thing at a time," Gwenn firmly addressed the room. "I only have two hands. I'll get back to you on Saturday."

It seemed to Gwenn that she lived her life on weekends. That was the time she had for herself and her house. Those two days of work made her feel she was accomplishing something, even if the renovation of her grandmother's house was taking forever.

"Saturday I'll finish stripping the molding. Maybe by that time the wallpaper will arrive. Until then, you wait. I'll be waiting, too." Gwenn neglected to inform the room that her own anticipation was for a phone call from the play director, Randal Cochran.

CHAPTER 2

The telephone woke Gwenn just past nine on Tuesday morning. She sighed, realizing half her morning was gone. Her plans would have to be altered; her grocery shopping would be rushed.

"Hello." Gwenn tried not to sound sleepy; as she spoke she nudged Westminster from his place on the pillow next to her head. He was not amused as he abdicated his throne for his cat-bed in the corner.

"Gwenn, I've got a problem." Shirley's voice sounded mildly excited. "I won't be able to open the office."

"Hello, Shirley. Have an enjoyable evening at Bennie's?"

"That's not fair, Gwenn. I didn't stay out late this time. Honest. It's Robin. She's pretty sick; got a fever and everything. I'm taking her to the pediatrician right now."

Gwenn threw back the covers and let her nightgown slide over her slim body and onto the floor. Her morning grocery shopping wouldn't be rushed after all; it would be eliminated. "Why didn't you call sooner? You know how I feel when we don't open on time."

"I know, Gwenn. But I thought Robin was faking again, until she threw up her breakfast all over the place."

"Okay, I'll take care of the office. And I want to know how Robin is as soon as you get back from the doctor."

"You're a life-saver, Gwenn. Thanks. Oh, yeah, there's a prospective buyer dropping in this morning. Early, he said . . ."

"And Carol's not due in till ten. Terrific. Talk to you later."

Gwenn raced down the hall to the bathroom. She hated to be rushed. But she knew she could be dressed and out the door in six minutes, if she pushed herself.

This morning it took her eight minutes. Gwenn would have an angry customer to contend with at the office. That was if he waited long enough for her to arrive. "If only our secretary worked full-time, there wouldn't be any of this trouble," Gwenn thought as she drove across town to Shirley's house, which also doubled as their real estate office.

A flashy silver sports car waited outside the office, the converted two-car garage attached to Shirley's home. Quickly Gwenn worded an appropriate apology in her mind. She walked past the other car without looking into it. As she unlocked the door with the gold letters, DUO REAL ESTATE, the sports car's door slammed shut behind her.

"I'm terribly sorry about this," Gwenn said over her shoulder. "My partner had to take her little girl to her pediatrician."

"If you plan to be a success in the business world," the man said, "you'll have to do better than that, Ms. Nichols." It was Randal Cochran.

"Oh. I didn't know you . . . ," Gwenn stammered, and then gained control of her voice. "Aren't children important to you, Mr. Cochran?" she asked without thinking. "I'm sorry. I shouldn't have said that. But I believe there are things more important than business or money. People, for instance."

"I suppose there are," he admitted. "But not many. . . . There wouldn't be any chance of a hot cup of coffee, would there?"

Gwenn doubted that Shirley had had time to make her usual tasty coffee before leaving. "Only if you have a few more precious business minutes to spare while I brew up a pot." Gwenn felt that her tongue was on its way to ruining a sale along with a part in the play. But she couldn't stop the words from falling out.

Randal eased himself into a chair across from the receptionist's desk. "I have the time, today." Though he was on the wrong side of the desk he commanded the office.

Gwenn turned up the thermostat slightly before tossing coffee into the percolator to be brewed. "A cold office, a cold customer," Gwenn thought. "Today isn't going to be one of my better days."

Ignoring the cool room temperature Gwenn slipped out of her coat and hung it on the coat rack by the door. The eight minutes she had taken at home had transformed her into the businesswoman she was. In her navy blue blazer, white silk blouse and navy slacks she could only be considered a professional.

"Shirley didn't have time to fill me in on your situation, I'm afraid. What exactly are you in the market for? A condominium?"

He pushed back a curl of brown hair from his forehead. "No. I'm looking for a large Victorian house."

"Near a school?"

"Why would you assume I need a house near a school?"

The smell of coffee drifted up from the warming pot. "I would think if you wanted a large old house you had a family to fill it."

He almost smiled. Even this slight change brightened his stern appearance pleasantly. "Please don't assume anything when it comes to me, Ms. Nichols. . . ."

"Gwenn, please."

"Gwenn, then. I don't have a family, or even a wife, if that matters. The house could be construed as an investment, or maybe as a getaway from chrome and plastic. . . . It doesn't have to be in perfect shape."

"Oh, you plan to remodel?"

"I intend to do whatever is necessary. I'll have to remodel anything I purchase, I'm sure. You see, I have this rather large piece of . . . of furniture that, well, allowances will have to be made for." Randal sighed. "Is that coffee ready?"

"Just about." Gwenn mentally ran down their inventory of homes. There weren't many that seemed suitable for Randal Cochran.

"Will we be able to see any houses this morning, Ms. Nicho . . . Gwenn? I mean, can you possibly afford to leave your office unattended and risk missing a prospective buyer?"

"Don't worry, Mr. Cochran. By the time you finish your coffee we'll be able to leave. Our secretary is due in soon."

"Fine. Fine. I hate to see even poorly managed businesses miss any money-making opportunities."

It took all the self-control Gwenn had not to react to Randal's rude remark. "I'm sorry we've given you such a bad first impression, Mr. Cochran. You realize this was an extraordinary day. I hope you'll soon change your mind."

"You'll find I'm a hard man to convert. You and your partner will have to do some fast dancing to get me to change my opinion of your operation."

"Then maybe it's useless for us to show you anything."

"You're not doing very well if you plan on changing my first impression. Let me be the judge if any of the listings you have are suitable for my purpose, if you don't mind. Now what about that coffee?"

The coffee was ready; for that Gwenn was grateful. It wasn't going to be easy working for or with Randal Cochran.

For the next few minutes they quietly sipped at their steaming cups. Gwenn hoped Carol would pick up her telepathic cry and come in early.

"What can you show me today?" Randal finally asked. "Shirley gave the impression that you had quite a lineup to see."

"Quite a lineup, huh? Well, we do have a couple of houses that might suit you."

"I suppose that's a start."

"Let me make some phone calls. Usually we give the sellers more notice before showing a place. But I just may be able to accommodate you this morning with a couple of fine old houses."

Randal nodded as he crossed his arms on his broad chest and looked around the office. His eyes went from the potted palm tree beside Carol's desk to the well-used Underwood typewriter, to the pen-and-ink sketch of the Rocky Mountains on the wall. He ended his examination with Gwenn, looking her over from her shiny long brown hair down to her sensible black leather shoes.

His meticulous appraisal of the office unnerved her. No one had ever studied the room, or her, so thoroughly. That kind of look should be saved for the listed properties, not the real estate office, and especially not her.

Gwenn found relief from Randal's gaze when she retreated to her small office in the back. There she rang up two clients in private. Both were more than ready to greet a prospective buyer.

"I'll send the kids next door and have the living room vacuumed in five minutes," was the first woman's answer.

The other owners were on their way out the door. "Miss Nichols, the front door's open. Show all you like. We won't be back till midafternoon."

When Gwenn came back to Randal with the news, Carol was walking in the door. It was ten o'clock.

"I'll be out for a while, Carol," Gwenn said as she put on her coat. "I don't think Shirley will be available at all today. See if you can get those letters ready for this afternoon's mail pickup, okay?"

Randal's beeper sounded as he walked toward the door. He sighed. "I'll only be a minute. May I use your office?" Without waiting for an answer, he did an about-face and walked into her private office.

Gwenn was left open-mouthed, pacing in front of Carol as she waited.

The telephone conversation started out in muffled tones but Randal's voice soon grew in volume.

"Not one more day! I want those chemicals out of there by tomorrow afternoon at the latest or you'll be hearing from my lawyers! When they're through with Millin Industries you won't own a barrel to store chemicals in. . . . Well, if you're not the man who makes those kinds

of decisions, you'd better put me in touch with the person who does!
. . . Fine. I'll be waiting for his call."

Randal strode out of the back room.

Gwenn rushed ahead of him and whisked the door open. "We'll take
my car, Mr. Cochran."

"You will start calling me Randal soon, won't you? Customers usually like to be on a first-name basis with real estate dealers."

"Somehow I felt you were different. More the busy executive. But
that's fine with me, Randal." Gwenn snapped her seat belt closed and
looked at Randal, who had ignored his own. "I don't want to offend,"
Gwenn said, "but would you mind buckling your seat belt? It's a rule of
mine. I know some people think it's silly of me to tell all my passengers
to buckle up, but I believe in being safe."

Randal raised one heavy eyebrow, then obliged. "I hope this doesn't
have anything to do with your driving ability," he said.

"No." Gwenn laughed a bit too nervously. The scar just past her
hairline was invisible to others, but she remembered it was there. It and
the memory of the accident with Fred were vivid to her. "My driving
record is spotless. It's just . . . well . . ." She saw no reason to explain her past to Randal. Instead she smiled and said, "The manufac-
turer did put the belts in the car to be used, so why not use them?"

As Gwenn drove down maple-lined Main Street toward the first
house she tried to relax with some small talk. "What do you think
about this weather? Kind of early to be so cool. Even for Wisconsin,
don't you think?"

"Cool? It's downright cold," he said.

"Though I haven't seen such spectacular fall colors in years."

"Haven't had time to notice."

"I'm sorry."

Randal laughed. "Sorry? Why should you be sorry?"

"You surely must be busy if you haven't had time to enjoy the fall
colors. It's the best time of the year. Don't you agree?"

"Only if you consider Christmas."

"Christmas? Christmas is months away. Don't tell me you're doing
your shopping early?"

"I'm speaking about retail sales. The Christmas season gets most
retailers through the rest of the year."

"Oh, business. I was referring to the fall colors." Gwenn motioned
out the windshield at the oranges, golds and reds that cascaded over the
street. "Don't they impress you?"

"I guess they're okay, for photographers and calendars."

Gwenn sighed another "I'm sorry," without saying a word.

Randal looked at her and laughed heartily. "Don't worry about me, Gwenn. I'll survive even if I don't appreciate your fall colors. At the moment my mind is on other matters."

"Of course. . . . Anyway we're approaching the first house. The neighborhood's quiet, well off the main traffic pattern."

She turned the car west on Greenfield. The houses that lined the street had been there for years. Most were painted the same white shade they had been painted when they were built.

"The first house we'll be looking at is another block down, on the right." The orange For Sale sign in the yard pointed out the house for Gwenn. There, a large rectangular two-story sat snug in its nest of green lilac bushes. A modern two-car garage took a 45-degree angle off the back completing a letter L. "The family in the house right now uses all six bedrooms. They have nine children."

"Don't tell me, they're moving out for a place with more room."

"Nope. The husband's been transferred to Orlando."

"At least they can count on a lower heating bill. I bet that barn really soaks up the fuel."

"Most larger older homes of this vintage do use a fair amount. But this one has good insulation. I'd say it holds the heat better than many, mine for instance. Now, if it's economy you're looking for, a modern . . ."

"No. I'm not in the market for any little cracker-box house. I'm looking for one particular old house. I'll know it when I see it. And I'm afraid this is not the house I want."

"But you haven't even stepped inside," Gwenn protested.

"I'll go in, if you insist. But this isn't the place for me."

As Gwenn and Randal walked up to the house the door swung open. Gwenn wished the woman had gone next door with her preschoolers. She was too anxious to sell the old house, circling over Randal's left shoulder during the entire tour.

"My husband's already in Florida," the woman said as she held the door open for them to leave. "I really hate to part with this place. Ralph's having a terrible time finding another home for us down there. I wish I could move this whole place with us. But we can't and we have to keep the family together."

Gwenn's car was half a block away from the house when Randal began to laugh. "I never had such a feeling of claustrophobia with so few people in such a large building," he said.

"She did make things a bit difficult. I'll have to have a chat with her before I bring over another prospective buyer."

"You know, of course, that if the house was right for me it wouldn't have mattered what your client did or didn't do. Silliness will never affect my judgment."

"Somehow I knew that. The other house I thought you should consider is only three blocks from here."

As they drove up in front of the second house Randal sighed. "That's not right, either. It looks like an old farmhouse."

"It *is* an old farmhouse. The town kind of grew up around it. Do you want to go in?"

They took a quick tour of the house. Randal asked no questions. Gwenn gave no statistics. It obviously was another no-sale.

"Well, that's all the older homes we have at the moment, Randal. I'm sorry I've not been able to help you." As Gwenn started the car she noticed that Randal had neglected his seat belt. If she had taken her own advice the night of that so-called business cocktail party with Fred, she might have missed out on a lengthy hospital stay.

Gwenn had learned a great deal from that car ride, about seat belts, about herself . . . and about men. "I do hate to be a bother, Randal," she said, "but your seat belt. Please?"

"Sorry. That's one good habit I'll have to work on."

They were close to her own home now, where she should have spent the morning. "Would you mind if I stopped by my place before taking you back to the office? I was in such a hurry this morning that I forgot an important file."

"Just as long as it doesn't take you an hour to find it."

"One minute. Guaranteed."

Gwenn drove the last few blocks to her home and parked in the driveway near the back door. "I'll be just a second," she said as she leaped from the car.

The crammed file was on the kitchen counter. Gwenn grabbed it. As she turned to leave she ran into Randal coming in the back door.

"This is the house!" he said.

"I'm sorry my place is in such a state. I'm working . . ."

"No. No. This is the house I want," Randal said, walking past Gwenn into the kitchen.

"I'm afraid there's a slight misunderstanding. This house isn't for sale," she said.

Randal looked at Gwenn. His face was sober. "Everything has a price tag on it. I'm willing to pay yours." He continued through the kitchen into the living room. "Your carpenters seem to have taken an early lunch," he said, looking at the surrounding clutter.

"The carpenters are right behind you, Mr. Cochran. I happen to be doing the remodeling myself. Now if you don't mind, the door is . . ."

Westminster woke from his nest on the drop cloth at that moment and stepped in front of Randal. Lurching sideways, Randal tried to avoid tromping on the cat, but failed.

With a shrill screech the cat darted out of the room. Randal's arms waved windmill fashion in the air as he tried to regain his balance. To save himself he flailed about frantically and grabbed the ladder. "Damn!"

"Are you all right, Randal? Westminster's always underfoot."

"All right? First I almost took a swan dive into that pile of junk, then in saving myself I grabbed this . . . this wooden monstrosity," he said, shaking the old wood ladder with his right hand. "And look what I get, stabbed."

"Stabbed? Let me see." Gwenn took Randal's left hand in hers. A large wooden sliver penetrated the center of his palm.

"I hope your insurance is up-to-date," he said.

"It's only a sliver. I'll take care of it. Why don't you have a seat in the kitchen while I get the first-aid kit."

Randal cradled his left hand with his right as he went mumbling back to the kitchen.

Gwenn smiled to herself. Mr. Know-it-all got what he deserved, coming into her house as if he owned it.

After retrieving the first-aid kit from the bathroom Gwenn looked into her bedroom for Westminster. The cat was perched on her calico bed pillows as she expected, with only his pride hurt.

But Gwenn didn't find Randal seated at her kitchen table as she expected. Instead, he was in the corner near the stove examining the woodwork. "I suppose you did this room all by yourself, too."

"Yes, I'm proud to say."

"How long did it take you? Your business must not allow too much free time. And considering you're a . . ."

"Don't say it."

"Say what?" He turned to face her, a bit astonished.

"That I couldn't do the work because I'm a woman."

Randal laughed as he came to sit by the table. "On the contrary. I just thought you were too, let's say, meticulous to dirty yourself with such a demeaning job."

"Now you're assuming too much about me, Mr. Cochran. . . . I try keeping this world separate from my business."

"You can be proud then. You've truly accomplished that."

"Let's take care of that sliver now." Gwenn took Randal's hand and reexamined it.

He gazed not at his hand but at her glossy brown hair. "Maybe I should drop in at the clinic and have it removed professionally."

"It's not in very deep. I'll have it out in a moment."

"Ouch!"

"All gone. Want to see?"

"That's disgusting. Just slap a bandage on it and be done with it."

"First some antibiotic."

Randal winced as Gwenn dabbed a clear liquid on his palm. He continued looking away until the bandage was firmly in place.

"Maybe I should moonlight as a nurse instead of a carpenter?" Gwenn smiled.

"Nah. Poor bedside manner. Now, about this house . . ."

"The house isn't for sale. I told you that already," Gwenn said as she tossed the first-aid kit back together. "I believe it's time for me to get back to the office. I don't want to miss any *real* customers."

"Have it your own way. But don't think I'm finished with you and this house yet."

Gwenn and Randal drove back to the office in silence. She fumed to herself, "What nerve he has. He doesn't know anything about me or the house, yet he thinks he can grab my home up like it was a loaf of bread on the grocer's shelf. What about Grandma and her life there? That's nothing to him."

Finally, as they were leaving her car, Gwenn spoke.
"I'll keep an eye out for a house for you, if you like."

"I already know the house I want."

"That's one home that will never be on the market." Gwenn wished he would give up.

"We'll see. You can keep my name on file, just in case you run across an identical building." He handed her a white business card. "You can reach me through my office. The service always knows how to find me. Otherwise I'll see you Thursday night."

"Thursday?"

"The play. Really, I was surprised you didn't bring up casting before."

"It honestly slipped my mind."

"It didn't have anything to do with our business today," he said. "So, of course, it shouldn't have interfered."

"Yes, I know the cliché about business and pleasure."

Shirley pulled into the driveway behind Gwenn's car, honking and waving. "Have you made your choices yet about the cast?" she called to Randal from her car window.

He waved politely but waited until she ushered nine-year-old Robin into the house and joined them before answering. "Yes, I have," he said. "I hope you won't be too disappointed, Shirley. You were good, but I didn't choose you. I can tell your strong point is comedy. One's scheduled for winter. You should try out again."

"Sure. Remember me, the comedienne. So what about Gwenn?"

"You will still help with the production?" he asked, ignoring her question. "Behind the scenes?"

"Sure, sure. You can count on good old, funny Shirley. So what about Gwenn?"

"We were just getting around to that," said Gwenn. "When you tooted in on us."

Randal looked at Gwenn. He said, "I want you to play Edna."

"The mother!" Shirley exclaimed. "Who's the daughter? I didn't think any third-graders tried out."

"JoJo's playing Natalie," said Randal.

"Oh, you're rewriting the play for sisters instead of mother and daughter," said Shirley.

"No rewriting." Randal tried to step between Shirley and Gwenn. "Makeup will take care of your aging. Will you do it?"

Shirley popped up next to Gwenn. "Of course she won't do it. Who would expect a young woman to play an old lady?"

"I don't know," Gwenn said, biting her lip. "It might be fun."

"Fun! Wait until the crows-feet, wrinkles and grey hair. It won't be fun then." Shirley winced at the idea. "How could you think of turning her old?"

"I know you can handle the part," said Randal and for Shirley's benefit he added, "and the makeup."

"If giving me the part of Edna's your way of getting on my good side, it won't work."

"This has nothing to do with your house. If it did you'd be the daughter. I had my mind made up about the cast last night."

"Then why didn't you say so last night?" Shirley asked.

"It's better to let everyone think the decision was a difficult one," he said.

"Yeah," said Shirley, "or people like me wouldn't come back and work as peons."

Randal took a play book from his inside jacket pocket. "You'll be needing this. I'll have everyone's schedules ready at rehearsal. . . . I'd better be on my way. See you Thursday at eight."

Shirley started to walk into the office. "Oh, did you find a house?" she asked.

"Yes." He smiled.

"No!" Gwenn nearly shouted back.

"Yes? No? What gives?" Shirley looked from one to the other.

"We'll talk inside." Gwenn turned her partner away from Randal and forced her into their office.

"Gwenn," he called.

Gwenn fought the urge to turn around, but lost.

Randal's handsome face was smiling. "I'll be in touch with you later."

"Thursday, I know."

"No, this is business."

She knew he hadn't given up on owning her home.

CHAPTER 3

"Now you must believe me that Robin was really sick," Shirley said as she rummaged through her purse on the receptionist's desk.

"Must believe you?" Gwenn looked puzzled.

Shirley brought out a silver rectangular case from her leather bag and took out a cigarette. "You think I'd give up the chance of being alone with Randal Cochran if it wasn't absolutely necessary? He's simply beautiful."

"He's okay, I guess," Gwenn admitted. "But you should have heard the way he spoke to some poor person on the phone. Heads are sure to roll somewhere today."

"Who cares. As long as it wasn't you or me on the other end of the line. . . . I knew you should have gone to Bennie's last night." Shirley pointed an unlit cigarette at Gwenn.

Gwenn coughed.

"Don't worry your pretty little nose about this little smoke-maker." Shirley held the cigarette up. "I'll give myself cancer in my office. . . . You should have seen the show JoJo gave us last night. She performed better at the bar than at the theater."

"So? What has that got to do with me?"

Shirley fingered the cigarette as she spoke. "JoJo was all over Randal. Bet that's when he made his decision to make her Natalie and you the old woman. Or it could have been when he drove her home."

"He drove her home?" Gwenn looked surprised. "Well, nothing would have been different if I went to Bennie's, I'm sure. First off, I believe Randal made his decision on our acting abilities. Second, I wouldn't want the part if I had to act like JoJo. I couldn't anyway."

"If you don't warm up a little, the next play'll have you cast as the Wicked Witch of the West."

"That's not a bad idea. I look great in black and I could have a great big wart right here on my nose." Gwenn touched the tip of her button nose.

"If you're ready to trade in that sweet little nose of yours I'm first in

line. You can have my honker any day. Now, what was that bit about
Randal finding a house or not finding a house."

"First, how's Robin?"

"She'll be fine. Just picked up some bug goin' 'round school. She
should be back at her books by Thursday."

"Then you should be with her in the house."

"I'm heading there. I have to tie up some loose ends around here
first, then I'll go and hold her hand like a good mother. Now tell me
about the house."

"There's nothing to tell. Randal Cochran thinks he can get me to sell
my house to him. That's all."

"You're kidding. Your castle? And you told him where to get off.
Right? No wonder he made you the old lady."

"Shirley, go tie up those loose ends of yours and take care of Robin."
Gwenn scowled at her partner.

"Keep making faces like that, girl, and you'll have all the wrinkles
you'll need for the part. You won't need any makeup." Shirley patted
Gwenn's silky cheek and then retreated to her office.

The smell of Shirley's cigarette smoke made Gwenn's nose itch as she
gathered the morning paper from Carol's desk. After checking for messages she went into her own office and shut the door; but her sensitive
nose still detected the smoke.

As Gwenn thumbed her way to the classified section a brief article
caught her attention. According to the inch-square notice a tropical
storm was beginning to brew in the Caribbean, south of Puerto Rico.
She thought about her mother for a moment, then continued turning
the pages.

Methodically Gwenn searched the ad section. Maybe there was a new
private listing she hadn't heard about. Gwenn didn't feel comfortable
having Randal Cochran circling her home like a vulture. She would find
another house for him even if she had to forego her commission.

To her dismay she found nothing suitable on the market.

She looked up from the paper to a faded framed photo sitting on her
desk. Her house overwhelmed the background, the same, yet different.
A family was seated formally in the front yard. Gwenn's grandmother
sat straight-backed on a wooden kitchen chair, holding a baby, Gwenn's
mother. Her husband stood at her left shoulder and surrounding them
were five older boys.

"Don't worry, Grandma. I'm not going to let the house go. I know
how hurt you were when you lost it."

Gwenn took the empty newspaper and threw it across her office. It hit the opposite wall; pages fluttered like dry leaves around the floor.

As the paper settled there was a light knock on the door. Carol stuck her head in and said, "Gwenn, there's a lady to see you." The secretary ignored the newspaper litter.

"Give me a minute to pick up, then show her in." Gwenn shot up, scooped the paper off the floor and crumpled it into a large ball in her arms. Hurriedly she pulled open the top file drawer and stuffed it inside; the following instant the office door opened again.

"This is Mrs. Blomerich, Gwenn," Carol said before disappearing. She left the woman standing in the middle of the office doorway.

"Please have a seat, Mrs. Blomerich," Gwenn said to the large woman who almost completely filled the opening. Politely, Gwenn offered to take her mink coat but instead of shedding the warm covering the woman gathered the fur closer about her neck.

The chair creaked as Mrs. Blomerich and her mink sat in it. "My aunt wants to . . . *has to* sell her house," she said. "Can you take care of it?" As she spoke she stroked the soft fur of her coat. "Aunt Mae has lived alone since her husband died ten years ago. I'm afraid she can't any longer. I'm seeing to it that she's moved into a suitable retirement home. I'm all she has left, so I guess I have to be the one to look after her interests."

"I see. What's her address?" Gwenn took out pencil and pad for notes.

"She lives at the end of Briar Road, the little house in the pine grove. Been there for years. Her name's Jenkins, Mae Jenkins."

"Oh, I know that place. Pretty location, always reminded me of a fairy tale cottage," Gwenn said. "Do you live in town, Mrs. Blomerich?"

"Heavens no! Beverly Hills, that's where my husband and I live. I have his card here." She rummaged through her black handbag for a white card which she handed to Gwenn. "I'll be flying back this afternoon. How soon can you dispose of the house?"

Gwenn laughed. "I think it might take longer than a few hours, Mrs. Blomerich."

"Don't be silly. I didn't ask if you could sell it today," she huffed.

The smile on Gwenn's face faded. "I can't give you a definite answer, I'm afraid. It all depends on when a buyer shows up ready to pay your price."

"Well, get rid of it any way you can. But get rid of it fast. The

furniture, too. Have an auction. I can't be bothered with this nonsense.
. . . Aunt Mae has to be moved to a home, a retirement home, soon,
before another winter cuts her off from the outside world. . . . It's for
her own good."

Gwenn noted the asking price Mrs. Blomerich considered reasonable
on her pad. At that figure the house shouldn't be on the market long. It
was agreed that Gwenn would visit Mrs. Jenkins that same afternoon.

"Aunt Mae never goes out. You don't have to call. I told her to
expect you around two." The woman hesitated. "You'll have to have
her sign your papers. She wouldn't give me power of attorney," Mrs.
Blomerich grudgingly admitted. "But she won't give you any trouble.
Mae Jenkins knows what's good for her. And don't let her gruffness
intimidate you. She likes to bark a lot." With that Mrs. Blomerich pried
herself out of the chair and she and her mink left the office.

As Gwenn showed Mrs. Blomerich out, she met a delivery man from
Nancy's Flowers on his way in.

"Gwenn Nichols?" he asked. When she acknowledged that she was
he handed her a long white box.

Gwenn turned toward Carol. "I can't imagine . . ." was all she had
a chance to say before Shirley came barging in via the back door that
lead to her kitchen.

"Hey! That wouldn't be for me, would it?" Shirley said.

"No, Shirley," said Carol. "It's not your birthday or anything, is it,
Gwenn?"

"Nope."

"Good," Carol said. "I hate forgetting people's birthdays."

Gwenn continued looking at the unopened box. "I just can't imagine . . ."

Shirley started to take the box out of her hands. "Enough with imagining. If you don't open this, I will."

"All right, already. I'll do it myself. It's not everyday I get . . ."
Gwenn gasped when she opened the box, dropping the lid. Two dozen
long-stemmed red roses looked up at her.

Shirley gave a low whistle.

Lifting the box Gwenn let the delicate scent tickle her nose.

"Where's the card?" Shirley demanded.

"It's stapled to the top of the box," Carol said, retrieving the top
from the floor.

Shirley ripped off the envelope and handed it to Gwenn.

Reluctantly Gwenn released the box of flowers to her partner and opened the card. As she read the message her fine brows rose and her cheeks flushed nearly as red as the roses. Then Gwenn's expression changed and she began to laugh.

"What is it?" Shirley smiled without knowing why. "Give me that." She took the card from Gwenn's hand. "It's an offer for your house!"

Gwenn could barely speak. She was still laughing. "Mr. Randal Cochran thinks he can sweep my house away with a few roses."

"These aren't just a few roses," Carol cut in. "Bet these babies cost a hundred bucks."

"So? I didn't ask for them." Gwenn gained control of herself.

"You know, Gwenn," Shirley said, studying the card. "This is a fair price for that place of yours. You should consider . . ."

"I'm not considering anything."

"That ridiculous house is costing you a fortune. Just wait. When winter comes your fuel bills will be astronomical. How do you intend paying those, young lady? You haven't been in this business long enough to be financially well off. And we'll soon be in the middle of our annual winter sales slowdown. Tell me how you intend to survive then."

Gwenn wasn't affected. "You know how long I bargained to get that property. My grandma lived in that house. . . ."

"I know. Your mother was born there. But your grandmother is long dead and your mother is in Florida. Gwenn Nichols needs a medium-sized apartment, not an old drafty barn. You can't continue to support your mother and buy your own groceries with that house draining every extra cent you earn. You'll go bankrupt before you're forty."

"Since I have over ten years before I reach forty, unlike some other person I could mention, I won't start filing for bankruptcy, yet. Really, Shirl, the remodeling is coming along better than I expected. . . . It won't be drafty when I'm finished. It'll be cozy."

"And what century might that be?"

"I'm in no hurry," Gwenn said, taking the flowers from Shirley. "I'd better put these in water."

"What! You're going to keep them? I thought you were insulted by Randal's offer."

"I may be insulted, but I'm not stupid. Carol's probably right about the hundred dollars." Gwenn looked at the flowers. "If you have a few vases in your house, we can each have roses for our desks."

Shirley smiled. "That's eight each!"

"That's four each," Gwenn corrected. "I'm taking the rest home."

Gwenn joined Shirley at her kitchen table to properly arrange the flowers. Carol's four were placed in white porcelain, Shirley's in cut glass and Gwenn's in a heavy handmade ceramic vase. The other roses waited in a pitcher on Shirley's kitchen table for Gwenn to take them home.

"Mom! MOM!" Robin called Shirley from the other end of the ranch house.

"Take Robin a rose, too. She needs it," Gwenn said as she plucked one flower from the pitcher.

"She'll like that."

"Mr. Cochran will never know how many people these flowers of his cheered up today." Gwenn smiled.

"You *are* going to thank him. Aren't you?"

"I'll think about it," was all Gwenn said. And she did think about Randal, his roses and his offer all the way to Mrs. Jenkins's later that afternoon.

Gwenn enjoyed the drive to the Jenkins house. The sun had broken through the clouds after lunch and warmed the bright autumn countryside enough to tempt Gwenn into leaving her coat at the office.

The dead-end road was sparsely populated. After turning off the highway onto Briar Road Gwenn saw a Holstein dairy farm. It sat far off the gravel country road, a community in itself. A quarter of a mile down was a hairpin curve; soon after that came another dairy operation, one that housed brown cows. Another half a mile and Gwenn was at the end of the road and at the Jenkins place.

A weathered split-rail fence outlined the gravel driveway and the flagstone walk up to the doorstep.

The weathered redwood-shingled cottage was nearly surrounded by forty-foot-tall Scotch pines. Only a postage-stamp lawn remained green in the sunny clearing in front of the cottage.

Window boxes splashed color against the house with yellow and orange chrysanthemums. Dark shutters accented the windows of the house. One such window near the door was open. The tail of a lace curtain whipped about its dark shutters, free in the autumn breeze.

As Gwenn approached the shaded cottage she discovered a coolness in the air. She shivered slightly, chiding herself for leaving her coat.

Gwenn was about to knock when an old woman stuck her head out the opened window, squinted at Gwenn and said, "Who's there? Come, come. Tell me who you are."

"I'm Gwenn Nichols from Duo Realtors. Your niece, Mrs. Blomerich, spoke to me this morning, Mrs. Jenkins. She said you'd be expecting me."

"Yes, yes. I know. I suppose you'd better come in then." Mae Jenkins drew her grey head back inside the house. A moment later Gwenn heard the lock click and then the door opened for her.

Inside, the house was dark except for the light from the opened window. The scent of mothballs assaulted Gwenn. Heavy wood furniture was everywhere. Gwenn judged most of the pieces to be turn-of-the-century. All were dusted, oiled, obviously well cared for.

Mae closed the door behind her. She was a tiny thing, barely coming to Gwenn's shoulder, maybe weighing ninety pounds. Her dress, in a print of faded purple lilacs, was covered by an off-white apron. The old woman shuffled to Gwenn's side, took Gwenn's right arm for support and said, "We'll sit and talk by the window. I need some fresh air. People don't get enough fresh air these days with all that air-conditioning."

"I guess you're right," said Gwenn as she let Mae ease her onto an overstuffed swivel rocker. Mae then sat across from her in a well-aged Boston rocker.

"My niece never gets any fresh air. I think that's why she's become so stuffy. She never was like that until she moved away from here and hitched herself to Mr. Moneybags."

Gwenn couldn't help laughing at the old woman's remark.

"It's true. Don't think this old lady's fooling you. If you don't get enough fresh air you turn stale like week-old bread." Mae reached over to a wood plant-stand that she obviously used as a table. There her hand found a pair of thick-lensed glasses. "Now let's see what you look like, girl."

Mae put on her glasses and leaned nearer to Gwenn. "Toward the light, girl. Tip your face toward the light."

Gwenn obliged.

"You're a baby!" Mae exclaimed, hitting both hands hard on the rocker armrests. "How's a bit of a bean like you going to sell my house?"

With a light laugh Gwenn settled back in the rocker. It moved back and forth as if it had a will of its own. She cleared her throat and said, "Mrs. Jenkins, you know I'm no baby. I can certainly sell this house for you, if that's what you want me to do."

"You are a baby," Mae said firmly. "And it's my niece that says this place has to go. So I guess it has to. She always gets her way."

"I only want to help."

"How about some tea?" Mae offered.

"I would like that."

"There's a pot on the stove. Water's nearby. Tea's in a tin by the cookie jar." Mae looked out the window as she gave Gwenn directions.

An eight-foot-high wooden hutch dominated Mae's kitchen. The modern conveniences were a stained porcelain sink, a green combination wood and electric stove, and a shiny white refrigerator which stood apart from the rest of the room by the back door.

Gwenn set a sparkling brass kettle on a burner to warm. She had trouble finding the tin with the tea. On Mae's counter, near the cookie jar, were a dozen tins. One by one Gwenn opened them, finding rubber bands, buttons, and walnuts before she found the tea.

Soon she was back in the rocker, a spicy cup of herb tea in her hands. Mae left hers on the plant-stand to cool.

"Mrs. Jenkins, would you like me to appraise your house for you? I believe the price your niece quoted was somewhat low."

"Mae."

"You *may* want me to do an appraisal?"

"The name's Mae. Can't abide being called Mrs. Jenkins. Makes me sound like an old woman."

"Okay, Mae. Now about the appraisal . . ."

"If Clara set a price I guess it should stand. I'm tired of fighting her." Mae sighed. "She's set on putting me away."

"Mae, it sounds like you don't really want to sell."

"Have to. Doc says I'm going blind."

"I'm sorry."

"Don't be. I've been sorry enough for the both of us. Ain't any longer. . . . For now, I can still take care of myself."

"How do you do that? Take care of yourself?" Gwenn found herself drawn to the old woman. "I don't mean to pry but how do you get supplies way out here. You obviously can't drive."

"Never could drive, at least that was what my husband used to say. After he died I sold his car. No need for it anyway, what with my eyes. . . . Phyllis, down the road, takes care of my groceries. She goes to town a couple times a week trying to keep enough food on the table for her boys. She calls for my list before she goes and drops it off when she comes back. Except for this week . . ."

"What happened this week."

"Phyllis didn't call. Stan, her husband, went to the store instead. She had the flu or something. Guess he forgot 'bout me. Probably wouldn't have brought me what I wanted, anyway. You know how men are. Maybe he thought since my niece was visiting she'd get me my food. Ha! All she did was eat it."

"Maybe I could help you. I'll be coming back tomorrow, after I've typed up your papers. I could bring you what you need."

"No need for you to bother yourself about me. I can get by until Phyllis is better. But I could use some butter and milk and . . . No, it's too much trouble for you."

"Don't be silly. I have to pick a few things up for myself. And who knows, your neighbor might be laid up for days."

Mae grumbled for a few more minutes before handing Gwenn her scribbled shopping list.

"Can you read it? Make sure. I don't want any lima beans. Phyllis once brought me lima beans instead of green beans. I almost died. I hate lima beans!"

"So do I," Gwenn said.

"I guess you're not such a bit of a bean after all." Mae eased herself back into her chair and drank down her cold tea.

Gwenn took her time getting information about the cottage and room measurements. She sipped tea all afternoon and let the conversation veer any way Mae led it.

"My husband made that kitchen hutch, and the table, and even our bed. Len really had skilled hands, big hands, as big as his heart. He never was much of a businessman, though. Gave too much away."

Mae ran her hand down the table's grain. "I remember when he brought the wood home for this table. It took him a month before he cut into it. Not because he was lazy, you understand. The oak was just so beautiful. He wanted to look at it awhile and think about the tree."

Gwenn moved closer to the kitchen table. The wood was beautiful, even after years of use. "He must have been a very special person, your husband."

"Was. He built this house, too. He built it for me." Mae's voice cracked and the two women didn't say anything for a few minutes.

After finishing four cups of tea and filling her notepad with figures, Gwenn was ready to leave.

"What time should I come out tomorrow, Mae?"

"Time? Girl, do you see a clock anywhere in this house?" Mae asked.

Gwenn looked around the living room. There wasn't any. Nor did she remember seeing a clock anywhere in the rest of the house.

"I don't count minutes," Mae said. "No use. They're all the same. You come when you're ready. I'll be here. Got nowhere else to go."

"In that case I'll come on my lunch hour," Gwenn said. "As long as I don't get interrupted with another client."

"Fine. Fine. You'd better add some tea to my grocery list. Get a kind you like. Doesn't matter to me. I drink anything, except maybe chamomile."

It was much cooler when Gwenn left Mae. The sun was hidden completely behind the pines, leaving the cottage in a dark purple shadow. Gwenn looked at her wristwatch as she started her car. She was surprised that she had been with Mae Jenkins for three hours. Happily, she had not thought about the play, her house, or Mr. Randal Cochran once during the entire afternoon.

Gwenn sang along with the car radio as she drove back to the office.

The door was locked, Carol gone, when she returned. It had been a long day. But Gwenn wasn't finished.

Before her memory fogged, she typed out all the important information about Mae Jenkins's property. While she worked, Shirley opened the back door and came into the office. The smell of roast chicken drifted into the office too, reminding Gwenn that it was suppertime.

"You have any trouble this afternoon?" Shirley asked.

"No," Gwenn said. She shushed any further questions by holding up one index finger. She typed furiously, then slumped back in her chair. "There. Finished."

Shirley sat in the chair opposite Gwenn's desk, leaving the kitchen door ajar. "I expected you two hours ago."

"Oh, did you need me?"

"No. It's been quiet, too quiet, actually. But you don't usually take so long."

"Mrs. Jenkins lives alone. She likes to talk."

"So?"

"So, I talked." Gwenn dug in her purse for a tissue and pulled the scribbled grocery list from her pocket.

"What's that?"

"Oh, nothing," Gwenn lied.

"And what does Mrs. Jenkins have you doing? Picking up her laundry? Relaying messages?"

"No, I'm just picking up a few things at the store for her. . . . I have to go anyway. . . . Shirley, don't look at me that way."

"You're letting someone else take advantage of you, again."

"No, I'm not. . . . Honestly, I'm not."

"Gwenn, you're too kind-hearted. You let people walk all over you . . . like me. . . . Would you mind picking up some orange juice, too . . . for Robin . . . when you go to the store?"

The women laughed. "Sure, Shirl. Anything else?"

"Don't get caught up in someone else's problems. You have enough of your own."

"I don't have any problems."

"What about the play and all those lines you have to learn? What about your car? Didn't it just round the one-hundred-thousand-mile mark? What about making enough money to support yourself and your house, not to mention your mother? You ever catch yourself thinking about her and her bad heart? What about her wanting you to move to Florida? And what about Randal Cochran?"

"Okay, okay." Gwenn put her hands to her ears. "Enough problems already. . . . I think I'd better get moving so I can stop at the store. I'll have to arrange some quiet time at home to learn my lines."

Robin moaned from somewhere in the house. "Mom, supper ready yet? MOTHER!"

"I'll trade you that whine, for quiet."

"No, you wouldn't."

"You're right. . . . At least she's feeling well enough to eat."

"Need the juice now?"

"For breakfast. Why don't you come by early and eat with us? We can listen to Robin moan and groan together."

That evening Gwenn phoned Florida.

"Hi, Mom. How are you doing? . . . No, there's nothing wrong up here. I just wanted to make sure you saw your doctor this week. . . . Good. You just do what she tells you and you'll be fine. I can't keep track of your pills from here. Are you taking them every day? . . . I can worry about you if I want to, Mom. Is it warm enough there for you? Have you had a chance to visit your friend in Panama City yet? When you do, say hi from me. . . . Is that tropical storm going to rain on your new mobile home? . . . Of course I don't expect you to check the forecast in your crystal ball. It's just that Wisconsin newspapers don't tell us much about Florida's weather. . . . Okay, I'll try not to worry. . . . Oh, I meant to tell you. I got a part in a local play. . . . No, I'm sure the production isn't headed for Broadway. . . . I don't know if I'll be able to come down for Thanksgiving. We'll have to wait and see."

CHAPTER 4

Robin didn't moan at the breakfast table, at least not too much. She was her talkative self, though she still had a fever.

"Aunt Gwenn, how do you think I'd look with pierced ears?" Robin asked, holding her blond hair back away from her ears.

Gwenn looked over her half-eaten stack of pancakes at Shirley's frown, winked at her partner and then said, "I think your ears should grow a bit more before you pierce them. If you pierce them now your lobes get pulled all out of shape. Before you know it they'd be down to your shoulders."

"Oh, Aunt Gwenn, I should have known. You're so old-fashioned. Just like mother."

"How is *your* mother doing, Gwenn?" asked Shirley.

"I called her last night. She said she's fine."

"You don't sound convinced." Shirley looked closely at her friend. "Don't you think Florida's agreeing with her?"

"Oh, I'm sure she appreciates the warmer weather. She could never live through another Wisconsin winter. It's just so far if she needs me."

"Then move."

"Wouldn't work. We'd drive each other crazy in a week. And anyway, I like it here. Winter might bother mother. I, on the other hand, can't wait for snow."

Gwenn felt sleepy after eating Shirley's big breakfast. Her usual wake-up meal was a container of yogurt and a cup of coffee. She didn't quite feel her sharpest when she opened the office for business at nine and was ready for a nap by lunchtime.

But there wasn't time for a nap. She had to stop at home for Mae's groceries and drive them out to Briar Road.

She hurried home and packed the groceries into the back seat of her sturdy, but aging, tan station wagon. As she backed out of her driveway, Randal drove his sleek silver foreign sports car into the driveway and blocked the exit.

"Risky business parking behind a *woman* driver. How did you know I was here, anyway?" Gwenn called out through the open car window as he approached. Then speaking heavenward she added, "Just wait, Shirley. I'll pay you back."

"Don't blame your partner," Randal said as he leaned against her car. "I told her this was business. And you still are a businesswoman, aren't you?"

"I haven't found a house for you, Randal. I've checked the entire area. There aren't . . ." Gwenn turned off the engine.

"You don't have to bother looking any more, Gwenn. I've found the house I want."

"You have?" Gwenn was caught off guard. But when she looked in Randal's deep blue eyes she realized what he meant. "That building right there," she said as she pointed at her house, "belongs to me . . . and the bank. And that's the way it's going to stay. Period. . . . Until I can pay my debt, then it'll be all mine. End of discussion. Finished. Understand?"

"I don't think you understand. Once I've set my mind to something, I get it. And right now my plans are to own this house by Christmas."

"Is that a challenge?"

"Only if you consider it one."

"Okay. But I'm going to make up some rules."

"By all means."

"I've told you my home isn't for sale. You understand that?"

Randal nodded. "You received my offer . . . and the roses?"

Gwenn nodded. "Yesterday."

"They were beautiful, weren't they?"

"Yes, most roses are. Don't get off the subject."

"I'm not. The offer was fair, wasn't it?"

"I suppose so if it was on the market, but it's not."

"And I'm not giving up." He handed her a square envelope.

"What's this?"

"Open it."

Gwenn took out the card inside and read. It was another offer, twenty-five hundred dollars higher than his first.

"Well?" Randal looked hopeful.

Gwenn tore the card and the envelope into little pieces and placed them in Randal's hand. "Until Christmas. That seems like a fair amount of time for your project. Don't you think?"

"What are you talking about?" He stuffed the hand holding the bits of paper into his jacket pocket.

"Just setting a time limit, a rule, if you will. . . . If you haven't persuaded me to sell to you by Christmas, which you won't, you'll give up trying."

Randal removed his hand from his pocket and studied the destroyed card for a moment.

She felt comforted by his hesitation. "Or maybe that's too much of a challenge for you, Randal? You set the time limit yourself, you know."

"Okay, I agree." The card disappeared into his pocket again. "If I haven't convinced you to sell this house to me by Christmas I'll give up trying."

Gwenn held out her hand to seal the bargain. Randal took it between both of his and held it gently, warmly. He looked her in the eyes and smiled a mischievous smile.

Uncomfortable, Gwenn pulled her hand from between his and backed away.

"Oh, are there other rules?"

"Nothing sneaky or underhanded, that's all. Otherwise, I think I can stand your pestering until Christmas. It's sure you'll be the loser, Randal Cochran. Maybe you want to bow out now."

"Until Christmas. We shook. Can't back out. Now, where are we going?"

"We?" Gwenn looked puzzled.

"We, as in you and me. Lunch? Or are you heading inside with those groceries?"

Gwenn looked in the car window at Mae's food. She couldn't imagine Randal Cochran spending time with the old woman. "You'd be bored," she said. "I'm just taking this out to a friend."

"I won't be bored. How can you say that? I'll be in your charming company. . . . Face it, Gwenn. You're just going to have to get used to my smiling face. You're going to see quite a lot of it . . . until Christmas." Randal backed his car onto the street in front of Gwenn's house, then climbed into the station wagon's passenger seat.

"Why, if it isn't that bit of a bean," Mae said as she opened the door. "And she's brought a friend too." The old woman had been waiting for Gwenn. She had the door wide open before the car's motor had stopped.

"Hi, Mae. I've brought your groceries." Gwenn went to reach for the paper bags in the back seat, but Randal was there first.

"Allow me," he said.

"Only until Christmas," she answered softly as she grabbed her briefcase off the front seat.

Gwenn introduced Randal to Mae as he carried the bags into her kitchen.

Randal ran his hand along the wood table after setting his burden down. "Fine piece of furniture," he said, then turned to examine the hutch. "Handmade. Pegged together. You can't find anything constructed this strong these days."

"Len, my late husband," said Mae, "knew what he was doing when he worked with wood. Not fancy work, but he made things that lasted."

"I can see that." Randal examined the hutch, carefully opening each door and drawer in turn. "It must have taken him a good many hours to make this," he said.

"For a while, when we were first married, I thought he loved that piece of furniture more than he loved me," Mae laughed. "I almost walked out on him once because he spent so much time working on it."

"You didn't. Did you?" Gwenn finally spoke.

"Nope. Not for one minute. I soon learned how to share Len with his wood work. Now how about you two staying for lunch? Looks like my cupboard's not bare anymore."

Gwenn turned her back on Randal and the hutch. "Mae, we couldn't put you to the trouble. . . ."

"No trouble. The pots are in that cabinet by the sink. Bowls are up above. You know where the food's at. You brought it. Make what you like. I'll eat anything . . . except broccoli. I do absolutely hate broccoli. You didn't bring me any broccoli, did you?" Mae picked up her half-empty cup of tea and sat on a pressed wood kitchen chair.

"It wasn't on your list, Mae."

"I know it wasn't on my list. I hate broccoli. You two can make anything for lunch but broccoli."

Randal looked at Gwenn, a smile near his lips. "Well, how good a cook are you, Gwenn Nichols?" he asked.

"You'll soon find out."

"I'm not bad in the kitchen myself. I'll help, of course," he said as he slipped off his grey sport jacket and rolled up his shirt sleeves.

"You have time for this?" Gwenn looked surprised.

"Everyone has to take time to eat. Even me." Randal winked at

Gwenn. "Don't worry about the time. I'll let you know if there's a problem. Now, Mae, tell me about your husband. Did he make his living working with wood?"

Gwenn listened to Mae and Randal discuss Len and his lack of business sense as she emptied the grocery bags. Randal seemed honestly interested in the old woman and her stories.

Randal helped with the meal as he talked. He was at the sink washing lettuce when he asked, "Did your husband initial all the furniture he made?"

Mae looked puzzled.

"Initial. Carve or burn L. J. into the wood. Some master carpenters do that. It's their way of signing their creations."

"I see, Randal. I don't know. I never . . . Wait a minute. When I dust my table I feel something under the top." Mae left the kitchen and shuffled to the front window. She stopped at the plant-stand, swept it clear of some third-class junk mail and tipped the table over. "Well, what do you know. Len's initials."

Randal watched Mae's every move from his place by the kitchen table where he tore lettuce for their salad. "I thought so," he whispered to himself.

"Gwenn, come see this. I never even knew Len did this." Mae traced the two carved square letters with her finger. "Funny, after all these years . . ."

Gwenn shot Randal a look before joining Mae. Something about his curiosity bothered her, but she wasn't sure what it was, yet.

The tea was hot, the chef salad cold and the conversation stimulating as the three sat in Mae's kitchen for the better part of an hour.

At first Gwenn felt uneasy sitting across the table from Randal Cochran. But soon his easy manner and the light conversation made her forget why he had accompanied her that afternoon.

Gwenn started clearing the leftover food from the table. "Mae, I'm afraid it's time to end this chat and get on to business," said Gwenn. "I brought the listing papers for you to sign. We'd better clear the table and go over them."

"I'll get out of your way then," Randal volunteered. "If it's okay with you, Mae, while I'm waiting for Gwenn, I'd like to look at the other furniture your husband made."

"Don't mind at all. Not a locked door in this house."

Randal helped clear the few dishes from the table, then left the women alone, to roam the building.

"You've got yourself a nice fellow there, Gwenn," Mae said with a twinkle in her faded blue eyes.

"He's not mine. I mean we're business associates, kind of."

"He'll give you beautiful children. Len never could give me children. Be a fine father, I'll wager, that man of yours."

"He's not mine, Mae. We're just . . . Oh forget it. It doesn't matter. Now about these papers . . ." Gwenn took a file folder from her briefcase.

"I wanted at least six children. How many children do you and Randal plan? Six is a good number. Never have to worry about somethin' to do with six children."

"I believe that, Mae. But I'm not planning a family, yet. You don't understand . . ."

"Gwenn, you're not one of those modern women who doesn't want children! I'd have had a houseful if Len could have given them to me."

"Don't worry, Mae. When I find the right man, we'll probably decide to have children. It's just that Randal and I aren't . . ."

"Don't tell me he doesn't want children! He needs a son. A man should have sons to carry on his name."

"And what's wrong with daughters, Mae?" Gwenn half laughed at Mae's sexist remark.

"Of course daughters, too. Three of each. Boy, girl, boy, girl, boy, girl."

"That's some family planning, Mae. I don't know what Randal Cochran would say to your arrangement. But I'm guessing some day I'll have a couple of children, if not six."

"Good. You and Randal will have beautiful children."

Gwenn took a deep breath and pushed the papers in front of Mae. "I'll explain this contract for you."

Mae was silent as Gwenn thoroughly covered the real estate details.

"Do you have any questions, Mae?" Gwenn asked. "Want to change anything?"

Mae shook her head.

"You understand everything about the listing?"

"No. I never was one for business matters. But don't worry yourself. I trust you." Mae signed the paper with a shaking hand. The old woman immediately pushed her chair back from the table. "Where's that man of yours? Randal? Done with your looking?" She met Randal by the open front door where he was standing looking at the country-side.

"Yes," he said. "Just waiting for my ride. Thanks for letting me nose around. You sure have a nice location out here."

"I loved it the first day Len brought me here. . . ."

Gwenn straightened the papers in her briefcase as the two chatted. She didn't pay much attention to their conversation until she heard Mae saying, "Six is a good number to have. Don't you think?" and Randal giving a hearty laugh.

The papers were shoved into a file and snapped into the briefcase as Gwenn hurried to join the conversation. "Mae, you weren't listening to me. I said Randal and I weren't planning a family."

Mae looked blankly at Gwenn. "Family? We were talking about chickens. Six is a good number to have. Don't you think? I used to sell eggs. But I can't take care of a big flock anymore. I've been trying to talk Phyllis into lending me a few chicks, just for the summer, to keep me company."

While the old woman explained about the chickens Randal directed a raised eyebrow at Gwenn. His simple gesture helped redden her face. He withheld comment until they were in Gwenn's car and a safe distance down Briar Road.

"Six?" Randal's question affected Gwenn's complexion again. Immediately, she turned a bright shade of red.

"I don't want to talk about it," Gwenn said, keeping her eyes straight ahead on the road.

"But, six?" He chuckled.

"It was an honest mistake. Don't get the wrong idea, Randal."

"Yes, I imagine six would be a mistake these days." Randal laughed.

"Don't you like children?" When Gwenn finished the question she knew she had been drawn into a trap.

"It all depends, Ms. Nichols. Are you talking about six children in general? Six of my own children? Or six of our children, yours and mine?"

"Yours and mine?"

"I agree with Mae. We would make great children together. Your beautiful brown hair and my business sense . . ."

"No, we wouldn't! And I thought Mae and I were having a private conversation."

"Maybe there's a recessive gene I don't know about?"

"Don't be silly. There's no recessive gene to worry about."

"Good. Wouldn't want our six little rug rats to inherit anything from your side of the family."

"Randal!"

"Of course, six may be too much for you to handle."

"Don't worry about me handling six children."

"Oh?"

"There aren't going to be any children."

"Then you are one of those modern women. Mae was right."

Gwenn sighed. "I don't believe this."

"What is it you don't believe? That we're talking about having six children or that you're a modern woman?"

"I don't think I can stand you until Christmas."

"Giving up already? Good, I get the house!"

"Not on your life, Mr. Cochran. Don't plan Christmas anywhere but at your place. Mine's booked."

"Don't be so sure. . . . What about those six kids? What if we start working on making one of them."

"I couldn't imagine you and I . . . Any other man wouldn't say such . . . The idea of you and I . . . If I didn't know you were kidding . . . ," Gwenn stammered. "I'd make you walk home."

Randal touched her hand softly as it rested on the steering wheel. His fingers were gentle and warm, very, very warm. "There's nothing wrong with my imagination. . . . Who said I was joking?"

A shiver went through Gwenn. She quickly pulled her hand away from his which caused the station wagon to swerve sharply to the left.

"Whoa. So, I was joking! You don't have to kill us. Please control yourself. . . . And the car."

"You're the one that has to be controlled," Gwenn said as she slowed the car to make a left turn. "The bargain was to go after my house. Not after me."

"And that was rule number what?"

"No number. I just said nothing sneaky . . . or underhanded."

"You consider making love with me dirty? And you call yourself a modern woman. . . . Love is beautiful. And we could make love like no other couple." Randal reached out toward Gwenn again.

Gwenn slammed her foot to the brake pedal. "Want to walk?"

Randal took his hand back without touching her. "It is a fine fall day. Isn't it?" he said as he rolled down the window, allowing the cool wind to race across his face.

Gwenn humphed.

"What? I thought you liked autumn. It seems to agree with you so. When the sun caresses your hair it's streaked with red and gold. Did you know that?"

Gwenn humphed again.

The next few minutes of the drive were quiet. Randal hummed as the wind blew in his window. Gwenn tried to concentrate on her driving, although the back of her hand remained warm where he had touched her.

Then Randal broke the silence. "Will Mae have to sell all her furniture when her place sells?"

"Her niece insists everything has to go. Why?"

"I might be interested in buying a couple of the pieces. That is if you do your job and her property moves. I happen to have an affection for antiques."

Gwenn's eyes widened as she looked at her passenger. "Funny, I imagined you as an ultramodern person. I'm going to have to get a look at your apartment. It must be unusual."

"Any time, Gwenn. Always in the mood to show off my treasures. In fact that's why I want your house. My antiques need a suitable setting. They don't seem at home in my apartment."

"I can believe that." Gwenn wondered why Randal's antique collection deserved her home more than she did. For once she didn't voice her feeling.

"One particularly large piece would look fantastic in your house, that is, when it's completely remodeled. In fact, this antique came out of a building similar to yours. It would never work in an apartment. Right now it's in storage."

"What is it?"

He hesitated. "Oh, nothing that would interest you, I'm sure."

"But I'm fascinated by early American antiques, too."

"When Mae does decide to sell her furniture, let me know. If it would help, I could take all her furniture and save her the pain of an auction."

"That all depends on Mae and her feelings. First Duo Realtors has to sell her house. Wouldn't do to have the rooms empty and Mae sitting on a packing crate. That kind of thing turns prospective buyers off."

Randal's mouth fell open. "Boy, you do have a poor impression of me as a businessman."

"I've learned the hard way that practical business dealings don't necessarily consider people's feelings. Fred once . . ." Abruptly Gwenn stopped speaking.

"I suppose you're going to tell me that I haven't conducted myself in a proper manner concerning you and your house."

"My home and I are inseparable. I've told you that again and again. Yet, you insist on pestering me."

"But I do my pestering in an honorable manner, wouldn't you say? I assure you most of my business associates don't receive communications from me by way of the florist."

"It has been an interesting afternoon, Randal," Gwenn ended the conversation as she double-parked the station wagon next to his sports car. "I do have to get back to the office."

Randal didn't get out of the car, but gazed up at Gwenn's faded white house. "Going to take quite a bit of work getting this place in shape."

"Don't I know." Gwenn sighed.

"The longer you let the exterior go, the harder it will be to restore. Have you considered no-maintenance siding?

"I've considered it."

"Of course, vinyl wouldn't be quite right for this old beauty."

"That's what I thought," said Gwenn. "But it would help with insulation and then there's the heating bill."

"It would be a shame to change the siding so drastically, though." His comment made them both sigh.

Randal quickly snapped out of his revery. "I'd say there was enough space in there for those six kids we're planning." He winked mischievously.

"Randal! Good-bye. Work, remember?"

"Me too," Randal opened the car door. "See you tonight."

"Tonight? Oh, I forgot, the play."

"Never say, 'I forgot the play,' to the director. It wounds his ego. Don't you know everything is supposed to revolve around this play's production? . . . That was your director speaking."

"My, my, a man of many hats."

"You should see me in my cowboy hat."

"You ride?"

"No. I hate horses. I just look great in that hat. . . . See you later."

"Did he find you?" Shirley asked as Gwenn stepped into the office.

"He who?" Gwenn played dumb.

"You know. Mr. Director. Did he find you?"

"Yes."

"Well, have you sold your house?"

"You know I didn't. And may I ask, Shirley, why did you tell Randal where I was?"

"He said it was business. So, of course, I . . . Don't tell me it wasn't business, you lucky . . ."

"Don't you get the wrong idea, too."

"Too? Why Gwenn, has Randal . . ."

"Not another word, Shirley. All Mr. Randal Cochran wants from one Gwenn Nichols is her house. That's it. Period. End of conversation."

"Don't deny it so hard, Gwenn. You know me, the more you deny anything is happening the more I think something's happening. He's too gorgeous a man to ignore."

"There's more to a man than his body. . . . Oh, go ahead, imagine all you want. Nothing's happening concerning me . . . or my house, when it comes to Mr. Cochran."

"Of course, of course," Shirley said.

"Don't believe me if that's the way you feel, Shirl. You'll believe everything by Christmas, when Mr. Cochran walks out of my life just the way he walked in, empty-handed."

This time it was Shirley who winked and said, "Sure, Gwenn. Anything you say, Gwenn."

Gwenn stomped away from Shirley and into her office where she slammed the door.

As she sat down there was a knock at the door. Shirley opened it a crack and said, "You're denying it too hard, dear."

Gwenn threw a wad of paper at the door as it clicked shut again.

It was impossible for Gwenn to concentrate on the paperwork on her desk. Her thoughts whirled through time and space, landing more often than not on the image of Randal Cochran.

To compose her thoughts she took her portable radio out of a drawer and switched on an FM station. The usual soothing music didn't come on immediately; instead Gwenn heard the hourly news broadcast:

"Tropical storm Sam is now Hurricane Sam and is slowly heading in a northwesterly direction toward Florida. Movement of Sam is erratic making accurate prediction difficult. The entire Gulf Coast is under a hurricane watch."

The music that came on after the hurricane news did not soothe Gwenn's nerves at all. Her thoughts had been torn away from Randal and concentrated on her mother. She switched off the radio, picked up the telephone receiver and started dialing the 813 area code.

After twenty rings with no answer Gwenn hung up. She turned the radio dial to line up with an AM news program and waited for a hurricane update.

"Mother, where are you?" Gwenn's question couldn't travel the hundreds of miles across the country.

CHAPTER 5

"In case you don't remember me, I'm your director, Randal Cochran. I know this is an amateur production, but that doesn't mean we can't conduct ourselves like professionals." Randal spoke to the five people sitting in the first row of theater seats.

"I expect rehearsals to start on time. We're all working people, some with families. If we start at eight we can finish by ten and get home to those families."

He handed each person a piece of paper. "You'll find the schedule is like past plays. Tonight is the read-through. Monday we'll block the play. Because of the director change we have a severely shortened schedule, only four weeks until opening night. I expect everyone to be off the book by the end of week three. Now, are there any questions or conflicts with the schedule?"

JoJo waved her perfectly manicured hand in the air. "Randy, I can't possibly make it next Thursday. I'll be in New York, starting a *long* weekend. And as for being here by eight, well I'm not so sure I can always be here at exactly eight."

Randal's gaze went up toward the high ceiling. "Maybe, JoJo, you'd prefer someone else to have your part in this play." He flipped through his papers. "I could give my second choice for Natalie a call. . . ."

JoJo gasped. "But . . . but, Randy."

He looked up from his stat sheets. "I wouldn't want our schedule to inconvenience you, JoJo."

"Oh, Randy, you wouldn't do that. Would you? Not for just one Thursday?"

"Yes, JoJo, I would if I thought you weren't taking this production seriously. Now what about next Thursday?"

"Well," JoJo said, looking Randal in his steel blue eyes. His features were like stone. "I guess I could leave early Friday morning," she said.

"Good." Director Randal Cochran opened his dog-eared yellow play book. "Now let's get started. When the play opens, Gwenn and Lyle are onstage. Edna's fidgeting about the living room, straightening. Your daughter's coming home for the first time in years. She doesn't know Henry's your boyfriend. You don't know what to expect from her. You're nervous. Okay? Please begin."

Gwenn knew she wouldn't have any trouble sounding nervous tonight. She hadn't been able to reach her mother yet and was consumed with worry. But there was nothing she could accomplish from Wisconsin, except to sit and watch a very quiet telephone. Rehearsal, she hoped, would help take her mind off the hurricane.

Lyle shot Gwenn a crooked grin and winked. With one hand he smoothed back his very thin mousy blond hair, while using the other to flick his top shirt button open. He cleared his throat, then again, and again, all this before he opened his mouth for the first line.

Randal waited patiently.

JoJo didn't. "For heaven's sake, Lyle," she said. "The theater's empty. How nervous do you intend to be when there's an audience?"

"I'm not nervous."

"Then read, for heaven's sake!"

Lyle Thurst began to read.

HENRY: "Edna, if you dust that table any more you'll have the finish worn off it. Sit down."

EDNA: "I can't sit down, Henry. She'll be here any minute!"

HENRY: "Be like me. Won't catch me getting flustered. I'll just sit right here like I always do and . . ."

EDNA: "You can't sit there, Henry! She'll see you!"

HENRY: "Of course, she'll see me. That is unless she's blind."

EDNA: "You can't stay. I can't tell her about us, yet."

HENRY: "But I thought that's why you asked me over."

EDNA: "I changed my mind. . . . Oh, my God, a car turned in the drive. . . . Get up, Henry. Get up! No, no, not out the front door, out the back!"

HENRY: "Hey, I never had to sneak around like this when I was a kid. . . . It's kind of exciting."

At that point Lyle Thurst leaned over and kissed Gwenn on the cheek.

Gwenn touched the place on her cheek where his cold, wet lips had rested. "What are you doing?" she asked, dropping character.

"Well, that's what it says right here. I'm supposed to kiss you. See." Lyle pointed to the stage direction in his play book.

"Not tonight you're not."

"Oh, pooh. That was the best part of the scene."

Randal left his stool and walked toward Lyle. "Let's skip all the stage directions tonight, though I'll agree kissing Gwenn's pretty cheek is the best part." Randal's gaze was directed to the blushing face in the adjoining theater seat. "I'm afraid that'll have to wait until next week."

"Darn," Lyle whispered. "But I will get to kiss her next week. Won't I?"

Randal nodded. "It's in the script."

Gwenn felt her stomach lurch. Lyle Thurst was the local undertaker. Meeting, even speaking to him at social gatherings had always made her skin crawl. It might have been her imagination but his skin always felt cold and clammy when he shook her hand. The idea of nightly kisses— well, she didn't want to think about it. She was afraid she'd lose her supper. Anyway, she had other things to worry about.

JoJo straightened her long legs out, letting her light jersey skirt ride up high on her thighs. "You better get all your kisses in early, Lyle," JoJo said. "Gwenn won't look so cute when she's in makeup."

"Listen, JoJo, Lil and Randal typecast me for this role. A ton of makeup on Gwenn would only help even out our ages. Right, Gwenn?"

Gwenn slid down into her seat and rested her head back. "Can't we continue?"

"Good idea." Randal took control. "Lyle, pick up right before the kiss. . . . But skip the kiss."

"Oh, pooh," Lyle protested again but continued as directed.

HENRY: "Hey, I never had to sneak around like this when I was a kid. . . . It's kind of exciting."

EDNA: "Not now, Henry. She'll see. Now get."

(JoJo straightened herself in her theater seat as if she were making an entrance.)

NATALIE: "Mother."

EDNA: "Natalie, so good to see you."

NATALIE: "Traffic was absolutely hideous. Thought I'd never get out of the city. Then the ridiculously long drive here."

(Gwenn directed her lines to JoJo. JoJo, on the other hand, directed her lines to Randal.)

EDNA: "How about some coffee, Natalie."

NATALIE: "Fine. I brought some with me. It's a special blend, imported, of course. I'd just vomit if I drank anything else."

EDNA: "Oh?"

NATALIE: "Really, Mother, you'll love this coffee. And don't forget to make it the way I like it, strong enough to stand a spoon in."

EDNA: "I can't tolerate strong coffee anymore. I drink decaffeinated. Have to. The doctor . . ."

NATALIE: "That's not coffee! That's liquid garbage. No one who's anyone drinks decaf."

The scene continued. JoJo had absolutely no trouble playing Natalie. Gwenn couldn't help wondering if the playwright hadn't modeled the character after the woman.

Scene Two also came in line with JoJo's life or at least Gwenn guessed it did. Though JoJo wasn't married, she'd been known to collect engagement rings like boys collect baseball cards.

NATALIE: "Mom, I've met a man."

EDNA: "You already have a man. His name's Will. Or have you forgotten?"

NATALIE: "I haven't forgotten Will. He's there, like always."

EDNA: "You treat him like your pet, a dog."

NATALIE: "I do not. I care about Will. He's comfortable to be with. But . . ."

EDNA: " 'But,' 'but,' with you Natalie there's always been a 'but.' Since you were four and couldn't decide what kind of ice cream flavor you wanted. Your father would always end up buying you two different scoops. You never, ever finished half of what he gave you."

NATALIE: "Mom, don't be a fool. Will's not ice cream or a pet. He's a man, a very warm, compassionate man."

EDNA: "You're right there. Will couldn't be nicer. In fact, he's too good for you."

Gwenn's character finally found her way offstage when Natalie's boyfriend, Drew, arrived in Scene Three and Keith Gilford stepped into the role.

Gwenn watched as JoJo continued to direct her lines to Randal, even with cast member Gilford, Natalie's so-called lover, reading in the theater seat adjoining hers.

It was a sure bet: JoJo was out to get another ring for her collection. Gwenn felt a knot in her stomach, which she promptly attributed to the tuna salad she had had for dinner. She wondered if Randal was prepared for a total assault of JoJo's charms. Gwenn doubted if any man was.

"Ms. Nichols . . . Ms. Nichols . . . Gwenn? Have you dozed off? Your line please." Randal's voice brought Gwenn out of her reverie.

"Sorry," Gwenn apologized and fumbled through the pages of dialogue she had missed.

A bit red in the face, Gwenn continued.

EDNA: "Has he gone?"

NATALIE: "He'll be back."

EDNA: "How did it go?"

NATALIE: "Don't you know? Don't tell me your hearing's gone and you can't listen at keyholes anymore. When I was dating you could hear through concrete."

EDNA: "How did it go with Drew, Natalie?"

NATALIE: "Just fine!"

EDNA: "Oh . . . Then you can help me fold the laundry."

NATALIE: "I never do laundry. I send all my . . . Whose shorts are these?"

EDNA: "They're Henry's, I guess."

NATALIE: "Who's Henry?"

EDNA: "I was meaning to explain about Henry."

NATALIE: "This is disgusting! Not the guy who mows the lawn. You couldn't be having an affair with that dirty old man?"

EDNA: "Don't call Henry a dirty old man. And we're not having an affair. At least not the way you are. I'm not cheating on *my* husband."

NATALIE: "That's because Dad's dead. Are you sure good old Henry wasn't around, just a bit, before Dad died?"

EDNA: "Natalie! I loved your father!"

NATALIE: "Never said you didn't."

EDNA: "I never cheated on him."

NATALIE: "He was sick for a long time, Mother. You can't tell me you never once thought about . . . about seeking comfort in someone else's arms. Good old Henry must have been around then."

EDNA: "No! Natalie, how could you say . . ."

HENRY: "Sorry to interrupt but I finished with the garden and . . ."

NATALIE: "How very kind of you to help a lonely widow lady, Henry.
You take care of her every need. Don't you?"
HENRY: "What? Edna, what's wrong with your daughter?"
EDNA: "She knows about us."

"Okay, people, let's take a break before starting Act Two," Randal said.

"Good, I need a drink of water." JoJo stood up, smoothing her skirt by running her fingers down her slim thigh.

Charlie Harris, who was to play Will, nervously cleared his throat as he watched her stroke her body. "Funny, I haven't read one word of dialogue yet, but suddenly I'm very thirsty."

"Come on, hubby, walk me to the breakroom." JoJo took Charlie's hand.

"Can your lover come too?" Keith followed them out into the hall.

Using the stage floor as a desk, Randal scratched more notes on his clipboard. It helped Gwenn relax to know Randal treated his directorship as he did other business dealings. It was a separate matter and for a while, at least, she didn't have to worry about his designs on her home.

Lyle didn't move from Gwenn's side. "Next week I'll bring my coffee pot. I need more than water to keep me going. Like Natalie, I need coffee strong enough to stand a spoon in," Lyle said to Gwenn's neck.

His hot breath made the hair on the back of Gwenn's neck stand on end. "I'm sure there's a pot in the makeup room. I remember Lil had it going at the first tryouts."

"Then I'll bring some fresh coffee."

The thought of Lyle's coffee kept the back of Gwenn's neck tingling. Somehow she figured his brew would have the distinct flavor of formaldehyde. "Why don't we just have hot water in the pot?" she suggested. "That way we can have coffee, tea or instant hot chocolate if we want."

Lyle shrugged, stood up and looked around the theater. "I did a lot of work here," he said and paused for Gwenn to question him about his work. When she remained silent he continued without her. "Not acting. I mean work . . . when it was still a church." He giggled to himself at his joke. "I couldn't count how many customers of mine came and rested right there where you're sitting, Gwenn, right in the center aisle. The seating was quite different then. I'd arrange the flowers here around the altar, where the stage is now. . . ."

Quickly Gwenn left the center seat. She did not need talk of church or funerals. "I think I need some water before we start again." As she crossed in front of Randal he looked up from his notes. He smiled at Gwenn like a knowing parent would at a silly child.

Lyle continued his eulogy to the old church as Gwenn ducked into the hall. The queasiness in her stomach evaporated when she heard laughter coming from the makeup room. But when she walked in all laughter stopped.

JoJo looked deep into her glass of water and giggled like a high school student. "This stuff is terrible," she said. "There's little brown specks floating around in it. I think we should petition the theater group to put in bottled water."

"It's not in the budget, JoJo," Gwenn said as she opened the tap and filled her glass. "So the water's a little hard. A few extra minerals will do you some good."

"Really, Gwenn. You don't have to stay in character backstage. You're only my mother when we're up front." JoJo laughed merrily at her joke. Charlie and Keith smiled.

Gwenn could barely swallow her mouthful of water. When it finally worked its way down her throat she looked at Keith. "How do you plan to fit all this play business in with your college studies, Keith?" she asked.

"No problem." His slight chest puffed out as he answered. "I can read anything once and have it just about memorized."

"He's not the one you have to worry about," said Charlie. "I'm going to have to stay up past my bedtime to learn my lines. And we all know a sleepy junior high teacher is taking his life in his hands. I have to be on my toes all the time. One never knows when a spitball is going to fly." Charlie Harris pantomimed dodging a barrage of spitballs, then proceeded to pretend to pick one out of his ear.

"Oh, Charlie," JoJo chuckled. "I don't know how you do it. Those little brats would drive me crazy. . . . I don't have to twist my life around for this production. I'm free as a bird until mid-December. Then I'm off to Europe. I'll be in Italy for Christmas."

JoJo didn't have time to brag about her upcoming trip. As she finished making her announcement Lyle came to the door and called them back for Act Two.

Randal was not alone by the stage as the cast entered the theater. A huge muscular man stood next to him writing on a stenographer's pad. His upper arm muscles bulged, stretching his short-sleeved shirt in a pleasant manner, Gwenn thought.

The three male cast members reacted silently to the man. Lyle physically shrunk in stature as he crossed to his seat. Keith gulped so loud, Gwenn thought he had swallowed his Adam's apple. Charlie, on the other hand, straightened up out of his usual slouch and remained at attention in his seat.

Gwenn was the only cast member who chose a different theater seat for the second act's reading. She knew after her conversation with Lyle that she would never be able to sit front row center again.

The two men by the stage spoke quietly for a few minutes before Randal acknowledged the cast's return.

"This is Tank Lormar, as many of you may know," Randal said, tipping his head toward the mountain of muscles standing next to him. "He's the stage manager for this play. For the most part, Tank will have the set ready for blocking Monday. If any of you have any appropriate props and are willing to loan them to us for this production, Tank's the man to talk with."

"We're lucky this play has one basic room," Tank said in such a soft low voice that Gwenn had to strain to hear him. "The way it looks, the only thing our properties department doesn't have is a painting for over the mantel."

"You know me and my apartment, Tank." JoJo avoided looking at Tank by searching through her leather clutch purse for a lace handkerchief. "I wouldn't own anything tacky enough for Edna's living room. Why don't you ask Gwenn?"

"You're probably right, JoJo," Gwenn freely acknowledged. "Mom saved all my high school art projects. Why, I don't know. None warranted more than a C. Anyway I'm sure there's some kind of tacky painting stashed away in my attic you could use. I'll bring it Monday."

"If it's all right with you, I'll stop by this weekend and check it out. If you don't have a painting that's right I'll have time to go to a flea market or second-hand stores to find something."

"A flea market is the perfect place to look," Gwenn agreed. "I've found some great bargains there in the past."

"What do you know, Tank," JoJo broke in. "You and Gwenn have a lot in common. You shop at the same flea markets."

"Okay, *ladies* and gentlemen, time for Act Two," Randal said, his authoritative voice bringing everyone's attention to him.

"I've some work to do in the storage room and I want to check the light board tonight," said Tank to Randal. Then he turned back to Gwenn. "When you're finished stop back and I'll get your address and set up a time to look at that painting."

She nodded and Tank left.

Charlie finally took a breath and slouched down in his seat as the side door closed behind Tank. "That man scares the heck out of me every time I see him in town."

"Don't be silly, Charlie," JoJo said. "He wouldn't smash a flea at a flea market. Tank's all muscle and nothing else."

"Just the same . . . he's so *big*." Charlie dabbed at the beads of perspiration on his forehead.

Randal began speaking, "Act Two begins with Natalie on the phone with her husband."

Charlie Harris straightened his posture again. "Finally I get to say something. Isn't that the way it is? Husbands never get a chance to talk."

"JoJo, you'll have to practice talking with our dummy phone to get the timing right. Of course, no one will be onstage or off exchanging lines at this time."

"Randy, darlin', why don't you let me read the part first, before you correct my acting." JoJo smiled sweetly. "I know how to pace the telephone conversation, I assure you."

"So show me."

NATALIE: "Will? . . . Yes, I know I should have called you when I arrived at Mother's. . . . Only Mother and I . . . Of course, I know I'm still legally your wife. . . . Don't get so emotional. I love you, too. . . . I don't care if you believe me or not. . . . No, I don't think you should come out here. Having you here will only make me more confused. . . . Will, can't you understand? I need this time alone. . . . Don't hang up. . . . Will? Will?"

JoJo paced the telephone conversation perfectly.

Gwenn fought with herself not to think about her mother's whereabouts. She tried to focus her attention on JoJo. She was surprised and impressed by her timing and expression. She even caught herself wondering if JoJo had rehearsed the scene or if she was so versed at lying to men on the phone that she spoke automatically.

Gwenn was smiling to herself when Randal broke into her thoughts. "Ms. Nichols . . . Gwenn? Are you going to join us?"

"Sorry, again."

"I hope these lapses of yours are credited to a hard day at the office. I would hate for opening night to arrive and have a cue go by because you're off somewhere in Never Never Land."

"I said I was sorry."

Randal wrote on his notepad and gave directions at the same time. "JoJo, would you mind picking it up again with your last line?"

NATALIE: "Set another place at the table tonight, Mother. Will's on his way up here."

EDNA: "It's going to get pretty crowded here with both Drew and Will at the same table, isn't it?"

NATALIE: "Not for me it won't."

EDNA: "Doesn't that bother you, Natalie? Aren't you the least bit concerned about destroying your marriage? . . . I can't believe I gave birth to you. . . ."

NATALIE: "I've been meaning to ask you, Mother. Who was my father? I'd like to know if I should call Henry, or some other John, "Daddy." . . . Don't walk out on me! I'm talking to you, Mother!"

Randal stopped the dialogue. "At this point Edna grabs her sweater and exits by the front door and Natalie exits to the kitchen."

"Do you really think Natalie would go to the kitchen?" Gwenn asked. "I get the distinct impression she doesn't know her way around the room."

"She probably doesn't," JoJo agreed. "Maybe she went there to make herself a cup of instant coffee."

"But she wouldn't be caught dead drinking instant. Remember?"

"Well then, Gwenn, she's making herself a piece of toast."

"Nope. It would ruin her diet."

JoJo sighed. "Then she opened a bottle of sparkling water."

"I can live with that."

"I should hope so." Randal tapped his play book against the stage. "We'll get into character analysis next week. Please continue. . . . It's almost lunch. The doorbell rings. Natalie opens it for Will. JoJo, pick it up there."

Gwenn tried to listen to JoJo and Charlie Harris as they went over their big scene. But her eyes kept drifting away from the printed dialogue to where Randal sat on his stool. She had to be careful or he would catch her watching him.

Randal wasn't handsome in comparison to modern screen actors, but Gwenn decided his features were pleasant: square jaw, strong chin and blue eyes. Tonight he was dressed in denim slacks and a short-sleeved shirt that was the faintest pale lime green. The light color showed off his tan.

Gwenn looked a second time. Yes, Randal was definitely tan. How could he acquire a tan from behind a desk? It was her guess that he spent his leisure in front of a sunlamp.

What kind of man butts into people's private lives without revealing an ounce of his own? Gwenn wondered how much she would learn about Randal before Christmas. Too much, she was sure—this short-lived relationship would never do. The only way she would survive would be to continue like an actress playing a part until Christmas. She would be Natalie, taking advantage of one of her many men.

By accident Gwenn heard her cue and was back reading without anyone catching her lapse of concentration.

She was exhausted by the time the final scene arrived.

EDNA: "You're a damn fool if you leave Will!"

NATALIE: "Will, Will, Will, that's all you know. Maybe *you* should have married him and not me. You seem to be made for each other."

EDNA: "Drew has had enough of your dangling him. He's out of your life forever. Your only chance is with Will. You should go down on your knees. If you're lucky he'll take you back. . . . I don't need Will, darling daughter. You do."

NATALIE: "Yes, I forgot. You already have a live-in lover. Why don't you get married? Why doesn't Henry make an honest woman out of you, Mother?"

EDNA: "I don't have to explain my actions to anyone, especially you. . . . Who asked you to stick your perfect nose in here again? I sure as hell didn't."

NATALIE: "Don't act like an ass, Mom. You're getting old. You're going to need me some day."

EDNA: "The day I need you is the day I roll over and die. I've got Henry, now. He's all I need."

NATALIE: "What? Your lover? You'll need more than that dirty old man!"

EDNA: "Look who's talking about being dirty. Maybe I should get a husband and a lover like my big-shot daughter. Maybe I should get myself two or three lovers. How many have you had? Four? Eight?"

NATALIE: "I can't help it if men find me irresistible."

EDNA: "What happens when you're no longer irresistible? What happens when you're alone and I'm the only one you have left in the world?"

NATALIE: "If that day ever came, you'll be long dead and won't have to worry about me."

EDNA: "Go! Leave! Keep running with all those men that find you irresistible. After they've used you and tossed you over for some other piece of fluff you'll find me here, happy with my mundane life and with Henry."

CHAPTER 6

The first rehearsal was over. After Gwenn had used her last ounce of energy reading the final emotional scene, she rubbed the back of her neck and sighed. "I'm going to have to double up on my vitamins if I'm going to survive this play."

"Don't tell me you're tired, Gwenn," JoJo said as she bounced out of her theater seat. "The night's just begun. I'm ready for some dancing. What about you, Randy?"

"I wouldn't mind a nightcap at Bennie's," Randal said.

Charlie and Keith were quick to agree and rushed to fight for position at JoJo's right side. Keith lost and consoled himself with her left arm.

"Let's all go, Gwenn," said Lyle. "That way we can really get to know each other." Lyle Thurst was so close to Gwenn that his hot breath made her skin crawl.

Gwenn took a step back and shook her head. "I'm heading home, right after I talk to Tank. I've got work tomorrow."

"Don't we all." Lyle stepped forward and touched Gwenn's hand. "I'll save a seat for you . . . just in case you change your mind." He had to trot to catch up with the three other cast members at the main entrance.

JoJo stopped the group as Charlie opened the door. "You coming, Randy?" she called through the dark theater toward the lighted stage.

Randal waved them out the door. "It'll take me a few minutes to close up. Order me a gin and tonic. . . . What about you, Tank?" Randal called his question to the muscular man standing high over the trio's heads in the old choir balcony. "Bennie's?"

Tank looked down at the top of JoJo's shiny mane before answering. Softly he answered, "Sure."

As the noisy group left the theater Shirley entered. "Guess I'm too late to hear any of the reading," she said. Her mouth fell open as she watched Tank leave the balcony via a wall ladder and cross the theater to her partner's side.

Gwenn scribbled her home address on her business card and handed it to Tank. "In another minute the door would have been locked," Gwenn said to Shirley. "Is there anything wrong at the office?"

"No. I . . . I . . . I was on my way home from a da . . . from a meeting and thought since the lights were on in the theater, I'd stop and be nosy." The entire time Shirley spoke she didn't take her eyes off Tank.

"Some of us are going to Bennie's," Randal said. "You're welcome, too."

"Gwenn?" Shirley finally tore her eyes from Tank and turned to Gwenn. "You're going. Aren't you?" Her last question pleaded with her partner to say "Yes."

"I wasn't . . ." Gwenn started to answer. The painful expression on Shirley's face made her change her mind. "Oh, I guess I can go . . . for one nightcap. It might help me relax."

Gwenn wasn't happy to discover that Bennie's was far from quiet that particular Thursday evening. As she followed Tank and Shirley in she was nearly blinded by a silky rainbow haloed by a cloud of smoke.

The majority of the twenty-plus patrons mobbing the bar were wearing colorful bowling shirts, and it seemed everyone there was smoking. The smell was so strong it hurt Gwenn to breathe.

JoJo pushed past Tank, Shirley and Gwenn in a desperate effort to reach Randal as he stepped through the door. "Gin and tonic. Right?" She held out his drink.

"If I feel ill tonight," Shirley whispered into Gwenn's ear, "it won't be because of the booze. It'll be because JoJo's going to do her sickeningly-sweet act."

Gwenn only nodded. She thought she was going to be ill, too, but for a different reason. Lyle was smiling at her from his place at the bar, patting the only empty stool. He wanted her seated next to him.

Shirley nudged Gwenn when she caught the look Lyle was sending across the room. "I think you're being paged," she said.

Lyle called, "Come on, I'll buy you a drink. . . . Your friend too."

"Maybe later, Lyle. I . . . I have some . . . some real estate business to discuss with my partner." Gwenn steered Shirley into the coatroom.

Shirley shivered as she accompanied Gwenn into the small room. "That man gives me the creeps," she said. "How can anyone work with dead people all the time?"

"I guess somebody's got to do it." Gwenn slipped out of her brown suede jacket and hung it up.

"And to think you have to kiss him in the play. *Ish.*"

"Don't remind me," Gwenn said. "What's going on at the office that's so important?"

"At the office?" Shirley smiled a half smile. "Not a blessed thing. Business is always a good excuse to help get into a situation . . . or out of one, as you know."

"As long as you're talking business," Randal said, coming into the room carrying his black nylon jacket, "I'd like to know if you heat with oil, gas or electricity?"

"Oil. And if you intend to bug me about *my* house, the answer's still no sale," Gwenn said shortly.

Randal held up his hand. "One more question," he said.

Gwenn reached up to take her jacket back off its hanger. "I thought we came here to unwind."

"You're conclusion-jumping again. My question was, what are you drinking?"

"I'll have a rosé, thank you," said Shirley. "Hang your coat back up, Gwenn!" Shirley forced the wood hanger back into Gwenn's jacket. "And my impatient friend will have a sangria."

"Fine. There's no room at the bar. I'll let Tank escort you to a table while I get your drinks."

The arrangement suited Shirley. She smiled broadly as Randal walked out of the coatroom.

Gwenn hesitated, holding onto her hanging coat sleeve.

Shirley took a firm grip on her friend's elbow and pleaded. "Tank's waiting for us. It won't hurt you to pair up with Randal for a couple drinks. Will it? I mean, he *is* your director."

"You don't have to break my arm. If all you want is to be introduced to Tank Lormar, I can arrange that as I'm heading out the door."

"And how would it look if you leave and I stay? He'd think I was after him."

"Well, aren't you?"

"Yes, but I don't want him to know that yet."

"Then I suggest you keep your mouth from dropping open every time you look at Tank. That is if you want to keep your wicked intentions secret."

"My mouth doesn't drop open," Shirley protested. "Does it?"

Gwenn nodded. "Just like a schoolgirl's." She finally released the coat sleeve and followed Shirley who followed Tank across the crowded bar to a table near the kitchen entrance.

Shirley didn't take Gwenn's advice. Her mouth dropped open the moment Tank was officially introduced to her. As he shook her hand she squared her shoulders and mumbled, "I'm enchanted . . . I'm happy . . . I mean, I'm pleased to meet you, Tank."

Gwenn giggled. Shirley wasn't so overwhelmed by Tank that she neglected to sweep her right foot under the table at Gwenn's shin. Along with the threatened kick, Shirley sent Gwenn a look so full of daggers that Gwenn nearly felt her skin prick.

She bit her lip trying to squelch the giggles that kept trying to escape. "Ah," Gwenn looked away from Shirley and straight into Randal's gaze. "Ah . . ."

"My, my, you do have a way with words," Randal said as he held up his glass in a mock salute.

"I told you I was tired. And anyway you didn't cast me to play a charming after-rehearsal conversationlist. You chose me to play Edna, a very down-to-earth woman, who . . ."

"Who always knows the right thing to say," Randal finished Gwenn's thought.

"Yes, but she had a playwright to help her. And he had hours, weeks, maybe even months, to mull over every line, every word."

"In other words, you need time to think before you can make small talk."

"In other words, I don't know why you singled me out to hassle when JoJo, at the bar, is more than willing to flatter you to death."

"I'm just a glutton for punishment, I guess."

"What is it with you two?" Shirley said. "Do you intend picking at each other throughout the production?"

"That's separate," Gwenn and Randal answered together.

Gwenn looked down at her full wineglass and ran her finger around its rim. She bit her lip, struggling not to smile. But the instant she looked up at Randal's twinkling eyes the laugh she was holding burst out.

"I don't know if I'm going to allow you to do that in the play," Randal said sternly.

"What?" Gwenn continued to smile. Her face flushed a warm rosy glow as she flipped her dark brown hair over her shoulder.

"Laugh," Randal answered seriously. "Probably not even smile. It'll ruin everything."

"Explain, please."

"I doubt we would ever be able to afford enough makeup to keep you looking old enough, not if you smile like that all the time. Not on our pitiful budget. No smiling for your Edna."

"Thank you for the compliment. I think. But you know, now that you've brought up smiling onstage I won't be able to guarantee a sour puss."

"Just think about *your* house becoming *my* house."

Gwenn's smile faded. "Why did you have to say that?"

Randal winked. "It worked. Didn't it?"

There was a moment of silence while everyone sipped their drinks. Then Shirley cleared her throat and said, "Gwenn, do you have any clients scheduled for Saturday?"

"Not this week. That special living room wallpaper I ordered was delivered today. I plan to spend Saturday hanging it."

"What kind of paper is it?" Randal asked. "I hope I like it."

"Why should the wallpaper matter to you?" Gwenn asked in mock innocence.

Randal didn't answer, but glared at Gwenn as he drained his glass.

"Since *my* wallpaper's so important to you, why don't you come over Saturday and help me hang it?"

"What time?"

"I was kidding."

"I wasn't. What time?"

"There's no great rush to have the wallpaper up. I can handle the job myself. . . . Look at the kitchen. I did that alone."

Randal shook his head. "You probably didn't have any volunteers when you were doing the kitchen. . . . It'll take you forever. If you accept my superb help you'll be finished in half the time."

"True, but . . ."

"But, but, but. What time should I come?"

"Well, if you're really going to work, I suppose you should come around nine."

Tank, who had sat silently since his hello to Shirley, opened his mouth. "I couldn't come that early. What if I show up after lunch?"

"Any time, Tank. It won't take long to give you that painting," Gwenn said, fighting back a smoke-caused cough.

"No. I mean, yes I want the painting, but I also want to help with your wallpaper."

"Nonsense, I couldn't impose . . . ," Gwenn said.

"Hey," Shirley cut in before Gwenn could dissuade Tank, "if you three are going to be working your fingers to the bone with Gwenn's wallpaper, why don't I make supper for everyone at my place?"

Tank gulped the last of his ginger ale. "Maybe you'd better not count on me for dinner. I can't . . ."

"Oh, you already have a date. I should have guessed, a man like you would be busy Saturday night." Shirley sounded disappointed.

"No, I'm free. It's just that I don't . . ."

"No date? Then there's no excuse. You'll just have to come. I won't take no for an answer. What about you, Randal?"

"I'll come only if you're a good cook and you don't force me to eat tuna casserole," Randal said.

Gwenn set down her glass of wine. "Shirley, you don't have to cook for all of us."

"What? You're a terrible cook?" Randal sounded shocked.

"I'm a master chef and I'll confirm that Saturday night at seven." As Shirley finished speaking the other cast members left the bar and joined them.

Chairs were drawn close to the small table. People shuffled and re-shuffled the seating arrangement until JoJo sat between Randal and Lyle, and Lyle had his arm around the back of Gwenn's chair.

"Randy, Randy, Randy, enough of this boring real estate business." JoJo spoke huskily into Randal's ear. "I'm sure Gwenn might be able to talk intelligently about something else. That is if she tried hard enough."

"There are a few other subjects I might, just *might,* mind you, be able to converse about, JoJo. What are your thoughts on acid rain and Wisconsin lakes? Do you think sulfur pollution is killing all our bluegills?"

"Acid rain? Bluegills?" JoJo huffed. "That's not normal conversation, Gwenn. That's a high school debate."

"I like bluegills," said Lyle.

All the men at the table agreed.

"I caught a pound-and-a-half bluegill in White Clay Lake once." Lyle whispered his fish story toward Gwenn's ear. "It was the best-tasting fish I ever ate."

Gwenn tried to move away from Lyle's hot breath and ignore his fish story. Randal watched her squirm and asked, "Did it put up much of a fight, Lyle?"

"Fight? The way that fish struggled you would have thought I had a hold of a walleye!" Lyle brought up his right hand from behind Gwenn in his effort to explain the fight the fish gave him. As his hand brushed past her, his wristwatch band got tangled in her long hair.

"Ouch!" Gwenn grabbed Lyle's hand as he struggled to free her hair. "Let me do that," she said as she slipped his watch off his wrist and untangled her hair.

"I'm sorry. I'm so sorry, Gwenn," Lyle said as she handed the watch back to him, loose hair still dangling from its silver links. "I scalped you!"

"Oh, Gwenn has enough hair for two people," said JoJo. "That hair's going to be a problem when you try to stuff it under a grey wig for the play."

"We could spray it grey, like we did Tom's in the last production," said Charlie.

"That spray was silver," said JoJo. "And Tom ended up looking like a museum statute instead of an old man.

Gwenn felt safe when the conversation steered itself toward the theater, the last play and its run, and past box office receipts. Finally, when JoJo's acting abilities became the center of the conversation, Gwenn thought it time to bow out.

"I think the wine has done the trick. I'm heading home," Gwenn said.

"But I haven't bought you a drink yet." Lyle caught her hand in his.

"Next time," Gwenn said. She had to pull her hand out of his. She set his hand back on the table and patted it as she would the head of her cat, Westminster. "See you all Monday night."

"Saturday, Saturday morning at nine," Randal corrected.

Gwenn nodded and turned on her heels as Randal explained about the wallpaper he had volunteered to hang. Quickly she wove her way through the noisy bowlers surrounding the bar.

The coatroom's quiet was a relief, though the cigarette smoke had a strong hold of the small room too. She stood facing the rack of coats, slowly buttoning her jacket, when someone entered the room behind her.

"I'll walk you to your car." Randal slipped his jacket off the hanger.

"It's not necessary."

"Nothing's necessary. . . . But I'll walk you to your car, anyway." She sighed and allowed Randal to open the door for her.

Outside Gwenn inhaled deeply. The sharp pungent smell of fallen leaves helped Gwenn clear her lungs of cigarette smoke. She stopped and looked up at Randal. "I'm surprised you don't smoke, Randal," she said.

"Now, why would you associate me with a disgusting habit like that. . . . I used to smoke, when I was a kid. I finally kicked it two years ago."

"I bet it helped your lungs when you quit."

"Maybe so. I figured the money I was smoking away wasn't doing anything profitable."

"Does everything you do always tie up with business and money?"

"Probably," he said.

"What about the play?"

"Contacts."

Gwenn couldn't see his face in the dark parking lot but she was almost sure he answered her with a smile.

"Buying my house won't make you any money. Just trying to get me to sell has only cost you, so far."

"Don't worry about my business deals. I know what I'm doing."

"I'm not worried. Why should I be? I'll accept gorgeous roses from you any day. Keep up your wheelings and dealings for all I care."

"How about a play?"

"No thanks. I already have one."

"No, honestly, the visiting artists group at the university is bringing in a one-woman show, *The Belle of Amherst.* I have two tickets for a week from Saturday. Would you like to go?"

"With you?"

"Of course, with me. . . . Unless you prefer Lyle's company?"

Gwenn gulped. "I'd like to go . . . with you."

"Fine. And of course I'll take you to dinner before the theater."

"Of course, but only the most expensive restaurant in the area."

"Nothing but the best."

"Randal, doesn't it bother you that I'm taking advantage of you? I'm not going to change my mind about my house, yet I accept your gifts."

"People have been known to change their minds."

"Yes, people have. . . . Would you like to reconsider bidding on my house?"

Randal shook his head as he held Gwenn's car door open. "Just chalk my offer up another thousand. Interested, yet?"

Without a second thought Gwenn said, "No."

"It will be intriguing to see who better survives this battle of stubbornness, you or me," he said.

"Well, my mother always said I was more stubborn than a grass stain on white jeans."

"*My* mother compared me to Sisyphus, in Greek mythology. He was condemned forever to roll a huge stone up a hill only to have it roll down again on nearing the top. I, on the other hand, though not condemned, would forever roll my stone up because of my pigheadedness."

Gwenn laughed. "Somehow, that's not hard to believe."

"Yes, that smile has to go. . . ." Randal's beeper sounded from his shirt pocket. "Darn . . ." he said as he switched off the annoying alarm. "Sometimes I wish . . . Oh well, good night, Gwenn." Randal slammed her car door and walked to his car where he picked up a telephone receiver.

Gwenn watched his silhouette as he spoke into the telephone. If only he was as serious about a personal relationship with her, she thought, as he was about buying her house. . . . She sighed heavily as she started the engine.

Friday was impossible at work. Not one prospective buyer called to rescue Gwenn from tons of paperwork, not even Randal. The only phone calls to the office all day were three from Mae.

"Gwenn," Mae said at 9 A.M. "You didn't bring me any cranberry juice."

"It wasn't on your list, Mae."

"But Phyllis always buys me cranberry juice. I need it for my plumbing."

"Plumbing?"

"I have to drink some every day or I can't go. . . . You know."

"Oh. Okay, Mae, I'll bring some out after work."

At ten-fifteen Mae called to ask Gwenn when she would be out.

When she phoned again at eleven Gwenn agreed to bring the cranberry juice out to her at noon.

After lunch Shirley started acting odd.

"What do you think about Italian?" Shirley came out of her kitchen door carrying a half-dozen cookbooks.

"Italian what?"

"Maybe Greek . . . or maybe French. . . . Oh, I don't know what to cook tomorrow night." Shirley dropped the books on Gwenn's desk.

"Why not a chef's salad?"

"A salad after working all afternoon on your wallpaper! No, it has to be something special, very special. I want to make a good impression."

"You don't have to go out of your way to impress me, Shirl," Gwenn said.

"Maybe I'll make a chocolate mousse."

"I don't think Tank's the kind of guy you have to impress with a chocolate mousse. He'd probably be happier if you didn't go overboard. I vote for apple pie."

"A lot you know about men. You haven't had a steady man since Fred left town."

"That hurt, Shirl."

"I'm sorry. I forget, you still have memories. All I remember about Fred was the pain he caused you. He was an A-1 jerk. I never could understand what you saw in him."

"Fred was a great dance partner."

"A great dance partner? Don't tell me that's why you almost married him. So the guy didn't step on your toes when you were waltzing. . . . Be reasonable, Gwenn."

"Maybe the trouble with Fred and me was me. I had stars in my eyes. All I saw was his handsome face, nothing else."

"Sure, blame it on inexperience."

"What else can I say. Fred was a jerk, but so was I for caring about him. . . . Look, Shirl, I'd rather not discuss Fred, if you don't mind."

"I don't mind. I'd much rather talk about scorpions, or rattlesnakes or this menu. . . . God, how I want this dinner to be perfect."

"Then have it catered."

"I considered that. . . . Men like it when women are domestic."

"Yeah, domestic like a dog or a cow is domestic. It's best to be yourself. Try the chef's salad."

Shirley was too busy looking through a thick cookbook to hear Gwenn. "French. Definitely French," she muttered to herself as she picked up the books and walked out of Gwenn's office.

A few short minutes later Shirley was back waving a long narrow piece of paper. "I'm off to the grocery store. I'll be gone for a couple of hours."

"Hours?"

"Well, you don't expect me to find the ingredients I need here in town. I'll probably have to stop at a few places in Green Bay before I find everything."

"What did you finally decide to make?" Gwenn's question hung in midair as Shirley whirled out the door. "Well, if Shirley can take off from here like that, I guess it's all right if I take some time to learn a few of my lines." Gwenn closed the file folder that had been open on her desk, took her play book out of her purse and started to study.

CHAPTER 7

Gwenn and Westminster were up and eating breakfast at eight on Saturday morning. A large cardboard box full of wallpaper rolls shared the kitchen table with Gwenn and her oatmeal.

"I can't wait for *him* to get here, Westminster." Gwenn put her empty bowl in the sink and picked up a plastic bucket of wallpaper sizing from the counter. "Why did I tell him to come at nine o'clock, anyway? I can have half the room finished by then."

She restirred the wheat concoction at the table with a wooden spoon. Suddenly Gwenn sneezed. "I hate the smell of this." She breathed through her mouth as she took the bucket into the living room.

The goopy mixture quickly brushed on the wall, covering the smooth painted surface with a grayish film.

When she was halfway around the room Gwenn's arms tired. It was ten minutes past nine. Randal was nowhere in sight. "Who needs Mr. Director anyway?" Gwenn said to the wall. "I'm not waiting any longer. I have to see what that wallpaper looks like up."

In the kitchen, she snapped the cover on the wallpaper sizing bucket and took out the first roll of rose-dotted paper. "Okay, the book says . . ." To refresh her memory Gwenn opened a thick library book and thumbed to the wallpapering chapter. "I already have a line on the wall where I want to start . . . so all I have to do is to cut the first piece."

Gwenn held the roll of paper under her arm as she dragged the infamous ladder close to the north wall and nimbly climbed up. She measured the first length of paper well beyond what the wall required.

As she sidestepped back down the ladder she rerolled the piece rose side in, then sloshed it through a water box on the floor and drew the wet paper up toward the ceiling again.

"This isn't so hard." Gwenn marveled at the way the paper attached itself to the wall. She only had to pull it away from the wall once before it lined up perfectly with her pencil mark. It took time and patience to find all the air bubbles and to brush them out, but Gwenn was satisfied with her first piece of wallpaper when it was finally secure in place.

"I knew I could do this myself," she said as she picked up her extra sharp utility knife and knelt to cut off the excess paper near the floor.

She started to slit the paper crease as her fluffy grey cat came up to investigate. "Not now, Westminster. I'm busy," she said, gently pushing the cat away with her elbow.

The cat didn't listen. It put its inquisitive nose first into the water box. Then, just as Gwenn put the knife into motion, the cat stuck its cold wet nose against her bare arm. *Zip,* the knife moved through the paper, sliced up the wall well past the intended crease and right across Gwenn's left index finger.

"WESTMINSTER! . . . OUCH!" Gwenn dropped the knife, sat back on the floor and grabbed her injured finger with her right hand.

"Look what you made me do!" She indicated the sliced wallpaper to the cat, who was on his way down the hall, heading for the safety of Gwenn's bedroom.

The pain in Gwenn's finger grew with each passing second. Also growing was the stream of blood oozing from between the fingers of her right hand.

The flow of red didn't slow even with pressure. Gwenn knew she needed her first-aid kit and help.

It was difficult to stand up, considering how her hands were occupied. As she uncurled from the floor Gwenn lost her balance, stepped into the water box and fell against the wall. Water drenched her tennis shoes, ran along the wall and formed a puddle by the kitchen entrance.

Gwenn stepped back and shook the water off her feet. There on the wallpaper in front of her were two bloody handprints where she had fallen.

"NO!" She kicked the almost empty water box and sent it sailing toward the kitchen. With one yank Gwenn tore the paper roses off the wall, crunched the sticky paper up into a ball and sent it flying after the water box.

"What's going on in there?" Randal came in through the back door. "Didn't you hear me knock?" He smiled broadly as he stepped over the water puddle.

"Why weren't you here at nine like you promised?" Gwenn demanded. "If you were here I wouldn't have done this." She held up her two very red hands for Randal's benefit.

His eyes riveted on the blood. All the color drained out of his face.

"What's the matter, Randal?" Gwenn stepped forward. "You don't look . . ."

"I've got to get out of here." Randal stumbled back into the kitchen and collapsed on the floor.

"Randal!" Gwenn raced to him. His face was as white as Gwenn's kitchen walls. She touched his cheek with the back of her hand. His skin felt cold.

"Think, Gwenn! What are you supposed to do when someone faints?" she asked herself, but couldn't remember. So she just called his name again and again. "Randal . . . Randal . . ."

He groaned and slowly opened his eyes. Gwenn's big brown eyes were only inches above his pale face. "Is this heaven?" he moaned.

"Hardly."

"Then where . . ." He looked blankly around the room.

"You fainted."

"What!" Randal slammed his fist against the floor. His color returned slowly as he pulled himself to a sitting position, using the white kitchen wall for a back rest.

"No kidding. You fainted."

"I remember seeing . . ." He looked at Gwenn's hands, then looked away as the color drained from his face again.

"Are you ill? Should I do something? Maybe I should call a doctor." Gwenn moved even closer.

"You don't have to call a doctor or anything. I'm not sick," Randal said, hissing his words out through clenched teeth.

"Oh," Gwenn backed away. "You need some water."

"I'll be fine." He continued facing away from Gwenn.

"But you fainted."

"I know *that*." Randal rubbed the back of his neck with his hands.

"Did you hurt your head when you fell?"

"No! Forget about me. I'll be all right in a minute."

"But . . ."

"Listen," Randal cut her off. "If all that red on your hands is blood, you're the one that needs help."

His reminder brought the pain back to Gwenn's consciousness. She unwound the fingers of her blood-caked hand and looked at the injured one. The bleeding had slowed, nearly stopped.

"Can't you do that somewhere else?" Randal shaded his eyes away from Gwenn.

"It's not as bad as it looks."

"You could have fooled me with all that blood."

"Blood. That's it. You fainted because of the blood!"

"I know what happened," he flared. "This is ridiculous. Every time I'm in this house with you I get hurt. You're a jinx."

"I am not. What do you think I did, cut my finger just so I could watch you faint. . . . Though I do admit you did give me a good show. But not quite good enough for this." Gwenn held out her finger.

"I've seen enough, Ms. Nichols."

"It's nearly unbelievable that the great Randal Cochran faints at the sight of blood."

"Now I suppose the whole world's going to find out."

"Not from me they won't, unless you intend to give a public demonstration on the courthouse steps. . . . On second thought it would be a great media blitz. You could stand in front of one of your business and have some little kid show you his skinned knee. . . . Prime time news would eat it up. Think of the free publicity."

"I think that's quite enough, Gwenn. The loss of blood must have affected your mind."

"But the businessman in you should be able to see the benefits of such a public display."

"I said, enough! . . . Now why don't you go clean up so we can get to work on the wallpaper."

"Is it safe to leave you? I mean, a man in your state . . ."

"Very funny. The fact is, I'm better off if you and your blood, your *visible* blood, were in another room."

"I'll leave only if I'm sure you're all right. . . . And if you promise not to sue me because of all this."

"Don't be ludicrous."

"I was only checking. You were ready to sue me for a sliver the other day."

"Get out of here, already!"

"I'm going. I'm going. You don't have to yell." Gwenn stood up, went to the kitchen sink and washed the blood from her hands. "Ouch," she gasped as the warm water ran over the open cut.

"Are you okay?" Randal asked from his seat on the floor.

"Sure. Just as okay as you are, Mr. Cochran."

"Then we're both in a lot of trouble."

"All I need is some antiseptic and a bandage. I'll be right back. . . ." She had to step over Randal's legs to leave the room. "Don't get up on my account," Gwenn said and smiled down at him.

"Ha, ha. You're such a card. Get out of here."

On her way out of the room Gwenn dropped a dishtowel on the floor to absorb the spilled water.

In the bathroom she drenched her finger with peroxide. For a brief moment the bubbling liquid made her finger hurt more. The room blurred. She grabbed the basin for support until the faint feeling passed. It wouldn't do to have Randal find her passed out.

When her vision cleared she opened the first-aid kit. Wrapping her finger wasn't going to be easy. The only bandage large enough to cover the cut was a pad that was held on by a length of gauze. She tried to cut the gauze with the little scissors she kept in the first-aid kit just for such emergencies.

Gwenn struggled to hold the material and work the scissors at the same time with her good hand, with no success. Then she held one end of the gauze between her teeth to stretch it to the proper tautness. The scissors only mauled the bandage material.

Gwenn wondered if Randal could help her.

Cautiously she went back down the hall and poked her head in the kitchen, hiding her left hand behind her back. Randal was standing by the sink drinking a glass of water.

"Feeling better?" she asked.

He turned to face her. "Yes. You?"

"I can't get the bandage on. Can you help?"

He swallowed the last of the water before looking at her straight. "You sure you can't do it yourself?" he asked. Gwenn nodded. "I'll try. Sit down by the table."

Gwenn obeyed, placing her hand on the wooden surface.

Randal took a deep breath before he walked across the room and took a seat next to her.

"You don't look well, Randal. Maybe I should call my neighbor. She . . ."

"I'm fine. Now just be quiet so I can get your finger properly covered."

"I don't want you to faint again."

"I'm *not going to faint again.*" Randal's clenched teeth told Gwenn he was trying to convince himself more then he was her.

He took the gauze and cut it to the needed length, without looking at her hand. Then he quickly picked up the square pad, placed it on her finger, wound the white material around and secured it in place with a knot the size of a walnut. "There. Good as new," he said as he wiped the sweat off his forehead.

Gwenn tried bending her finger. With the bandage in place her joints were immobile. "That's quite a Boy Scout knot you tied there, Doc." She touched the lump of gauze.

"At least it's tied. Instead of putting down my work, you should say, 'Thank you, Mr. Cochran. I'm eternally grateful.' "

Gwenn smiled, ceremoniously picked up his right hand and kissed the back of it. "Thank you, Mr. Cochran. I'll be eternally grateful."

"I'm counting on that." He put both his cool hands around hers and forced her to remain close for a moment.

The humor that twinkled in her eyes faded as she put his hand down and patted his clean-shaven cheek. "If you believe that lie, you're more gullible than I could ever imagine."

"Just waiting for you to underestimate me, Ms. Nichols. Now how about we try wallpapering again. Your finger up to some work?"

"My finger won't get in the way. I'm ready to go to work if you guarantee you won't faint again."

"Guarantee? You guarantee not to have your blood gushing all over the place and I'll guarantee not to fai—"

"Go on, say it. The word's FAINT, Randal. . . . You don't have to be embarrassed about fainting at the sight of blood, a lot of people do."

"I didn't notice you swooning. . . . And anyway, I'm not a lot of people."

"Yes, I know. You're Randal Cochran, super man."

"Make that super businessman and I'll agree with you."

Gwenn walked away from the table. "The wallpaper's waiting," she said.

She was on top of the ladder measuring a second piece of paper when Randal joined her with the freshly filled water box.

"I'll do all the cutting, if you don't mind," he said as he picked up the knife.

"I hope there isn't any of me still on that thing," Gwenn teased.

Randal held his breath and warily looked at the clean knife. "You'd better watch your tongue," he said. "Remember where you're perched. If I f-fell, I could possibly hit that ladder and knock it over. Then where would you be?" He shook the ladder for effect.

"Probably on the floor, on top of your pale body."

The second piece of wallpaper refused to cling to the flat surface. It wrinkled and slid everywhere but where Randal and Gwenn wanted it.

"Are you sure this paper isn't a second?"

"Second? Let me tell you something. I sent away for top-of-the-line paper. For over two months I waited for this stuff," Gwenn said from her ladder seat. "Maybe the problem's you. I didn't have so much trouble lining up the first piece. You sure you can see the pencil line clear enough? I mean, maybe you need glasses." Gwenn peeled the paper back from the wall and tried to realign it.

"I don't need glasses. It's probably your plumb line. It could be crooked. Or maybe the wall's not square." Randal brushed an air bubble out as he worked the paper toward the faint pencil mark.

Gwenn ran nine of her fingers along the paper feeling for air pockets. "Well, what did you expect in an old house like this," she said. "I could have told you the wall wasn't square. Nothing's square."

"I don't see how we're ever going to get this paper straight. You should hire a regular decorator to do the job."

"Sure. And who's going to pay this regular decorator? I'll tell you what, Randal, you go on home and leave my walls to me."

"Certainly not. I want the wallpaper in my house hung properly."

"Let's not get into that your house, my house argument."

"I'm not arguing."

"No, certainly not. I argue all by myself."

"At last we agree on something."

Gwenn pulled the crooked piece of paper from the wall, crumpled it into another huge ball and threw it at Randal.

He easily ducked away. "Temper, temper, Gwenn. Save all that emotion for the stage."

A third piece of paper was measured, put through the water box and ready for the wall when there was a knock on the back door.

"I'll hold the paper, Gwenn, while you answer that." Randal took the dripping wallpaper from her hands.

Gwenn was surprised to find Tank waiting outside the back door. "I thought you weren't coming until after noon."

Tank's heavy eyebrows rose upward as he stared at Gwenn. "It's already twelve-thirty," he said quietly.

"No. It can't be twelve . . ." Gwenn was sure Tank's watch was fast until she saw her own kitchen clock. It read twelve thirty-five. "Randal, you're never going to believe how long we've been working on that one piece of wallpaper," she called loudly to the living room.

When she entered the room she found Randal cutting off the excess wallpaper. The first strip of paper roses was finally in place.

"How did you manage that without my help?" she asked.

"It was because I didn't have your help that I managed to get the paper up. . . . What do you think, Tank? Straight enough?"

"Looks fine to me." Tank stripped off his heavy grey sweatshirt, revealing a white T-shirt clinging to his muscular frame. "Now what do you want me to do?"

The two men took over the wallpapering job. Randal delegated Gwenn to the kitchen to make him a sandwich. Then, after he had eaten, Gwenn was allowed to finish sizing the last two walls.

"This is *my* house," she said. "I want to wallpaper, too."

"You saw what happened when we worked together, Gwenn. I thought you wanted this room finished before Christmas," said Randal. "Tank and I have already pasted three strips of paper up in fifteen minutes."

Gwenn had to agree the wallpaper was going up quicker and smoother with the men working together. But she was disappointed at being left out. The entire kitchen had been finished without benefit of a man's help. If it weren't for Randal butting in, when the entire house was remodeled Gwenn would have been able to say she did all the work herself. Now she wouldn't.

After she finished applying the wallpaper size, Gwenn was allowed to measure and cut pieces of wallpaper for the men.

"The long strips we need now are all the same length. I think you can handle it," said Randal. "And make sure, when you cut, you use a blunt scissor."

At mock attention Gwenn saluted Randal with her left hand, her bandaged finger stopping at her dark eyebrow. "Yes, sir. No more blood, sir."

"That's enough insubordination."

She relaxed her stance as Tank left the wall, finally noticing her bandaged finger.

"Did you cut yourself doing the wallpaper?" Tank asked.

"My escapade with that utility knife you're holding wasn't half the fun Randal and I had this morning. You see Tank when Randal came in he . . ."

"Gwendolyn!" Randal threatened to stuff a smoothing brush in Gwenn's mouth. "You agreed."

She smiled. "I was only going to say if it wasn't for you, I'd never have been able to put this beautiful bandage on." Her smile faded when she added, "No one, *absolutely no one,* calls me Gwendolyn. And if you ever slip and call me *that* name again, well, you can guess what the world will find out about Mr. Randal Cochran. Get the message."

"No problem, *Gwenn,*" mocked Randal. "Let's quit this gabbing and get back to work."

The next piece of paper was up on the wall when Tank said, "Gwendolyn's a respectable name. You shouldn't be ashamed of it."

"I prefer Gwenn, Tank, if you don't mind. I think I enjoy Gwendolyn so much because of the way my mother used to call me when I was a kid. She kind of sang it out the back door and all the kids made fun. What about your real name? You couldn't have been christened Tank."

"My given name's Humphrey. The kids called me Humpty Dumpty Humphrey."

"Where did the name Tank come from?" asked Randal.

"Kids too. I was very heavy when I was young. When the neighborhood kids teased me I would chase them and sit on them."

Gwenn looked at Tank's muscular frame. "You're sure not that kind of tank now. But the name suits you, a lot better than Humphrey. Let's make a pact. I'll call you Tank and you call me Gwenn."

"Fair." Tank reached around the ladder and shook her hand.

"You must be hungry, after all this work. I'm afraid Shirley probably won't have dinner ready until after eight. How about a snack?"

"I could use a glass of fresh orange juice," Tank said.

"Sorry, no juice. How about a cup of coffee or tea, or maybe some soda?"

"No thanks. I like to stay away from caffeine and sodium. I'll take some ice water. . . . Uh, if it matters, I'm also a vegetarian. My sister calls me a health food junkie."

Gwenn's throat tightened. "Oh," was all she could say as she thought of Shirley up to her elbows in the flashiest, richest meal on earth.

Should she call her friend? No, it was too late to change the menu. Shirley had started cooking Friday night. Gwenn figured it would be best if she let Tank tell Shirley his own way. She guessed that no matter how things turned out, it was going to be an interesting dinner.

CHAPTER 8

"I have to admit, the wallpaper looks fantastic." Gwenn walked around her living room. She wanted to run the tips of her fingers over each strip of rose wallpaper, but didn't dare for fear the illusion would disappear.

"What else did you expect?" Randal said as he picked up slivers of paper scraps off the floor. "I wouldn't have my place anything less than fantastic."

Gwenn spun around to face Randal, but she was too tired to make an issue out of the subject. Her shoulders sagged as her brown eyes rolled up toward the ceiling.

"It was teamwork," said Tank. "Remind me to call you both when I start papering my apartment."

Randal stepped forward and put his arm around Gwenn's shoulders. "What do you think, Gwenn? Do you think we'll ever be a team? Have knife, will travel. . . . Oops, I mean scissors."

The telephone rang before Gwenn could think of an appropriate reply.

Gwenn peeled Randal's arm off her shoulder, wiped her hands on his sleeve and walked to the kitchen to answer the telephone.

"Hello. . . . Oh hello, Shirl. . . . I'm sorry, I didn't realize it was so late. We just finished. . . . Yes, I'm more than hungry. . . . No, I don't want all that food to go down your garbage disposal. . . . Now, why would I want to stay home and listen to my radio. . . . Oh, it seems gulf storms can be weird. This one's slow-moving, almost stationary at the moment. Guess the forecasters don't know when it's going to move or where. . . . Fine, when I reach Mom, I'll tell her you were worried too. . . . Don't get so excited about dinner. Give us a few minutes to wash up. Okay? If Robin's hungry, why don't you feed her. . . . No, you didn't tell me Robin was spending the weekend with her friend. . . . Calm down, Shirl. I've got some news for you about Tank. . . . Shirl, you may want to take time for this information. . . . No, Shirl, later will be too late. . . . Shirl? Shirley?" Gwenn hung up the telephone. "Well, I tried to warn her," she thought.

Tank and Randal had all the scraps picked up and tools stored away by the time Gwenn finished her phone conversation.

"We'd better hurry," Gwenn said. "Shirley's waiting for us. I'm afraid if we're not there in five minutes she's going to feed our dinner to her dog. And she doesn't even have a dog."

Randal combed his fingers through his hair. "Hope you don't mind, Tank, but I'm hungry enough to eat a horse."

"Maybe I should go home," said Tank. "I'm sure your friend isn't ready to entertain a vegetarian. I really tried to explain when Shirley asked me, but no one listened." He waited by the back door, eyes downcast, swaying back and forth on nervous feet.

"If you value my life at all, you'll come with us, Tank," said Gwenn. "I'm sure Shirley's prepared for anything. She'd feel bad if you didn't come. . . . And she'd probably blame me."

"I don't know. . . ." He hesitated.

Gwenn went to Tank and looked up, trying to catch his eye. "You're not ashamed of being a vegetarian, are you?" she asked, knowing his reaction.

Tank straightened up immediately. "Of course not. Why should I be?"

"That's right," Gwenn agreed. "Being a health-conscious vegetarian isn't a crime or a contagious disease. I mean, I could see your point if you didn't join us because of some uncontrollable phobia, like fainting at the sight of—" She shook her bandaged finger at Tank, and added "at the sight of a broken fingernail," then coyly smiled back at the man standing directly behind her.

It was Randal's turn to roll his eyes up toward the ceiling. "She's right," Randal finally agreed. He put his arm around her waist. "And think of the stimulating conversation you'd be missing if you didn't join us, not to mention our unabridged wit."

"Maybe you're right," Tank said. "And if all else fails I can always rely on my supply of wheat grass juice to get me through the meal."

Gwenn felt her throat contract. "Wheat grass juice? I'm not going to ask about your wheat grass juice, Tank. I have a weak stomach. And there's no more time for chit-chat. You bring your wheat grass juice and come with us right now. If we wait any longer Shirley may not have anything for you to worry about."

"Then everything's set." Randal sighed. "Should we all ride over together in my car?"

Tank shook his head. "I live in the apartment complex three blocks from Duo Realty. I'd better drive myself."

"I guess it's just you and me, kid." Randal squeezed Gwenn's slim waist.

She wriggled out of his grasp. "Maybe I should drive myself. I wouldn't want to put you out. I mean you'd have to bring me all the way back here."

"Don't be silly. You make it sound like driving you home would take me hundreds of miles out of my way. And anyway maybe I should check back on that wallpaper back there." Randal nodded toward the living room. "Who knows, we could have done something drastically wrong and it will all be on the floor when you return home."

"You're kidding. Aren't you?" Gwenn shivered as she pictured coming back to find the walls stripped bare.

"You never can tell. I've heard stories about just that happening to other novice paper-hangers. Right, Tank?" Randal winked at his male accomplice without Gwenn noticing.

"That's right, Randal," Tank said with a smile. "I even heard about one couple who had an entire wall collapse because of a poor papering job."

Gwenn looked at Randal, her eyes wide open with worry. "You are kidding. Aren't you?"

Randal struggled to keep a straight face. "We'd better get going," Randal said. "Don't want to keep Shirley waiting."

"Oh, Tank, don't forget that old painting of mine for the set." Gwenn pulled the two-by-three-foot still life from the pantry by the back door. "I hope it's tacky enough for the play."

"I like it," said Tank. "On that basis alone, JoJo will consider it properly tacky."

"Enough said," said Gwenn. "Let's go chow down."

Shirley met the wallpapering trio at the door with an overflowing tray of hot croquettes. "The ones with the blue toothpicks are chicken, the ones with the red toothpicks are ham and the others are liver. . . . I'm glad you could finally make it."

Gwenn and Randal both popped hors d'oeuvres into their mouths.

"This chicken's great, Shirl," Gwenn said, still chewing the food. "And your whole house smells fantastic."

Randal only could nod agreement as he ate a second and a third croquette.

Tank sadly shook his head at the tray Shirley held out. "No thanks."

Shirley shoved the tray into Gwenn's hands, twirled around and headed out of the room. Her black silk hostess trousers rustled seductively as she moved. "Don't overdo on the hors d'oeuvres. The best is yet to come. Gwenn, please show Tank and Randal where to hang their jackets."

Randal finally swallowed his croquettes. "I feel underdressed. I should have worn my tux." He brushed at the white splotches from the wallpaper paste on his slacks. The stains were almost identical to those Tank and Gwenn wore.

"I don't think Shirley's noticed how grubby we are," said Gwenn.

"She does seem to be excited," commented Tank. "Who else is coming?"

"No one. We're it," said Gwenn as she showed them the hall closet. "This meal is kind of important for Shirley. Do your best to show her that her company is worthy of her culinary efforts." Tank held the tray of food as Randal helped Gwenn with her jacket.

"In other words no crude noises?" smiled Randal. "Good thing I left my whoopee cushion at home."

"That's not a good start, Randal," warned Gwenn. "You probably don't even have one of those whoopee cushion things at your place."

"You'd be surprised what I have at my apartment. You'll just have to come over and see for yourself."

"Sure, I'll come to your place," Gwenn said out loud. "When roses bloom in January," she finished softly as she hung her coat in the closet.

"What's taking you three so long?" Shirley appeared at the end of the hall impatiently tapping her toe. "The whole meal's going to be ruined if you don't sit down this minute."

"Yes, Mother," Gwenn said as she followed her friend to the dining room. When she stepped into the room a long low whistle escaped from Gwenn's lips. Tall white candles burned in silver candlesticks on a brilliant white lace tablecloth. Four settings around the table had more pieces of china and silverware than Gwenn knew what to do with.

"I'll be right back," Shirley said as she disappeared into the kitchen.

Tank bent down and softly spoke into Gwenn's mop of brown hair. "I don't think my coming was such a good idea now," he said.

"Couldn't you eat one very rich, very unhealthy meal once in your life?" Gwenn whispered.

"I eat health foods because I'm allergic to much of that other stuff.

My body's oversensitized. I get sick. I break out. Maybe I should just say I have a headache. I really do feel one coming on."

"No! Shirley'll think you don't like her if you leave, after she did all this to impress you."

"Impress? Me?"

"I wasn't supposed to tell you . . ."

Gwenn stopped speaking when Shirley came back into the dining room with four shrimp cocktails. "What's all the whispering about? Sit. Sit. After this there's *boeuf bourguignon, oignons à la monégasque, céleris braisés,* and for dessert *tartes aux fruits avec crème pâtissière,* with wine for every course."

Tank cleared his throat. "Your French is very good, Shirley. And the meal does sound tempting. . . . Please don't think this is any reflection on you or your food, but I'm afraid I can't eat."

Shirley faced Tank. The light in her eyes faded. Her mouth opened as if she was going to speak, but no words came out.

He continued, "I'm a vegetarian who's allergic to dairy products. I know I should have said something before. But no one told me you were going to go to so much trouble. My sister said my eating habits would get me in trouble one day. I'm sorry this big lunk caused you so much trouble." He started to leave.

Shirley found her voice. "Wait. Don't go. Can you eat a fresh garden salad?"

"I don't want to put you to any more trouble."

Gwenn blocked Tank's escape route and made a futile attempt to push him in Shirley's direction. "If Tank can eat . . . or drink something he calls wheat grass juice, I'm sure he'd love your salad," Gwenn said.

"Wheat grass juice?" Shirley looked puzzled. "Are you kidding? I need a cigarette."

Gwenn's eyebrows went up as she slowly shook her head at her friend.

"Cigarette?" It took a moment before Shirley understood Gwenn's sign. "No, I suppose I don't need a cigarette."

"Why don't you and Tank work together on that fresh salad, Shirl?"

"I couldn't put a *guest* to work in my kitchen."

Tank needed no more coaxing. He took Shirley by her arm and escorted her into the kitchen. "You've never had a guest like me before, Shirley. And if you're going to the trouble to feed me, well I guess I can do my part and help."

After Tank and Shirley disappeared behind the swinging door, Randal held out a chair for Gwenn. "Somehow I don't think they'd mind if we started without them."

"Maybe we should wait a few minutes," Gwenn hesitated.

The sound of Shirley's and Tank's laughter came through the kitchen door.

"I have a feeling they've already forgotten about us," Randal said and continued to hold the chair for Gwenn.

She sighed and took her place at the table. "You're probably right." Gwenn dipped a chilled shrimp in the spicy red sauce and bit it in half. "I'm sure glad Shirley went with shrimp. I was afraid with the French meal she'd serve escargots. Snails are one of the few foods I've never been fond of."

"That surprises me. I enjoy them."

"Honestly, I've never had the nerve to taste one. When I look at snails on a plate I remember the times when I was a child and caught tons of the little black creatures in a friend's farm pond."

"Escargots are nothing like pond snails."

"I know that. They're bigger. I bet you'd feel different if the only thing you could picture when seeing *escargots* was a bucketful of smelly little black snails. We had a bad habit of leaving the bucket out in the sun for three days after filling it with snails fished out of the stagnant water. Images of *those* dead snails would change your notions about eating that French delicacy, too. I guarantee."

Randal gulped. "Mind if we change the subject? You're doing a great job killing my taste for any seafood with your exposé on dead snails."

"What? Don't tell me you have a weak stomach, too. Maybe you need a little healthy wheat grass juice."

"If I want to eat any grass, wheat, clover or, alfalfa, I'll take mine straight up and graze like all the good Holsteins do in the pastures around town."

"Randal, do you think Tank really drinks wheat grass juice?"

"I wouldn't doubt the man for a moment. His honesty is unquestionable. And besides, he's twice as big as I am."

Gwenn thought for a moment, a shrimp halfway to her mouth. "The way Tank watches his diet and health makes me feel guilty. Maybe I should reevaluate my own diet."

Randal nodded. "We probably all should," he said as he ate a sauce-covered shrimp. "But let's not start tonight. At least not until I'm finished with this meal."

The other couple remained in the kitchen. Gwenn and Randal knew Tank and Shirley were still in the house because the sound of sporadic laughter kept coming from the next room.

"I wonder if Shirley knows how wonderful this food is." Randal took another serving of *boeuf bourguignon* from a warming tray on Shirley's maple buffet.

"I don't think it matters to her anymore. She has all she wants right now, in the kitchen."

"And what is it that you want, Gwenn Nichols?"

"I want dessert." She looked at the assorted individual fruit tarts on a silver serving tray on the buffet. Gwenn finally sighed and chose a cherry.

"That's not what I meant," said Randal.

"I know. Let me think about that for a second. . . . Mother wants me to move to Florida, marry a doctor and have a houseful of grand-children for her to spoil. Shirley wants me to stay her partner and move into an apartment of a suitably small size, which would move me in the direction you want me to take."

"I asked what you wanted for yourself. Not what your mother or Shirley wanted for you, or me, for that matter. There's a difference."

"A big difference," Gwenn agreed. "I want to finish remodeling my unreasonably big house and live in it for the rest of my life. I guess I also want to continue my partnership and friendship with Shirley. We're a good team."

"Does a family of your own fit into your plans someday?"

"Only if I meet a man who has a future that can mesh with mine."

"And what if your plans don't come true? What would Gwenn Nichols do then? Run to Mother?"

"No. I love Mom, but she doesn't remember what it was like when we did live together. We get along so much better since she's moved to Florida and I've stayed in Wisconsin. Where's your mother, Randal?"

"Right at this moment she's in her New York apartment. Tomorrow she'll be in Paris, after that Rome. She loves to travel. Dragged me around the world with her when I was a kid. I sure was glad when I was finally old enough to say no and stay home. . . . Funny, we were never enemies but we do get along better when we only see each other once or twice a year."

"Some people would consider traveling around the world a plus. I've never traveled much. It's interesting to imagine flying from New York to Paris to Rome, but I don't think I'd care to live the life of a vagabond too long. . . . Is that why you want my house? To have an anchor in your life?"

"I'm anchored pretty well in this area with my work. What I want your place for is to house one particular piece of antique furniture."

"That's a bit out of the ordinary. Most people buy furniture to fit their house. But of course you have to be different. You buy a house to fit your furniture. What's so special about this antique of yours."

"Would you like to see it?"

Gwenn nodded.

"Then finish your dessert and I'll take you to it."

"Right now?" Gwenn looked at Shirley's wall clock. It was almost ten o'clock.

"You're not worried about offending our hostess? I believe we'd do her a favor if we were out of the way."

Gwenn put the last of the rich tart in her mouth and pushed her chair back from the dining room table. "I'm too full to move and we couldn't possibly leave Shirley with this mess." She gestured at the two sets of dirty dishes. "We should at least offer to wash these."

"Offer away. I'm betting they'll be glad to see us go."

Randal was right. Shirley wouldn't accept Gwenn's offer to help.

"Did you like the food?" Shirley asked. She sat at her tiny kitchen table, Tank at her side, his legs stretching halfway across the room. A mountain of raw vegetables was before them on the table.

"It was heaven," said Gwenn. "There's quite a lot left. We did our best to eat for four, but couldn't quite manage more than eating enough for three. Do you want me to put the leftovers in your refrigerator?"

"Nonsense. Tank will help me clean up. You both go on. I'm sure you're tired after all the wallpapering you did today."

The warehouse complex Randal drove Gwenn to was located on the west edge of town between a lumber company and acres of nursery trees.

Randal stopped his car so that its headlights lit up a small private entrance next to a twelve-foot warehouse door, one of ten large doors in the side of the long metal building.

"It's in here." Randal left the car keys in the ignition and took another set from his pants pocket. He approached the door, rattled the handful of keys for a moment before he found the correct one for the lock, and held the door open for Gwenn.

The warehouse area was deadly quiet. Gwenn hesitated, her car door ajar. "Don't you have to check in with a guard or someone before coming out here at this hour? We might be mistaken for thieves and end up with the police surrounding this place."

"Don't worry. The guard probably recognized my car. And anyway the police wouldn't be prompt to investigate. Bet it would take them hours to respond to a call. They're too busy directing traffic at the high school football game tonight."

"This antique better be worth my time," Gwenn said as she joined Randal at the door.

"It is. It is." He guided her forward into the black void and reached for the light switch, but didn't click it on. "You'll be surprised."

The few quick steps Gwenn took into the immense dark room made an eerie echo in the blackness, bouncing off an unseen wall and returning to her.

Gwenn stopped at the end of the headlight beam. Randal stood in the doorway, a huge shadow illuminated only by the car lights.

"Can't you find the light switch, Randal?" she asked.

He laughed menacingly. "Are you always so trusting, Gwenn? A man, a relative stranger, drives you to a deserted warehouse, and you expect him to switch on the light." Randal's voice had an unearthly tone.

Cold waves pulsed up and down Gwenn's spine. "Don't be ridiculous," she said with forced bravado. "Switch on the light, Randal!"

He blocked the exit, stretching out his arms, holding both sides of the doorjamb. "What if I didn't? What if I locked you in here for my own pleasure? You're a very beautiful woman, Gwenn Nichols, even with your wallpaper paste decorations."

This can't be happening, Gwenn thought as she backed into the darkness. One step, two, three. She could go no further; a huge canvas-covered object blocked her way. "Randal, you're scaring me."

"Good. You should be scared. You don't know me at all, Gwenn. Haven't you ever had the slightest feeling I was a bit crazy, trying to buy your house just for one piece of antique furniture? What if I was a maniac who brought his victims out here before killing them?"

"If you think this is going to influence me into selling, you couldn't be more wrong." Gwenn tried to swallow the lump in her throat. "And anyway, who ever heard of a murderer who faints at the sight of blood?

Don't make me laugh." The laugh she tried to squeeze from her throat never happened.

"There doesn't have to be any blood and if there was, well it's too dark to see it." He laughed a deep threatening laugh.

"You're kidding. I know you're kidding. You're just trying to get even because I discovered your secret when you fainted at my place this morning. . . . I don't like this, Randal. I'm going to scream!"

"Go right ahead and scream. No one would hear you. The guard's probably asleep or watching television."

Gwenn didn't care, she was going to scream anyway. She took a deep breath.

Randal laughed again, but this time it was natural, human. He hit the light switch. Twenty overhead lights lit the warehouse as if it were daylight. Shocked out of blackness, Gwenn had to cover her eyes so they could adjust.

"I'm sorry, Gwenn." Randal's voice sounded very ordinary. "It just occurred to me when you walked into the dark warehouse, you could have set yourself up for a lot of trouble. No one knew you were coming here with me. Think of this as a lesson. Never trust anyone."

She released the breath she had held for the scream. "That was a rotten thing to do. I don't think I want to take any more life-saving lessons from you. . . . I do have to say your performance was quite believable just now. Maybe you should be *in* the play instead of directing it," Gwenn said.

"My acting stinks. Chalk it all up to special effects." Randal switched the lights off and quickly back on. His smile broadened. "I couldn't help myself. I swear it wasn't premeditated, just a spur-of-the-moment impulse."

"You do realize that I have to get even with you for this—this *lesson.*"

"I suppose I should expect retaliation. But honestly, I didn't plan to scare you when I invited you out here."

Gwenn held her hand against her forehead. "I still can't comprehend that you did this to me. What if I had a heart condition and dropped dead right here in this warehouse? How well do you know *me*, Randal? What's written in my medical file? What would you tell your landlord when you were found here with my very dead body? That your practical joke got out of hand?"

Before Randal could answer, a heavy man wearing a grey uniform

came into the warehouse. "Mr. Cochran," the guard said, looking surprised. "You're not going to move that *thing* tonight?"

Randal slapped the man on his broad back. "No, Jake. The house
isn't ready for it, yet. But I'll have it moved out by Christmas, I'm sure.
Tonight, I thought I'd show it to a friend."

"You're not supposed to play bad practical jokes on friends," Gwenn
said in a near-whisper.

Jake touched the visor of his cap in acknowledgement of Gwenn and
turned back to Randal. "You sure do pop up at the strangest times, Mr.
Cochran," said Jake. "The other guys I worked for never showed up
anywhere near the business after quittin' time."

"Hope that doesn't bother you too much, Jake. I'm not about to
change my work habits. . . . I hear your wife had an operation. How's
she doing?"

Gwenn listened as the men discussed Jake's home life, his wife and
their five teenagers and their problems. She was more confused than
ever.

"Well, I best finish my rounds, or the boss'll have my head." Jake
chuckled and left.

"One more thing, Jake." Randal walked out with the guard. "Has
anyone from Millin Industries been here that you know of?"

Gwenn couldn't hear Jake's mumbled reply. Whatever he said an-
gered Randal.

Randal's last words were loud. "Doesn't anyone listen to me around
here? No more barrels from Millin, or some people will be looking for
new jobs. . . . Make sure everyone on the day shift knows that, Jake!
I'll be back tomorrow afternoon to make sure they understand my orders."

After the guard had disappeared Randal returned to Gwenn. "As I
was about to say, Gwenn . . ."

Gwenn put her hands on her hips. "Who the heck are you, Randal
Cochran?"

"Now that's the idea. But you should have asked me that question
hours, no, days ago. I guess I'm the landlord."

"Landlord? Of what?"

"Of these." He waved his hand upward toward the ceiling. "These
warehouses are just part of my business life, so is the Westside apartment building complex where I live and a few other odds and ends in
the area."

"Odds and ends? That's really telling me a lot. I don't care to be treated like a child, Randal. I think you should take me home."

"But you didn't see my antique treasure yet."

"That antique again. It's probably a figment of your very vivid imagination."

"This is no figment," Randal said as he tugged the canvas down and revealed an ornate oak bar.

Gwenn gasped. "It's beautiful." She ran her hand over on the glossy surface, touching the intricately sculptured wood. Her fingers traced the twists and turns until they stopped at the corner, fifteen feet from the other corner. There Gwenn touched the naked breast of one of the bar's two mermaids.

Her hand dropped to her side. "You want my house for *this?*"

"Yes. I plan to devote one whole downstairs room to this bar. I know where I can get an old gaming table and four chairs that would go perfectly with the decor I have in mind. Bookshelves would line the opposite wall and I also have a painting that would hang right above . . ."

"A painting! Just a second. Let me close my eyes and envision the painting you would put above a bar like this." Gwenn closed her eyes and cocked her head to the right. "A reclining nude draped in red satin. . . . Randal, where did this bar come from?"

"There's an antique dealer on the north side of Chicago who just became rich from the sale. . . ."

"I'm not talking about any antique dealer. You know what I meant. Where did it *originally* come from?"

"A house, kind of like yours."

"It did not come out of a house like mine. And it'll never be in a house like mine. Tell me, Randal. Where did this come from?"

"Okay, okay. What do you want me to say? That this beautiful, hand-carved, *expensive* antique bar came from a brothel? So what if it did? You have something against prostitutes?"

CHAPTER 9

"Then he had the gall to ask me if I had something against *prostitutes*? Can you believe it, Shirl? He wants my house for a brothel bar. A brothel bar!"

"Huh?" Shirley looked up from her cup of coffee. "What's that, Gwenn? Randal bought a brothel?"

"Something wrong with you, Shirl? Ever since Saturday you've been walking around in a fog. It's Monday afternoon, girl. Wake up. Randal isn't buying a brothel. He has this antique bar *from* a brothel. . . . Oh, what's the use. Why don't you go in your office and have a cigarette?"

"I gave up smoking."

"I can't believe it. Shirley, my partner, the person who has been a human chimney since she was fifteen, gave up puffing. When did all this happen?"

"What's the big deal. You know I've tried giving up that disgusting habit before. . . . I thought about it again Saturday night and considered it after lunch with Tank yesterday. But I finally quit for good after Tank took me for coffee this morning. He pointed out how unhealthy . . ."

"You mean you haven't had a cigarette since ten o'clock? Wow, a new record!"

"Go ahead, make fun. I know I've failed before, but this time I'm going to make it. Tank's helping me. Poor thing. The smoke makes his eyes water."

"Mine too. . . . But of course, my eyes don't count. I'm not Tank Lormar. . . . Boy, he must be something special."

"He is. . . . Do you think you could handle the office? I'd like some time off to do some shopping and I really could use the afternoon to get my hair done."

"I suppose so . . . if it's for Tank's benefit. Any guy that can get you to stop smoking is a miracle worker."

Shirley only smiled.

Blocking rehearsal Monday night was hectic and more.

Randal half frowned from his theater seat when JoJo raced into the theater five minutes late. "Not the best way to get on the director's good side, JoJo," Randal said as he glanced at his watch.

"I'm sorry. I'll do better. But if it's your good side I want to get on, I'll try this instead." JoJo leaned over and kissed Randal's right cheek. "Or maybe this side is better." She kissed his left cheek. "Or maybe . . ."

"I get the message. Now up onstage, JoJo."

The actress obliged by sliding her bottom up onto the stage and gracefully swinging her legs up to a cheesecake pose. "I'm onstage," she said.

Randal barely looked up from his clipboard. His expression didn't change.

"Hey, JoJo, how about getting on my good side?" said Charlie Harris. He held out his hand and helped JoJo to her feet.

"Me too," said Keith from his position in the left wing's shadow. "My good side could use a kiss or two. My bad side wouldn't mind it either."

JoJo chose to laugh at both men's requests. "Later," she said and brushed her hand over Charlie's five o'clock shadow.

A tan couch stood almost center stage, a pine coffee table directly in front of it. Off to the right, near the cardboard fireplace, was an overstuffed blue flowered armchair. A free-standing reading lamp and a knitting basket looked ready for a knitter next to the chair. Half of the set's walls were newly painted peach. The rest were still a faded blue color, a memento from the last play set.

Gwenn's high school painting rested against the couch. JoJo walked up to it. "This is perfect!" she said. "I'd even ask my own mother to hide this painting in the attic. . . . No, that's not quite right. I'd insist Gwenn's painting be hung right next to the furnace in the basement."

"Thanks, JoJo," said Gwenn. "I knew we could count on you to be the company art critic."

"Oh, Gwenn, don't be so sensitive. You can't tell me you expected me to say anything else. I mean, just look at it."

"No, you're right, JoJo. You said almost exactly what I expected you to say."

"Then it's settled," said JoJo. "We all agree this painting of Gwenn's is perfectly tacky and should hang over the fake mantel." She pointed a shiny silver fingernail stage right.

"The painting will hang on the back wall," Randal said without looking up from his clipboard.

"But Randal, didn't it say somewhere in the script about the painting being over the mantel?"

"Maybe. But the director said the painting will be on the back wall. Enough with set arrangement. Let's get started with blocking. Gwenn and Lyle are the only people on stage. Everybody else disappear." The mischievous prankster was again the able-bodied director.

"Edna will be dusting the coffee table when the curtain's pulled. Henry will be seated on the couch with his feet up on the coffee table. Before anything's said Edna will push Henry's feet off the table. Any questions? . . . No. . . . Lyle, start."

The first lines came easily. Gwenn automatically moved around the table, using her imaginary dustcloth. Then it came time for Lyle's first kiss.

She tried to sidestep away from Lyle.

"How am I supposed to learn to perform this kissing right if you won't let me near you?"

"I just thought for blocking we could skip . . ." Gwenn blushed.

"Ms. Nichols," Randal called her from his seat in the audience. "I'd like to speak with you for one moment."

When Gwenn went to Randal he spoke so softly she had to bend down to hear him. "We don't want to create hard feelings, Gwenn. We all have to work together if this play is ever going to come together. . . . You're going to have to let Lyle kiss you, sooner or later."

"But he's an undertaker."

"I believe he prefers the term funeral director. . . . I'm afraid you have no other choice, Gwenn. You'll just have to swallow your petty prejudices while you're acting in this play. Pretend he's a shoe salesman or something else safe."

"Like a director/businessman?"

Randal looked up from his notes for the first time and smiled. "Director? Businessman? You've got to be joking. We know they're not safe. . . . You're a good actress. Pretend your heart out when Lyle has to embrace you. Imagine the special man of your life."

"I'll try. But don't blame me if Lyle's kiss gives me hives."

"We'll just use more makeup." Randal stood up and spoke so Lyle could hear him on stage. "Ms. Nichols understands the importance of the kiss. Gwenn, pick up the scene with, 'Well, I changed my mind. . . .' "

This time through Henry kissed Edna. Lyle put his arms around Gwenn's shoulders and soon his moist lips crossed hers.

Inside, she cringed. But the actress won the battle. Gwenn pretended Lyle was someone else. To her surprise her imagination substituted the director for Lyle Thurst.

The kiss didn't bother her one bit after that. In fact, it was kind of pleasant. Afterwards, Gwenn decided it would have felt even better if Randal Cochran weren't trying to buy her home for his godforsaken brothel bar.

Thoughts about the bar stuck with Gwenn throughout rehearsal. The more she thought about the antique in her house the more wrong turns she made on stage.

"It would be better if you walk to the left of the couch," directed Randal. "Stand closer to Lyle. . . . Closer." "Exit through the kitchen. . . . No, that's the closet door, Gwenn. Pay attention." Gwenn's pencil broke twice as she tried to keep up with all Randal's directions.

Gwenn was so wound up in her own thoughts she didn't hear all the floor marks and advice Randal gave to the other cast members until Charlie moaned, "Hey, give me a break. I can't write that fast. My hand's cramping." He shook his right hand to relieve the cramp.

"I know this is taking forever tonight," said Randal. "But after this rehearsal I don't want to have to do any more blocking. In fact, I'll probably never look at my blocking notes again. It'll be up to you to remember where you're supposed to stand and through which door you're supposed to exit."

"Isn't that your job?" asked Charlie. "Aren't you supposed to tell us where to go?"

"I'll tell you where to go, Charlie," said Keith. "It'll be my pleasure to tell you to go to he—"

"Only your character can tell my character that," laughed Charlie.

"Maybe it's time for a short break," said Randal as he stretched up from the theater seat and walked toward the stage. "Be back here in five minutes. Gwenn, I'd like to ask you something."

Gwenn sat on the edge of the stage and scribbled a blocking note in her play book. "No, you cannot put that brothel monstrosity in my house."

"Can't you think of anything else but your precious house? I wanted to know if you could knit."

"Oh. No, I can't."

"Learn. There's a part in the second act where Edna has to actually sit and knit."

"Can't I fake it?"

"Knitting isn't that hard to learn."

"You know how to knit? Then you can teach me."

"I don't know how to knit. And I'm surprised you asked me to give you another lesson."

"Forget the knitting. I don't have time to learn. It's a struggle enough to find time to learn my lines. What if I crochet? I know how to crochet."

Randal scribbled a few words on his clipboard. "I guess that will have to do. But I did have my heart set on a handmade sweater when this play is over." He looked up from his notes, a twinkle in his blue eyes.

"If I knitted you a sweater one sleeve would be four feet too long and the other sleeve twelve inches too short. Would you settle for a scarf?"

"I don't think I'd care to have you wrap anything around my neck right now. Thank you. I might not survive the giving."

"It's not the gift, but the thought that counts."

"Yeah, and I know what you're thinking." Randal cocked his head and held up his loosened tie in a mock hanging.

"Hold it right there." Gwenn leaned back and used her hands to frame Randal. "I'd like to immortalize you in just that pose. I only wish I had my camera with me. It would be an honor to properly hang the great Randal Cochran, on my wall, of course."

He released the tie and chewed on the eraser end of his pencil. "Before you get too carried away, I have another question."

"Is this question from Director Cochran, Businessman Cochran, Buyer Cochran or Practical-Joke-Player Randal?"

"Which would you prefer—A, B, C, or D?"

"At the moment, none of the above. . . . I'm going to miss my break." She started to walk away.

"What are you doing for lunch on Thursday?"

Gwenn stopped walking and spoke without facing Randal. "I don't know. Who's asking?"

"Just little old me. . . . I swear I won't open my mouth once about your house."

Gwenn turned and faced him. "And not one word about that *thing* you're keeping in your warehouse."

Randal raised his right hand. "Not one single solitary syllable about the bar."

"Well . . . I did promise to see Mae."

"More groceries?

Gwenn nodded.

"If you ask me," said Randal, "Mae has stocked enough provisions this last week to open her own store."

"I feel sorry for her. Mae's all alone. She only wants company."

"She could move to town."

"How would you feel if you lived most of your life in one house and everyone you talked to said to move like it was nothing? That house of hers is filled with memories. You just don't understand. You never really had a home like that."

"Maybe you're right. But I am trying to rectify that situation by acquiring your home."

"You promised, Randal."

"I said I wouldn't say a word at lunch on Thursday. And I won't if you'll just give me an answer. Yes or no?"

"If you want to come with me to Mae's and visit, I suppose it'll be all right. She likes you, for some unknown reason."

"I'll pick you up at eleven-thirty."

The other actors wandered onto the stage, each carrying a cup of hot coffee.

JoJo was the last to walk in. She moved slowly, juggling two full cups of coffee. "I thought you might like a drink too, Randy, dear." She leaned forward to hand Randal the coffee, allowing her partially buttoned shirt to give him an ample view of her full breasts.

"Just what I needed." Randal smiled while accepting the coffee and the offered view.

Gwenn felt a bit self-conscious at the other woman's boldness. Automatically her hand went to her own plaid shirt's neckline. Every button was in place. She couldn't help but wonder if Randal's eyes would widen so large if she revealed as much flesh as JoJo.

The second act brought Lyle's and Gwenn's lips together again. The kiss was not to be abrupt, ending as the first one had, with Lyle being pushed away. It was written to be a kiss of passion, with both parties participating.

Lyle's arm was heavy on Gwenn's shoulder as they sat center stage on the couch waiting for a cue from the director. "I like the way this guy wrote this play," said Lyle as he pointed out the next scene in his play book for Gwenn. "At least his stage directions make sense. 'Kiss with feeling; passion.' Now that's my kind of smooching. How about if you and I rehearse a little on the side, Gwenn? How about Saturday?" He tightened his hold on her shoulder.

Gwenn leaned forward, shielding her eyes from the stage lights. "Sorry, Lyle. I'm busy Saturday. . . ." Gwenn searched the theater shadows for Randal. "Can't we get this over. . . . I mean, what's holding us up?"

"I'll be right with you," said Randal from the last row of seats. "I'm afraid we're going to have to move the chair to the right more, so we don't block the audience's view for the last scene."

"Move the chair wherever you like. Let's just get finished before midnight!"

"What's wrong, Gwenn? Anxious?" Randal's teasing voice was coming nearer.

"*I* sure am," said Lyle.

"Lyle, we're supposed to be actors," said Gwenn. "Kissing in a play isn't supposed to mean anything to us."

"Don't go taking the fun out of this play for me." Lyle bowed his head. "Pretty soon you'll have me thinking of it as work."

"Please don't talk to me about your work, Lyle," said Gwenn. "Even in passing. . . . Are you ready, Mr. Director?"

"Yes, proceed."

The two actors on stage read their lines of love. Gwenn closed her eyes when Lyle's face neared hers for his kiss of passion.

She tilted her head to an appropriate angle and prepared to imagine her way through another kiss. But Lyle surprised her.

Lyle wrapped his arms around her, trapping her arms to her sides. His mouth was all over hers, smothering the breath out of her. Lyle even tried to insert his tongue, but failed.

Instead of the feeling of "passion" that was written for her, Gwenn felt mauled.

She opened her eyes and started to struggle. It took all her strength to pry her arms free and push Lyle Thurst off her, onto the floor.

"Lyle!" she screamed. "What do you think you're doing?"

The actor looked stunned as he rubbed his elbow where it had smacked the coffee table. "It said with passion," he whimpered. "I was only trying to do what the scene called for."

She was on her feet, above his prone form. "That wasn't passion! That was . . . That was . . . RAPE!"

"Gwenn, let's not get carried away," Randal said as he walked up on to the stage and offered Lyle a hand up off the floor.

Lyle cradled his arm. "She called my kiss *rape*. Did you hear her, Randal? Rape. The idea."

"It sure wasn't passion, Lyle." Gwenn's voice was lower, but still distressed.

Randal turned his back on Gwenn and faced Lyle. "As director of this play, Lyle, I can say I honestly don't think the scene called for as much . . . as much enthusiasm as you read into it."

"It said to kiss her with passion, didn't it?"

"Yes, but I'm the director and I have the last say on how much passion you should exert. Right?"

"Oh . . ." Lyle stammered. "I was only acting."

"Maybe so. But I think your *acting* took Ms. Nichols off guard. It probably would make her feel better if you apologized."

"Apologize?" Lyle's eyes never came up from investigating a knothole in the floor. "Oh, okay. I'm sorry, Gwenn. . . . I only want to do a good job. I thought if I kissed you like they do in the movies . . ."

"Lyle, we're in Wisconsin, not Hollywood," said Gwenn. "And if you ever forget that fact again while you're kissing me onstage I'll stop you with my knee, and it won't matter if it's during a rehearsal or a performance for a packed house. Do you understand?"

He winced. The idea of Gwenn's knee hitting a sensitive part of his anatomy was not a pleasant thought. "I understand, all right. What I'm not quite sure about is how I'm supposed to kiss you." Lyle looked at Randal. "Tell me, exactly what is a passionate Wisconsin kiss, Mr. Cochran?"

The entire cast was onstage by this time, intently listening to the discussion.

Charlie elbowed Keith. "Go on, Keith. Show Lyle how he should kiss Gwenn. But watch out for her knee."

Keith hid behind Charlie. "No thanks. I'm not kissing anyone passionately tonight. I may want kids some day."

JoJo stepped center stage. "Randy, you're the director. You're the one who knows what kind of kiss this scene calls for. Why not show all of us what you want? I'll even volunteer. Kiss me the way Lyle should kiss Gwenn."

Lyle agreed with JoJo. "Yeah, go on, show me how I'm supposed to kiss. My Mama never taught me the proper way to kiss. I guess I'm ready to learn from an expert."

JoJo went to Randal's side. "Should we sit on the couch?" she asked as she walked her fingers up his shirt sleeve.

The director looked from one cast member to another. "You really want me to demonstrate what kind of kiss I want?"

It was unanimous, except for Gwenn who abstained from voicing her opinion.

"Okay, if you think it will help clarify the situation."

JoJo took Randal's hand. "Let's sit on the couch just like they were," she said enthusiastically.

But Randal didn't allow himself to be led. "I think it would be better if I kissed Gwenn," Randal said. "She's the one who has the most at stake here."

"Oh . . ." JoJo's lower lip came out in a childish pout as she stepped back.

"We're all waiting, Mr. Director. Show us all how to kiss," said Lyle.

Randal looked at Gwenn. "You willing?"

Gwenn folded her arms across her chest and looked him straight in the eyes. "As I understand it, this is supposed to be a demonstration of a passionate Wisconsin kiss. Right?"

The director nodded.

"I'm willing then."

The two sat on the couch. Gwenn moved tight against the armrest. Their audience, three men. JoJo had disappeared.

"Watch out for her knee, Randal," warned Charlie.

Randal's arms reached out toward Gwenn. She shivered and leaned away. Randal wasn't deterred. His hands touched her shoulders and slid around to her back. Each slow movement pulled Gwenn closer and closer toward him.

In a moment their bodies were against each other. Randal's lips met Gwenn's. They were soft, inviting. Gwenn's arms automatically found their way up to Randal's muscular shoulders. Pleasure tingled through her body.

As the kiss continued, Randal's hands stroked her hair and her back. Gwenn had never felt more alive.

Then his lips parted from hers. A sigh escaped from Gwenn. Randal's face remained inches from hers. He smiled, then winked.

"There," said Randal as he turned away from Gwenn and faced the three male cast members. "I think that about does it for passion, Wisconsin style."

The warmth of Randal's touch cooled quickly. Too quickly for Gwenn. His abrupt departure made her feel like she had been dropped into an icy pond.

Randal, the prankster, the actor, had again given her an unwanted lesson. He had shown her in less than half a minute that he could make her feel like a woman, then release her as if she were a manikin.

Gwenn was shaken. She remained on the couch, reeling from the feel of his flesh against hers, trying to hide her flushed face from any spectators.

While Gwenn worked at controlling her feelings, Randal walked across the stage, joking with Charlie about allowing him to rehearse a kiss with JoJo.

As the others left the stage Lyle came to Gwenn's side ready to do his imitation of Randal's kissing scene. Gwenn didn't want his hands on her. She preferred to let her body remember Randal's warm touch. But she was an actress and she was determined to treat Lyle as a set prop, nothing more.

Two lines led up to the kiss. Lyle gently put his arms around Gwenn and cautiously set his lips on hers. She closed her eyes briefly and imagined Randal's arms working their way around her body, exciting every nerve they touched, and more.

But this time the embrace was different, hesitant, wary. There was nothing there to make her body warm.

Halfway through the kiss Gwenn opened her eyes in a vain effort to find Randal's face next to her own. Lyle's questioning gaze met hers.

The kiss concluded. Lyle released Gwenn as if he were handling a china doll. "Was that acceptable?" he asked.

"It was an improvement over your first attempt." Gwenn wanted to add, "But you'll never kiss as well as Randal Cochran." Instead she held her comment to herself.

Their kiss onstage was nothing to the director, Gwenn was sure. His body movement as he walked away from the couch told Gwenn he had forgotten what her body felt like, how her perfume smelled, the second his arms freed her. But Gwenn remembered his hands on her shoulders, in her hair and on her back even after she had slipped between the sheets of her bed later that night.

"Westminster," she said to the cat sleeping on the pillow next to her head, "I'm beginning to think doing this play is a big mistake." Gwenn yawned. "He's too close. Randal's just too close. Worse yet, I like it. Too bad I don't mean anything to him."

CHAPTER 10

The tropical storm had moved and gained strength; at least that was what Gwenn's Wednesday afternoon newspaper said. It had become a full-fledged hurricane, Hurricane Sam. What worried Gwenn was that the storm continued to travel toward her mother.

Gwenn dialed Florida when she read this last report. There was no answer at three o'clock—or at four—or at five.

"Come on, Mom. Be there," Gwenn said to the unanswered phone. "Your daughter's worried about you and your very first hurricane."

Shirley walked into Gwenn's office, gnawing her pencil's eraser, as the phone was hung up after a fifth try. "No luck?" Shirley asked.

Gwenn solemnly shook her head. She reached up and pointed to Shirley's pencil. "Don't forget yourself, Shirl," said Gwenn. "Out of habit you might try to put a match to that pencil. Puffing on lead or graphite or whatever's in a pencil would probably be worse for your health than a cigarette. . . . And I'm sure Tank wouldn't approve." She checked her watch and lifted the telephone receiver again.

"Tank didn't force me to quit smoking. I wanted to. . . . You realize the hurricane's still hundreds of miles away from her," Shirley said as she looked at the newspaper. "Those things are so unpredictable. Sam could fizzle, kind of the way my ex-husband did."

The phone was clicked back onto its cradle. "I know I'm overreacting. But Mom doesn't know anything about hurricanes. She may think she should hide in a basement, like we do for tornadoes. And maybe she should. I don't know. What I do know is that she'll get excited. She'll go absolutely crazy when she remembers she doesn't have a basement under her mobile home."

Shirley plucked the pencil out from between her lips and popped a piece of strawberry gum into her mouth. "Tell me, Gwenn, how many hurricanes have you been in?"

Gwenn smiled weakly. "So there aren't many hurricanes coming west off Lake Michigan."

"Then how do you expect a telephone call from you to help your mom?"

"I don't know what I want to tell her. Maybe she doesn't know the storm is coming. . . . Maybe she lost her car keys again and can't go inland. . . . Oh, all I know is that I have to talk to her."

"Your mom's been around, Gwenn," said Shirley. "She's probably made hundreds of friends down there already. People living in those trailer parks look after one another. Someone's bound to tell her where to hide or what to do."

"I have to talk to her," Gwenn said as she picked up the telephone to try one last time from the office.

Gwenn dialed from her home every fifteen minutes until it was time to go to rehearsal.

"What if Mom phones when I'm gone?" She looked hopelessly at Westminster who was curled into a ball and purring on her lap. "You sure can't take a message, can you?" she said as she stroked his soft fur.

Gwenn considered incurring the wrath of the play director in her effort to remain close to the phone. She giggled out loud when she thought about the phone call to Randal.

"Sorry, I can't come to rehearsal tonight, but there's a hurricane moving toward Florida and I have to talk to my Mommy."

"Well, well, well," said JoJo as she lazily stretched her leg over the couch armrest onstage. "Look who's late tonight."

Randal was checking his watch when Gwenn walked in fifteen minutes late. "I was almost ready to call the police to see if you weren't waylaid by some stranger . . . other than myself." He gave her a half smile.

She didn't answer his smile. "I'm late. Shoot me." Gwenn's nerves were too tight for teasing.

The director's lips uncurled. "Something wrong?" he asked.

"Nothing you can do anything about, I'm sure." Gwenn carelessly tossed her coat on a theater seat. "And since everyone has been waiting *patiently* for my arrival, I won't waste another precious minute. Let's get started now."

"Gwenn, could you open this first?" Lyle handed Gwenn a small box wrapped in silver paper.

"Thank you, Lyle, but you didn't have to go to all this trouble just to apologize again for that kiss."

"It's not from me," said Lyle. "I apologized Monday night. And once is enough. This was sitting on the stage when I arrived."

The handwriting was familiar. Gwenn didn't want an audience when she opened the package. "It can't be anything," she said as she slipped the package into her sweater pocket. "I'll open it later. I don't want to delay rehearsal any longer."

Randal allowed Act One to be completed before he stopped the play and gathered the cast onstage. "Gwenn," he said as he checked his notes, "your volume isn't quite what I expected. Project more. . . . Lyle, you're moving stiffly. Relax. If you learn to relax during rehearsals you'll have less trouble when we have an audience. . . . JoJo, I know you're supposed to be snippy, but hold the big guns for Act Two . . ."

"But, Randy," said JoJo, "I was having so much fun picking at Gwenn. She's the perfect target tonight. I'll be even nastier later, you'll see. I don't have to tone down, do I?"

"Too heavy for the first act, JoJo, even if you can get meaner. Remember, I'm the director. Let's take a short break before continuing."

Gwenn walked to the back room without saying a word. She wished there was a pay telephone in the theater as she plopped a teabag in a cup of hot water. A noisy chatter filled the room as the others joined her. Gwenn left before anyone had a chance to speak to her. She needed to relax in the shadowed theater.

As she waited for her tea to cool she remembered the package.

Her name was printed boldly on a card on the top of the little box, but nothing else was written there. She opened it. Inside she found a gold chain with a pearl pendant. Under the tiny white globe was Randal's card and another offer on her house, five thousand dollars higher than his last.

She looked up to find Randal watching.

Methodically she picked the paper out of the box and tore it up into as many pieces as she could manage, before placing the offer back in his hand.

He let the paper scraps dribble through his fingers onto the floor. "Does this mean I can't take you to lunch tomorrow and visit with Mae?"

Gwenn rubbed her temples. "Randal, you're giving me a headache. . . . How can I possibly have lunch with you? You promised not to mention buying my house."

"I said I wouldn't bring up the subject tomorrow and I won't. Tonight's a different matter."

The necklace caught the stage light and glittered in the box. Gwenn took it out and drew the ends together at the back of her neck. "I wonder if I'm going to have to declare all these gifts on my taxes."

"Maybe I should claim you as a dependent," said Randal as he took the necklace from her struggling fingers. "Hold your hair to one side," he said as he fastened the clip for her. "Somehow I don't think the IRS would go for me claiming you unless I manage to get a signature on a marriage certificate first."

"A marriage certificate? I thought all you wanted was my signature on a bill of sale. . . . No matter. I'm not signing anything. I'll just consider this an early Christmas gift," said Gwenn as she fingered the pearl.

Randal's fists went deep into his pants pockets as he moved the pieces of paper on the floor with his foot. "You might be sorry some day, destroying my offers so quickly the way you do," he said. "The time will come when you'll be eager to sell to me. When that happens, and it will, I'll probably have forgotten about all these generous offers I've made to you. Then you'll have to settle for my original . . . or less."

"If you ever forget the offer, it will because so much time has passed. Senility will have set in by then and affected your mind."

"I wouldn't count on my reasoning abilities going downhill that fast before Christmas, Gwenn." Randal smiled. His eyes sparkled in the light as the necklace had.

Gwenn didn't want to look at his handsome face a moment longer. "If you don't mind, I don't feel like worrying about your state of mind, no matter how pleasant the thought of your senility might be." Gwenn leaned her head back and closed her eyes. "I happen to have a splitting headache that's fighting for my total attention."

"Will five minutes of quiet help?"

"Probably not, but I'll take it." Gwenn did not fake the headache. The pounding at her temples felt as if the cannons from the *1812 Overture* were being fired point-blank at her head.

The stage and the actors were ready for Act Two.

Gwenn was about to open her mouth for her first line when JoJo marched across the stage to where Gwenn sat rearranging Edna's knitting basket. "Gwenn," JoJo said, "that necklace won't do, no it won't do at all. Edna would never wear anything like that. You'll have to take it off."

"No one could possibly see that necklace from the audience. I can barely see it from here," Keith commented from the dark wings. "And anyway, JoJo, this is a rehearsal. The necklace isn't important."

"It is to me," JoJo said with a toss of her blonde mane. "It throws off my concentration."

"Was that what was in the package?" asked Lyle.

Gwenn nodded.

"Who was it from?" Lyle walked closer to view the necklace.

Gwenn looked at Randal who was watching the stage from the audience. "No one, at least no one important," she answered matter-of-factly. But silently Gwenn wondered if her answer was honest, especially regarding Randal's significance in her own life.

"I would think, if the necklace isn't important and the giver isn't important, we should forget about it and him and move on to Act Two," said Randal.

"But my concentration," whined JoJo.

"You're only concerned because the necklace wasn't left for you, JoJo," said Keith. "If the package was marked with your name we wouldn't be having this silly discussion."

"This isn't a silly discussion. . . . And if I was wearing that necklace it would be suitable for my character. Edna would never own anything so elegant—so Gwenn shouldn't wear it."

"JoJo, you're not helping my headache," Gwenn said as she took the necklace off and set it on the coffee table. "Does that make you feel better?"

A slim smile was JoJo's answer. "Randy, I'm ready to start Act Two."

As Gwenn took her place onstage she wondered what JoJo would have said if she knew the necklace was from Randal. Probably JoJo would have put on a dramatic scene that would make this last episode pale in comparison.

It was sure JoJo would never understand Randal's odd attempts to win the old house from her.

Gwenn wasn't sure if she herself understood them—or her peculiar reaction to the man himself.

Half way through Act Two Tank and Shirley showed up with paint-brushes and a gallon of paint. There was a brief whispered discussion in the audience with Randal before the actors were stopped onstage.

"Excuse me," Randal said as he strode up to the stage. "Would it bother anyone if Tank and Shirley painted the back wall while we rehearsed?"

"I'm sorry," said Tank. "But I've been working overtime and this is the only time I'm free to do the work."

Everyone said the painting wouldn't bother the rehearsal, except JoJo.

"How can I concentrate if I'm tripping over paint cans and painters?" she said as she looked down at Tank in the audience. "I think they should wait until we're finished. . . . But I'm only an actress. I'll leave the decision up to you, Randy. You're the director."

"Thank's for noticing, JoJo," said Randal. "Go ahead with your painting, Tank."

JoJo spun around on her pointed heels and walked off the stage. Randal sighed. "I said you can paint, Tank. Get started. Remember, I'm the one in charge. . . . I think." He followed JoJo to the back room.

When JoJo and Randal returned a few minutes later JoJo was beaming. "Well, what are you all standing around gawking at? Let's get on with the act. I have a date afterward." She looked at Randal and smiled.

Randal didn't look directly at anyone. "You heard the direct . . . JoJo. Pick up the action with Gwenn's last line." As he talked he disappeared into the back of the theater.

For ten minutes the rehearsal went along quietly. It wasn't until paint fumes filled the stage area that JoJo reverted to her normal self.

From offstage she whispered too loudly, "Where did you ever find such awful-smelling paint, Tank? Some kind of bargain basement sale, no doubt."

Tank and Shirley ignored her comment, silently painting side by side.

When JoJo entered the stage for her next scene she held a tissue over her nose and mouth.

"I can't understand you, JoJo," said Randal. "Is that really necessary?"

"Yes it is." JoJo walked across the stage to the footlights. "My stomach is doing flip-flops. I'm a very sensitive person. I can't tolerate foul smells. You're out there. You don't know what it's like up here, Randy."

"What about the rest of the cast? Paint smell too much for you?"

The men shook their heads.

"Gwenn?" Randal asked.

"I'm not thrilled with the paint smell. But it's only for tonight. I'll survive."

"Then let's not waste any more time. Keith, repeat your last line. Continue."

"The painting too?" JoJo looked as if she was about to cry.

"Yes, the painting too," answered Randal.

"Then you'll have to move in closer if you want to hear me," said JoJo through the white tissue. "I plan on using this the rest of the rehearsal."

Randal did not move. "Keith . . ."

The play advanced, even with the tissue over the lower half of JoJo's face. Gwenn decided she'd prefer it if JoJo held the white material over her whole face. That way she wouldn't have to watch her eyes either. The daggers JoJo was throwing toward Shirley and Tank every time she neared the painters were almost unbearable.

Gwenn caught her friend's attention after JoJo managed to kick Shirley's foot while crossing to the kitchen door.

Shirley smiled and winked at Gwenn.

Maybe that wasn't Shirley kneeling next to Tank after all. Gwenn checked again to see if some even-tempered person was impersonating her friend. The old Shirley would have given JoJo a vicious tongue-lashing for remarks hurled at Tank. The new Shirley continued painting.

After the final scene was finished, and after Director Cochran advised the cast of his feelings about their interpretation, Gwenn went up to the impostor. "The person I work with wouldn't have let JoJo's remarks go unchallenged. I don't think I know you, madam. Let me introduce myself; I'm Gwenn Nichols."

Shirley stood and wiped her peach-spotted hands on her peach-spotted jeans as she moved away from Tank. For Gwenn's ears only she said, "I considered decking the witch. . . ."

"You are Shirley then. I wasn't sure," said Gwenn.

"Tank thinks JoJo isn't worth my trouble. He's probably right." Shirley handed Tank her paint-soaked brush. When he walked off the stage, a familiar gleam popped back into Shirley's eyes. "It'll take Tank a while to clean up. Let's hurry outside and let the air out of all of JoJo's tires."

"Or dump sugar in her fuel tank," Gwenn said quitely.

"Now you're talking."

"But, like Tank said, she's not worth it."

"Right. . . . Have you heard from your mother, yet?"

Gwenn sadly shook her head.

"I think you need a Shirley cure-all, Gwenn. Why don't you go home, run a hot bubble bath, listen to soothing music, relax and let the rest of the world . . ."

"Worry itself to death." Gwenn finished the sentence before Shirley could finish it with one of her crude expressions. "Best idea I've heard all day. See you tomorrow."

As Gwenn walked to the back door she heard JoJo giggle. Gwenn couldn't help but glance over her shoulder to the dark corner where Randal and JoJo stood.

It was definitely time for her to let the rest of the world worry about itself.

On the kitchen table at home Gwenn discovered her mail and a note from her neighbor. "This was left in our mailbox by mistake. Thought I'd bring it over in case it was important."

Gwenn picked up one white envelope. It was an insurance bill. Behind it, almost ignored, was a postcard with a photo of a long white beach. She quickly read the short handwritten message on the back. "Gwenn, I finally drove north to visit my friend Ada. It has been cloudy here. But I'm still managing to have a good time. I'll be home in a few days. Love, Mother.

"Is this supposed to make me feel better, Mom? I still can't call you. I don't even remember your friend Ada's last name." The card was from Panama City, Florida. Knowing the city did not jog Gwenn's memory.

Not expecting an answer, Gwenn dialed Florida. The phone kept on ringing. "So what else is new, Mom?" she asked silently. The receiver made a hollow click as Gwenn replaced it.

Gwenn tried pacing to release some of her nervous tension. The pacing only made her nerves tighter. She searched for another solution.

Fifteen minutes after she had walked into the house, water was surging into Gwenn's monstrous old claw-footed tub, making mounds of perfumed bubbles.

As the water filled the tub Gwenn stripped out of her clothes and slipped into the silk robe Fred had bought her in Tokyo. She hadn't been able to wear the flowered robe for months after he left, but now the memories weren't quite so sharp. Gwenn knew he was gone forever.

Would she have any pain after Christmas? No, Gwenn told herself adamantly. There were no feelings between Randal and her, yet. There would be nothing to miss.

Gwenn prepared for her ritual bubble bath. At the back of the refrigerator she found a half-full bottle of dry white wine.

"White goes with fish. Doesn't it, Westminster?" she said as she tossed a withered hot dog down to the waiting cat. "It's time to forget about Mother's storm and Randal's pestering. . . . Tonight I'm going to be a mermaid, a mermaid in an ocean of bubbles. Red wine wouldn't be proper for a mermaid. Anyway, I'm out of red."

She chose a crystal wineglass from her keepsake cabinet, collected at least a dozen assorted candles from around the house and brought everything to the bathroom.

Lavender, green, blue and white candles were placed on every flat surface available, even on the windowsill. Gwenn lit each candle with a long fireplace match. That was part of the ceremony.

Click, she switched off the bright electric light. Instantly the room lost its modern atmosphere; instead it possessed a golden glow reminiscent of times long gone.

"Something's missing," Gwenn said out loud. She snapped her fingers as she remembered. In a moment she had her portable stereo in the room blasting one of Bach's Brandenburg Concertos. She hid the black stereo box partially in the closet, so its plastic image wouldn't interfere with the golden atmosphere.

Slowly, Gwenn allowed the robe to move down her velvety skin. When it lay in a heap on the floor she stepped into the white mound of bubbles. Her moves were deliberate, cautious. She did not want to upset the glass of wine she carried into the tub with her.

It took many minutes of warm water, bubbles and Bach, but finally Gwenn cleared her mind of all physical and mental torment. She became one with the music, one with the regal strains of the violin, one with those of the flute. For a short time at least Gwenn Nichols felt free of earth itself, until the bathroom door was banged opened.

"Randal! What in heaven's name are you doing here?" Gwenn instantly sunk further into the water, her chin beneath the bubbles. She had no trouble making her voice loud enough to be heard above the loud music.

He opened his mouth to answer but closed it again. Randal walked into the room and turned the Bach concerto down. "I thought teenagers were the only people who blasted their eardrums out with music. You shouldn't abuse Bach so, Gwenn."

"Randal, I'm in the tub!"

"Obviously. . . . I knocked on the back door for what must have been five minutes. All I could hear was that music."

"So you decided it sounded so great, you'd come and join me?" Suddenly the tub water turned icy. Gwenn shivered.

"I thought maybe you were in trouble or something. Remember when I walked in last Saturday. . . ."

"And you thought you'd rush in here and faint for me?"

"I don't know what I thought. Do you always leave your door unlocked?"

"The back door lock has been broken for as long as I can recall. But that doesn't matter. Randal, why are you standing in the middle of my bathroom?"

"You left this tonight." He held up the pearl dangling from the gold chain.

"You could have left it on the kitchen table or given it to me tomorrow at lunch, or better yet, not given it to me in the first place. I don't care for all the strings attached." The bubbles tickled Gwenn's nose. She sneezed. "If you don't mind, Randal . . ."

He looked around the candlelit room. "Very interesting bathroom you have, Gwenn. I never realized you liked candles so much. . . ."

"I am not conducting an open house, Randal. Please leave."

He finally obliged. But he only left the bathroom. When Gwenn emerged from her bath, wearing her silk robe, she found him seated by the kitchen table. The necklace was still in his hand.

"I thought you and JoJo had an appointment after rehearsal," said Gwenn as she poured herself a second glass of wine.

"She's at Bennie's, waiting. You see, I had this errand to run."

"Your errand is over. You may go on your way." Gwenn walked away from the table to stand in the doorway leading to the rest of the house.

Randal gently placed the necklace on the flat wood surface. "I'm in no hurry. You could offer me a glass of wine."

"Please, don't make things difficult, Randal. I don't want to have to force you to leave."

"What makes you so certain you could force me to do anything?"

"Please . . ."

He stood and slowly walked toward Gwenn. When he stopped he was inches from her still damp body.

Gwenn's breath came in short gasps, but she didn't retreat.

His hands came to her shoulders. Gwenn didn't look up. She stared straight ahead, though her eyes didn't actually see his opened jacket. Her vision blurred as she whispered, "No."

Randal didn't stop. He brought a hand to her chin and tilted her face upward. Then he brought his face to hers and kissed her, slowly at first. But as his mouth moved over hers it grew hungry and warmth turned to heat. Soon his strong arms lifted her off the floor.

All the breath left Gwenn's body. She felt too weak to fight Randal. But deep down she knew she didn't want to struggle. She enjoyed the touch of his hands, his lips on hers. Gwenn Nichols knew she was in love again with a man who would walk away from her as if she were invisible.

"Stop." Gwenn turned her face away from Randal. "Put me down." Her whispered protest sounded weak even to her ears.

Slowly, Randal released Gwenn. She held onto the door frame as he backed away. Randal ran a shaking hand through his thick brown hair. Gwenn imagined he was clearing thoughts of her out.

"God, I'm sorry. I never meant to do that," he said.

"What did you mean to do when you came barging in tonight?"

"To hand you the necklace. Nothing else. Honestly."

She held out her hand. Randal retrieved the necklace from the kitchen table and put it in the center of her bubble-scented palm. "Now you can leave, Mr. Cochran. Your errand is completed." Gwenn's fingers formed a fist around the necklace and brought it to her breast.

"Don't let this incident bother you," Randal said as he backed to the door. "Treat this kiss like the last. Just an acting lesson."

"You were better off when you didn't say anything. . . . Good night, Mr. Cochran."

"Until tomorrow, Ms. Nichols."

CHAPTER 11

"Don't you believe in locks?" Randal asked as he put his head around the door to Gwenn's private office.

Gwenn closed the file she had been working on. "I never thought much about locks until you walked into my life. The next time I'm at the hardware store I'll have to check out their display and install their most secure model on my back door."

"Don't worry. It shouldn't be too expensive. The contractor I brought out to your house last week said . . . ."

"You had a contractor at my house! When?"

"I didn't want to bother you. We only looked around, took some measurements, that was all. Honest, we didn't hurt anything. . . . Do you realize it's going to cost twice what I'm offering you to properly remodel that house. Two main support beams in the basement need replacing and . . ."

"And . . . and nothing! You and your contractor don't have to worry one more minute about *my* house or *my* beams."

"Weak supports can't be ignored. . . . I thought you'd like to know, that's all."

Gwenn frowned. "You've done your duty. I'll give those beams the proper amount of worry and care that are due them. And I would appreciate if you wouldn't take strangers on tours of my house without permission."

"Sean isn't a stranger. I've known him for years."

Gwenn pursed her lips the way her mother had done when she was upset with her little girl Gwendolyn.

"Okay, no more tours. I'll make myself a note on that." He took a pencil from his breast pocket and wet the sharpened tip with his lips. "All set for lunch?" he asked.

Randal's voice sounded normal to Gwenn. It was obvious he had put last night's incident in the kitchen out of his thoughts. The kiss hadn't mattered to him.

Gwenn was angry. The kiss had disturbed her more than Randal's

unannounced tour. His touch, his physical presence affected her so.
. . . It was exasperating. She had tried to wipe the feel, the taste of
Randal from her lips, but the kiss lingered on in her memory.

"Maybe I should go alone to Mae's today," said Gwenn.

"I promised not to mention buying you-know-what. I swear," he
said, bringing his right hand into the office so she could see it, "I won't
even open my mouth once on that forbidden subject. In fact, it won't
even cross my thoughts. All you have to do is say you don't want me to
bring up a particular subject, you'll find I'm more than willing to oblige.
Any time you want me to drop . . ."

"Randal! That's enough."

"What? You mean I'm not allowed to talk about not talking about
buying your house? Okay, you got it, kid. For you, I'll zip my lip. I'd
like you to know, not everyone gets Randal Cochran to shut up. . . ."

"Have you been drinking? Because if you have you can forget lunch."

"It's too early to drink. . . . Can I go with you to Mae's if I give
you these?" Randal stepped into the office. Out from behind his back
came a bouquet of flowers. He smiled and winked at Gwenn.

She didn't look at the colorful blossoms but searched through the
red, pink, and white flowers.

"No card today," Randal said. "It's my day off."

"Are you sure you're Randal Cochran?"

"I think so."

"Then this must be a dream."

He leaned closer. "Want me to pinch you and wake you up?"

"No, thank you. If you're giving me flowers just for the heck of it,
and you're not drunk and I'm not dreaming then *you* must be sick."
Gwenn touched his forehead with the palm of her hand. "Nope, no
fever," she said. "Then I must be the one who's crazy."

"If the flowers are bothering you so much, I'll take them back."
Randal put his hand over hers and they held the bouquet together for a
moment.

"I'll keep the flowers, thank you." Gwenn took total possession of the
bouquet again. "If there was no offer, then why bring me flowers?"

"No big mystery. As I walked to my car I passed a little old woman
selling flowers on the street corner. Her tattered shawl and shabby dress
got me right here." Randal touched his tie below his gold tie tack. "I
bought her entire stock."

Gwenn sighed. "I've never seen an old lady selling flowers on a street
corner in this town before."

"I should think not. She said she was from Pembine and was working her way south for the winter."

A smile crept across Gwenn's lips and finally turned into a laugh. "You don't give me a chance to be angry at you. Do you?"

"I take it, from your reaction, you don't believe me. . . . Well, maybe I got her story wrong. Maybe she was an undergrad working her way back to UCLA. Anyway, all my friends will benefit from her ingenuity today."

"God bless that little old lady then. . . . If you don't mind, I'll share these with Carol and Shirley."

But Gwenn couldn't share her bouquet. Shirley had daisies on her desk and Carol violets. She shot a questioning look at Randal.

He shrugged. "I told you I bought out her entire stock. That old lady probably hopped a bus with the proceeds from the sale and is halfway to Chicago by now."

Randal yawned as he set Mae's groceries in the back seat of his car next to the bouquet of orange mums he had for her. "Didn't get much sleep last night," he admitted.

"Oh? . . . JoJo and you had a good evening?" Gwenn couldn't hold back the question. Now the flowers had meaning. They meant guilt.

"JoJo? Oh, I guess so. Mostly a business call . . ."

Gwenn didn't wait for him to finish explaining. "She's very pretty," she said as she took her place in his car.

"JoJo? In a flashy sort of way, I guess."

Gwenn shook her head. "I could never be like her."

"And why would you want to imitate JoJo?"

"She's got style."

"Some people might think JoJo has style. But you have something she will never have. You have . . ."

Gwenn interrupted again, "And JoJo has money. Or at least her family has money."

"Money. Flash. I'll grant that JoJo has both. But you have . . ."

"I know. I have an old house you want to own."

"That's not what I was going to say. And I would prefer if you didn't put words in my mouth, if you don't mind. . . . What I was about to say was that you have sensitivity. . . . Why in the world are we wasting our lunch talking about JoJo, anyway?"

"Then what should we talk about? What do we have in common, Randal?"

"A great deal. We both admire antiques, good acting and Bach. I'd say that's more than most couples can claim."

"I should hope other people start a relationship with more than that."

"Relationship? Are we starting a relationship?"

Gwenn tried to laugh lightly. It was difficult. If she closed her eyes she could feel his lips on hers, feel her body warm to his touch. "You can hardly call what we have a relationship, Randal."

"What would you call it then?"

"I'd call it trouble."

"Then why did you let me come with you today?" he asked.

"Honestly, I don't know."

"The play is coming along fine, Mae," said Randal before putting a forkful of tuna casserole into his mouth.

Gwenn watched from across the table, as he swallowed a glutinous mixture of tuna and noodles. He didn't even flinch. Randal's acting abilities were coming in handy again.

"Your tuna casserole is wonderful, Mae" said Gwenn. "You'll have to give me your recipe. It would come in handy when unexpected company drops by." She smiled as Randal graciously turned down a second helping.

Randal sipped at his steaming cup of coffee. "Any luck finding a buyer, Mae?"

"Gwenn brought some people out here the other day," said Mae. "They were a real nice couple; wanted to get out of the city. They seemed kind of interested until I got talking to them."

"Mae," said Gwenn, "if you're ever going to sell this place you're going to have to stop telling prospective buyers your tall tales."

"Tall tales nothing. I only told 'em the truth. There was a bear outside my back door once."

"When was that?" Randal asked.

Mae looked thoughtfully at the ceiling as she tapped her chin with her finger. "I just can't seem to remember the exact date. . . . But I sure do remember that bear a-gruntin' and a-growlin' out there."

"Mae." Gwenn sounded stern. "You told me that bear turned over your garbage barrel some time during the Depression."

"See. I told you it wasn't so long ago." No one could let that lie pass, not even Mae. They all laughed.

Randal caught his breath first. "I'd like to help you, Mae," he said.

The old woman patted his hand. "You are. You can bring my Gwenn out here any time. I'll take all the company I can get."

"My pleasure," he said. "But what I meant was when you do sell and move to a retirement home, let me make things easier. I'll happily buy all your furniture."

The color drained from Mae's cheeks. "Buy my Len's furniture?"

"Yes, but only after you sell your home, of course."

"Don't worry, Mae," said Gwenn as she looked at the lines of distress in Mae's face. "You don't have to sell anything or move into that retirement home, yet. It could be months, years, before I find anyone who wants to live way out here."

"You think so, Gwenn?" Mae's face brightened slightly.

"Sure. I'll even wager you'll be able to get a couple chickens next summer to scratch up your yard."

Mae gazed out the window. "I'd like that. They don't allow chickens at any old people's home."

Gwenn threw Randal a look that warned him not to open his mouth again. "I wouldn't start worrying about moving yet, Mae," she said. "Spring and summer's when people usually buy homes. We're way past the moving season. Kids are in school. No one wants to move in the winter."

"But my niece said . . . ."

"Your niece isn't in the real estate business like I am. She doesn't know how long it can take to sell a home these days."

Mae shook her grey head. "She acts like I ring her up every half hour asking her for a favor, or money, or something. I can't go calling California but once or twice a year: Christmas and her birthday. . . . She wants to put me in a home, so I can die. Then she wouldn't have to be bothered with me any more."

"Don't say that, Mae." Gwenn knelt in front of the old woman and held her hand. "You're not ready to die. There's too much life left in you. Right, Randal?"

"I . . . I didn't mean to upset you, Mae. Gwenn's right. Don't worry about selling the furni—"

"See," said Gwenn. "Randal agrees with me. And anyway, you're tough as shoe leather. No home would want you."

It took ten minutes for Gwenn to bring Mae out of the depression Randal had inflicted with one sentence. By the time they were leaving she was back to her old talkative self.

"Remember I want more cranberry juice the next time you visit. And if you bring grapefruit juice by mistake, you'll just have to drink it yourself. I can't tolerate the stuff. Every time I drink grapefruit juice little red bumps pop out all over my neck."

"What in God's name were you trying to do back there?" Gwenn's question flew across the car as Randal turned onto the highway.

"What was I doing? I thought you were trying to sell the house for her! You brought out prospective buyers, didn't you?"

"Those people needed a much larger house. They would never even consider Mae's place."

"Then why bother?"

"I have to show Mae's California niece I'm trying. She expects a weekly report. If Mrs. Blomerich gives the listing to someone else at that ridiculously low price, the house would be snapped up."

"Isn't that what you're here for, to sell the house?"

"Randal, I'm convinced, after talking to Mae and her neighbor Phyllis, that old woman would rather die than move. I wish you hadn't said anything about buying her furniture."

"How was I supposed to know?"

"You should consider people's feelings first. Mae has feelings. JoJo has feelings. I do too. For that matter I guess even you have feelings. All humans do."

"Thanks for at least classifying me as a human."

"Humans also think, Randal. You didn't back there."

"I'm sorry."

"So am I. You can forget coming on these luncheon visits from now on." Gwenn leaned over and switched on the car radio, bringing their conversation to an end.

After the music concluded a news broadcast began. "Hurricane Sam has hit the coast of Florida south of Tampa. . . ."

With great effort Gwenn managed to listen to the news report without including Randal in her silent hysteria. The man driving the car was too much into her life already. She would not allow him to get another handhold. Gwenn also knew that when she was emotionally drained she was vulnerable, very vulnerable.

A pocket radio went with Gwenn to rehearsal that evening. She listened to it every time she was offstage.

The hurricane was ravaging Florida but national news broadcasts in

Wisconsin gave only scant thirty-second reports on its status. Certainly not enough information for Gwenn.

During an unscheduled break in play practice, after Lyle tripped over the floor lamp and they stopped to sweep up the shattered light bulb, Gwenn ran coatless to the corner gas station pay phone to dial her mother again. Since Sam's arrival all telephone lines in the greater Tampa area were down. All she heard was a recorded temporarily-out-of-order message.

Lyle stopped Gwenn as she raced back onstage. Her cheeks were flushed and her hair windblown. "Aren't you feeling well?" he asked. "You look sick, Gwenn."

"Oh, I'm fine," she lied. "I had to make a call to the—the office. I forgot to tell Shirley about a new listing."

"Nothing's worth ruining your health over. And I should think a message like that could have waited until morning. No one's calling your business at this hour."

"You get calls at odd hours, don't you, Lyle?"

"Of course, I do. But we're speaking about two entirely different operations."

Gwenn shrugged and took her place onstage. "The call *was* important."

Sleep was a stranger to Gwenn that night. She spent most of her time pacing through the unused rooms of her large house, estimating the thousands of dollars needed to finish remodeling.

But nothing could take her mind away from the hurricane.

"Mom, I hope you're still in Panama City with your friend What's-Her-Name," Gwenn thought. "They say Sam wasn't so bad up there. . . . Oh, be safe, Mom."

By morning Sam had lost his spunk and was raining on Georgia. Damage reports along the coast of Florida were extensive.

Gwenn unlocked the real estate office door red-eyed and exhausted. It took a moment before her eyes could focus on Shirley, who was standing by Carol's desk, dressed in a long lavender robe. "What are you doing here, Shirl?"

"What do you mean, what am I doing here?" Shirley snapped at Gwenn. "I work here."

"Oh," Gwenn said. "You need a nicotine fix." She plopped herself into the first chair she could drag her weary body to.

"I do not *need* a cigarette." Shirley straightened her disheveled hair. "I have not *needed* a cigarette since Monday."

"Of course, you always come in here and rummage through Carol's pencil drawer in your bathrobe. . . . What, no Tank last night?"

"No, he had to work." Shirley sagged into the secretary's chair and sucked on the end of an unsharpened pencil.

"I think you should give Tank a call, Shirl. You definitely look like you need him . . . or a few quick puffs on a filter tip."

"I'm up to my armpits with your advice, thank you. . . . And you should talk about appearances, dear. You don't look your usual Miss Mary Sunshine self this morning. I wouldn't throw stones if I were you. . . . No word from your mother, I take it." Shirley's last words were marked by deep concern.

Gwenn shook her head.

"Sleep at all?"

"Once I nodded off. I distinctly remember because when my head hit the kitchen table I woke up." Gwenn gently touched a round purple mark near her right temple.

Shirley picked up the telephone receiver. "I guess I'd better cancel my appointment at Karen's Kountry Kurl. They will have time to fill my time slot if I notify them right away."

"I thought you and Tank had a spectacular weekend planned."

"We do."

"Then why cancel? You've got the entire day off to baby yourself."

"I can't leave you here in that condition. You need sleep."

"Yes, and you need a cigarette."

"Great-looking partners we make," said Shirley. She thought a moment, then threw the pencil across the room. *"I don't need a cigarette!"*

"Way to go, Shirl. Now move your rear out of that chair and make sure you get the works at Karen's. You deserve it."

Shirley stood up and looked at Gwenn. "You need sleep."

"But I'm not going to be able to close my eyes until I hear from Mother. So I might as well be at work as at home. Here I might accomplish more than pacing."

"Only if a client isn't frightened away by those blood-red eyes of yours."

"So, I'll call Carol and tell her to pick up some eye drops when she comes in. . . . Get! I'll be fine, Mommy."

"Don't call me that! I feel old enough when Robin calls me Mom."

"Then get over to Karen's and make yourself look and feel young,

Ma. I'll be fine. Promise." Gwenn pushed herself out of the chair and gave her partner a shove toward the back door. "Don't worry about me. Think about Tank."

"And who will you be daydreaming about to make your day go quicker? Randal?"

"Sure. I'll dream about Randal, if that will make you happy and get you to Karen's."

"Really, Gwenn. He'd be a good catch."

"So you've said, many times. . . . But I'm not fishing."

"Not even with string and a safety pin?"

"I don't believe there is a season for someone like Randal Cochran."

"I'll say. He's a rare one, an endangered species."

"Shirley, you're stalling."

"No, I'm matchmaking. I'm happy with Tank. I want to see you happy, too."

"I don't need a man to be happy."

"I don't either, but having Tank around doesn't make life any happier, it's made it blissful."

"Then take your blissfulness over to Karen's and get it overhauled." Shirley saluted. "Yes, sir. . . . I mean, Yes, ma'am."

Carol woke Gwenn at her desk with the phone call at three-thirty. "I think it's your mother. The connection is terrible," said Carol.

"Mom? Oh, Mom! I was so worried. Are you all right? . . . I'm glad you stayed at your Ada's place." Gwenn pulled a tissue from her desk drawer and dabbed at the tears spilling out of her eyes. "Oh, no, the hurricane destroyed your beautiful mobile home? . . . A tornado? I thought you had a hurricane? . . . No, I didn't know they could come together. I thought we only had tornadoes in the Midwest. . . . But you're all right and that's all that counts now. Don't worry about the rest. . . . What do you mean you didn't have a chance to buy insurance on the home! Oh, Mom! Didn't I remind you enough times about insurance? . . ."

Gwenn ended the conversation thirty minutes later. "Keep calm, Mom. It could have been worse. You could have been in the mobile home when it was blown apart. . . . I'll be down as soon as I can hop a plane to Panama City. We'll drive back and pick up the pieces together. . . . I love you, too, Mom."

Wide awake again, Gwenn spun into motion. As she rummaged through her purse for her checkbook she called loudly to the outer office. "Carol! See how soon I can fly to Florida. . . . Panama City. I want to leave immediately."

The checkbook balance didn't please Gwenn when she found it. Enough for the air fare but not much more. Her savings account book was in her desk drawer, somewhere.

She pulled out paper clips, dry pens, notebooks, and hundreds of other assorted scraps before finding the little blue book hidden under the desk blotter. Six hundred fifty-three dollars and forty-seven cents wasn't going to help to reestablish her mother in Florida, but it was a start.

Carol came into the office with Gwenn's seven o'clock flight reservation.

"Great. That will give me time to pack. Carol, would you be a doll and keep Westminster company while I'm away?"

"Sure. I love that old hairball. Where can we reach you?" Carol asked.

Gwenn laughed. "Don't have any idea. It all depends what we find when Mom and I drive to what's left of her place. From what her neighbors told her there isn't much salvageable. . . . We may stay with her friends, we may have to find a hotel. Don't worry about calling. The telephone lines will probably take awhile to repair."

"What about Shirley?"

"Tell her I'll be back as soon as possible. I'll call and tell her when to pick me up at the airport. . . . Carol, don't let anyone else know what has happened. If a client asks about me, say . . . say I'm out of town, that's all. I'll explain everything after I see Mom. I don't want any mixed-up rumors floating around town."

"You mean like the rumor about you and Shirley opening an exercise salon here instead of this real estate office?"

"Isn't that how you got your job here, Carol?"

"Yeah, all I was calling about was your aerobic class schedule." Carol patted her own well-developed hips. "I'm still in need of that exercise class. Think we could branch out, use your living room or something?"

"Don't joke about my living room. I may not have one very long," Gwenn said sadly. If her mother's world was blown away she might have to reevaluate her own future and goals. That included owning her grandmother's house.

"What are you talking about? You're not planning to remodel your living room into something different, are you? Like a billiard room?" Carol looked confused.

"I'm just babbling again. Forget it, Carol. I'll be my cheery self once I see Mom. . . . Don't forget, don't tell anyone, *absolutely anyone,* where I've gone. . . . I'll ask my neighbor to drive me to the airport."

Gwenn raced home, threw her nightgown, a pair of jeans and a blue blouse into her overnight bag.

"Westminster, I'm going to leave you with Carol again. You be a good boy this time. Leave her parakeet alone or not one Kitty Cat Cookie when I come home."

She grabbed the box of dry cat food from under the sink, tucked it under one arm with her leather bag, and with Westminster securely in the other arm she left the old house.

Gwenn was back in Wisconsin late Tuesday afternoon. Shirley met her at Austin Straubel Airport.

A cool breeze off Lake Michigan made Gwenn shiver and hug her coat tightly as she walked to the car. "Shirley, Mom's fine," she said. "Right now she's sharing a bedroom with an eighty-year-old retired schoolteacher from Des Moines. Half of a double bed will have to do until a new home can be set on the foundation."

"Were there a lot of houses destroyed?"

"Mom was one of the few unlucky ones. The tornado touched down. Blew away one block, then it went back into the clouds. The government didn't find enough damage locally to consider it a disaster area. . . . There goes Mom's low interest loan."

"How's she taking everything? Has all the excitement bothered her heart?"

"Mom surprised me. She was relatively calm and composed when she picked me up at the airport. But I made her stop at her doctor's for a checkup before we went to see the rubble. Her blood pressure was up, but not much, considering. The doctor said not to worry. . . . Sure, it's not *her* mother. Not worry? She's got to be kidding."

"Could much be salvaged from the house?"

Gwenn shook her head. "Probably find half her stuff floating in the Atlantic, things were blown so far. Found two thirds of her sofa in the neighbor's carport, or what was left of the carport."

"It sounds absolutely terrible. . . . I'm glad it wasn't my mother. She falls apart so easily, I'd have to sweep her up with a dustpan."

"Mom's furniture was ruined, really everything. What wasn't blown apart was drenched. . . . . You know what upset her the most? Her photo albums. We didn't find a sign of them. When she realized they were gone, that's when she broke down and cried."

"I expected to see her come back to Wisconsin with you," said Shirley.

"We discussed the possibilities. Mom weighed all the options, benefits and drawbacks, including the hurricane, and decided she hadn't felt so physically well in fifteen years. She chose to stay and leave the winter and the snow to me. . . . Have there been any calls for me?"

"Calls? The phone hasn't stopped ringing. Mae called about every half hour. I finally had to tell her where you went. I didn't want her having a coronary or anything."

"Mae. I should have told her myself. I didn't think . . ."

"And tell me what you were supposed to do. Your mother had almost been blown out of the U.S. and some old woman wants you to bring her cranberry juice. . . . I do believe you *love* to worry about other people."

"Mae needs cranberry juice for her plumbing."

"So she told me."

"You brought the juice out to Mae's, didn't you?"

"I didn't do it because I'm a *nice* person, like Gwenn Nichols, Mae's bit of a bean. I did it for a purely selfish reason. I wanted her to stop phoning."

Gwenn winked at Shirley.

"Stop that!" said Shirley. "You know I'm not a nice person."

"Okay, Scrooge, then let's change the subject. What else happened while I was away?" Gwenn noticed her play book slipping out of her purse, and automatically she tucked it in deeper.

"Of course, you know you missed rehearsal last night."

"Not much I could do about that. I did manage to memorize most of my lines this weekend. Studying seemed more constructive than wearing a hole in the hotel rug."

"I was your stand-in at rehearsal last night. Did pretty well if I do say so myself. . . . How in the world do you stand that man, Lyle Thurst? When he kissed me his hands were all over. And that JoJo!"

"What did JoJo say now?"

"She said I should be Edna, that I was better suited for the part than you, that I wouldn't need nearly so much makeup to look old enough to be Natalie's mother."

Gwenn smiled sadistically. "Did you deck her?"

"Tank held me back." Shirley tossed her head. Her newly cut hair danced about her face.

"That's one time I wish Tank wasn't around you. . . . What did the director say . . . about me not being at rehearsal?"

"He hardly said two words to anyone last night, except JoJo. The woman was all over him, a female Lyle Thurst."

"Wasn't Randal curious where I was?"

"I believe he used up all his curiosity and spent not too little of his anger Saturday night. Did you two have a date or something planned?"

Gwenn's hand went up to her open mouth. "Oh my gosh. We were supposed to see a play. I forgot."

"Stress does tend to make a person lose her memory. I guess you've had more than your fair share."

"What did you tell him?" Gwenn asked.

"Nothing. That's what Carol said, 'We don't tell a living soul anything.' Wasn't that what you ordered?"

"Yes, but I had forgotten about Randal."

"Well, he certainly didn't forget about you. He's at your house right this minute, waiting."

Suddenly Gwenn felt a tightness in her throat and stared out at the browning countryside.

What was she going to tell him? If he knew about her mother's urgent money problems he was sure to jump on Gwenn like a vulture on a carcass and force her into a quick sale. She didn't need any additional pressure.

First Gwenn had to review her financial options. There had to be another avenue she could take for help aside from that of giving up her home.

She closed her eyes and thought.

CHAPTER 12

Randal met Gwenn and Westminster at the back door of her house. He crossed his arms over his broad chest as he watched her walk up the stairs. "So you're home," he stated sternly.

"It looks that way. Doesn't it, Westminster?" Gwenn said, squeezing past Randal into the house.

The man looked almost as bad as Gwenn felt. She realized that it was the first time she had ever seen him unshaved. His thick dark whiskers made it appear as if he hadn't used a razor in a week.

After releasing the cat Gwenn set her overnight bag on the table. "I didn't expect a welcoming committee to greet us," she said.

"Where have you been? You missed rehearsal last night . . . not to mention our date Saturday."

"Sorry."

"Sorry? That's all I get?" Randal paced the floor. "I came in here Saturday and waited for you to come home. I waited for . . . for . . . forever. . . . Your car was in the drive. I thought you were next door or somewhere in town—or at least in the state."

"Sorry, again. Didn't you ask Shirley where I was?"

"I tried asking. Some kid said she was on a date with Tank?"

"What about Carol?"

"She was out too. The whole darn world was out on a date Saturday."

"Except poor Randal Cochran." Gwenn sat down and kicked off her shoes. She felt the little strength she had left ooze down her slight frame and out through her toes.

"When I finally did get hold of Shirley she wouldn't tell me anything." Randal stopped pacing and faced her.

Gwenn felt her body tense. "What do you want from me? I said I was sorry."

His shoe tapped on the floor. "An explanation would be nice."

"It was a personal emergency. . . . The details don't concern you."

"Someone sick or something?"

"Something like that, I guess. . . . Look, what do you want to hear, that I was out rescuing an old lover from the jaws of bankruptcy? If that's the kind of explanation you want, fine, you've got it. If not I'll make up another one for you. My imagination is very active, as you know. . . . Really, Randal, I'm exhausted. I haven't had much sleep this weekend. If you go now I can grab a nap before rehearsal tonight. You wouldn't want me to miss another play practice, would you?"

"No, I guess not. There's not enough time, even counting every rehearsal. . . . Have you eaten?"

"I'm too tired to eat." Gwenn stood and moved across the kitchen. Her feet felt almost too heavy to lift. "I'm going to bed. You can show yourself out."

Gwenn was dumbfounded when she went into the living room. The paint-spattered dropcloth had disappeared and the pile of wood molding was no longer on the floor, but stripped, varnished and nailed in place. The room was empty except for her two pieces of living room furniture. Sitting near the window were Gwenn's worn maroon couch and pine coffee table. Together, against the new wallpaper, they made the room look livable again.

In bare feet, Gwenn walked diagonally across the room. Even the wooden ladder had been removed. She sat when she reached the couch and looked at Randal who was standing in the doorway.

He shrugged. "I think a decorator would call this room airy . . . ," he said. "Well, don't look at me like that. I just couldn't sit here waiting for you and do nothing."

Tears spilled out of Gwenn's eyes. She tried to hold them back, but she was too weak. The salty drops ran down her cheeks, smearing her makeup.

"What did I do now? I can't believe you're crying. Don't tell me, the varnish is the wrong shade."

She shook her head. How could she explain? Gwenn wasn't even sure why she was crying. Without another word she went to her bedroom.

Gwenn awoke to the smell of frying bacon and eggs. Her stomach growled. Part of her wanted to remain in her warm bed and sleep for a week. Another part of her wanted to eat and eat and eat. The latter part won.

Tossing back the bed covers Gwenn forced herself up. She threw a well-worn quilted robe over her scantily clad body and shuffled toward the kitchen.

"Shirley, I told you not to come over here and baby me," Gwenn said as she approached the kitchen. "I can take care of myself. I'm a grown woman. . . ."

"I've noticed." Randal turned from his place at the stove, scratching his chin thoughtfully. "I believe I noticed you were a grown woman the very first moment I saw you."

Gwenn tightened the belt of her robe and smoothed back her rumpled hair. "I . . . I thought Shirley was here."

Randal quickly scanned the room, opened a cupboard and even looked under the table. "Nope, no Shirley. . . . I was about to wake you. I hope you like your eggs scrambled. They started out sunny-side up but, well, now they're scrambled."

"The food smells great, Randal, but I wish you wouldn't sneak in here like this. It makes me nervous."

"You make me nervous waltzing around here dressed that way. And, I didn't sneak in, I never left."

"You're impossible."

"That's what I keep telling you. Now sit down and eat."

"I'll go dress first."

"Eggs wait for no woman. They get cold too fast and I don't think Westminster could hold another mouthful." Randal nodded to the sleeping cat, its fat belly turned skyward. "He ate the first batch I sort of burned."

Randal set the steaming meal on the table and even buttered Gwenn's toast.

Gwenn sighed after swallowing a mouthful of food. "I could get used to treatment like this."

"I know what you mean. When a person lives alone there's no one around to bring you coffee or scratch your back or wash your back for that matter or . . ."

"Or butter your toast," Gwenn finished his sentence. "You could hire a housekeeper to answer most of your requests, no doubt. . . . I guess it would all depend on who you hired with the back-washing, though."

"I have a housekeeper. There's a big difference when someone butters your bread because they want to or because they're paid to."

Gwenn agreed. It would have been ten times more pleasant if Randal wanted to do for her without trying to coerce her into selling.

They ate in silence for a few minutes. Finally Randal spoke. "I have a business proposition for you, Gwenn."

Quickly Gwenn picked up her napkin and held it to her lips. After forcing herself to swallow she said, "Randal, do you have to ruin my . . . my breakfast?"

"It's too late for breakfast. This is supper, even if it is eggs. And, as always, you're jumping to conclusions."

Gwenn raised one eyebrow. "Oh, am I?"

"You do appraisals, don't you? Real estate appraisals?"

She nodded.

"I have this . . . this *friend* who wants his cottage appraised. Could you go out to his place a week from Saturday?"

Gwenn stared at Randal, not answering.

"Honest," Randal said. "He needs money for a business investment and has been thinking about selling for some years. Poor fellow never gets a chance to use the cottage. He must have been there twice this entire year. It's a waste of capital."

"Don't let me be the one to help waste capital. Where is the cottage?"

"I'll drive you there."

"You'll drive me?. To some deserted cabin? No thanks. I fell for that one at the warehouse."

"We'll file flight plans this time. You can tell Shirley where you're going. Tell Carol. Tell the world. I'll even give you a telephone number where you can be reached. If it'll make you feel safe, I'll inform the local authorities that you're in the company of a despicable villain who should be watched."

"Well . . ."

"My friend expects to pay you for your appraisal."

"I guess I can trust you, for one afternoon."

"Great. . . . Oh, did I mention that it takes almost three hours to drive to my friend's cottage?"

"I'm sorry, Miss Nichols," the young bank manager said sadly, shaking his head. "The bank won't be able to loan you any more money on your house. If it was a new building things might be different. . . . We wouldn't hesitate lending you money for a new car. You have a good credit rating. I'm afraid your house isn't worth what you're asking."

One used car dealer offered to give Gwenn six hundred for her station wagon. He buffed the paint on a red showroom car as he spoke. "On a trade-in for a new car, I could do a lot better. We'd be taking a licking, but for you I'd go as high as twelve hundred toward this hot little number. . . ."

"But I don't want to buy another car. I want to sell a car." She drove to two other dealers. The best offer she received was five hundred dollars.

The inevitable was fast approaching. Gwenn decided to put off selling to Randal for as long as she could. With luck, in the next two weeks, a real estate boom would hand her all the money she needed.

Gwenn's mother phoned collect three times in three days.

"So did the bulldozer come, Mom?" asked Gwenn. "Don't cry. You'll have a new mobile home up before you know it. . . . I'm sorry your roommate snores like a gorilla. . . . Then sleep on the couch if you can't sleep with her. . . . Don't get upset about the money, Mom. You'll end up in the hospital instead of your own home, if you don't calm down. . . . It's not going to be that bad for me. Business has been picking up, really. I'll have the money wired down to you before you know it."

Work, rehearsal, life in general, became a blur to Gwenn. She went from one to the other, doing what she was supposed to, smiling and acting friendly but nothing extra. Somewhere along the way Gwenn had lost her energy, her enthusiasm, her heart.

A whole weekend went by without Gwenn making even one tiny improvement on her house. That hadn't happened since she signed the purchasing agreement.

Saturday she didn't even bother to dress, preferring to sit in her *airy* living room and pet Westminster. She did manage to attend church services Sunday morning, but only because it was expected and her absence would have been questioned.

After Monday night's rehearsal Gwenn looked into her mirror. Makeup couldn't hide the circles under her eyes. Her usually peach-colored skin had lost its glow. "Good God, Gwenn Nichols, it's not the end of the world! It's only a house, *a house.* An almighty wind could come tomorrow and blow it away like it was made of cards. . . . It will cost too much to remodel anyway."

The pep talk helped a little. She went to bed and fell into a restless sleep.

In her dreams she was walking and walking. She was going away, away from something, but when she turned she didn't see the house. She saw a faceless man standing alone on a hill. He turned away when Gwenn moved toward him. No matter how many steps she took forward, the shadowy man never was close enough to identify. Gwenn awoke exhausted.

By Wednesday, Gwenn was tired of her self-imposed isolation. It was her suggestion that the cast meet at Bennie's after play practice.

"Now I can finally buy you that drink," said Lyle.

An actress's smile crossed Gwenn's lips as she looped her arm through Lyle's. "I was hoping you'd say that," she said. "I could use a drink . . . and some good news. Tell me some good news, Lyle."

The older man pushed back a wisp of hair off his high forehead and looked at Gwenn. "Good news?" His entire forehead wrinkled. "Good news, you say. . . . I do happen to have some news. We're breaking ground for an addition to the funeral home in two weeks. It's exciting. I designed the wing myself. . . ."

Lyle continued his monologue about the addition when they were all seated at Bennie's. He even drew a diagram of it on a napkin.

It wasn't quite the kind of good news Gwenn was searching for, but she continued to smile. After half an hour of funeral home news Randal caught Gwenn's attention. He rolled his eyes heavenward and Gwenn laughed out loud.

Lyle stopped talking. "Did I say something funny?"

"You?" Gwenn could barely speak. A hysterical laugh was desperately trying to escape her throat. "Lyle, I'm sorry. It wasn't anything you said. Go on, what about . . ." The battle to control the laugh was lost when Randal rolled his eyes again.

Gwenn couldn't say another word. She sputtered, choked, and grabbed for a napkin to laugh-cough into. When she pulled the napkin a good portion of her drink spilled onto JoJo's lap.

While the men scurried to help JoJo, Gwenn moved away from the table, still laughing. Her body was shaking and nearly doubled over as she stepped out alone into the cool night air.

Taking in deep breaths, Gwenn fought to gain control. She was not quite back to normal when Randal walked out of the door.

"Are you all right?" Randal asked, a smile on his lips.

"Only as long as you don't bring up the subject of funeral homes." She giggled. "Oh God, I wish I didn't have to kiss Lyle in the play. I know from now on I'm going to bust out laughing when things between Edna and Henry are supposed to be getting hot and heavy."

"That would be a scene the audience could understand. You and Lyle

. . . together . . ." He choked and tightened his lips, struggling not to join her in hysterical laughter.

She wiped away a tear on her cheeks with the back of her hand as she sagged against the brick building. "I haven't felt so good in days."

Indeed Gwenn felt alive again. She couldn't help wondering why. Her world was being torn apart, yet she felt relieved, as if an evil spirit had been exorcised from her body. How odd, she thought, considering her decision to sell Randal the house. She would tell him about the sale on Saturday. After that her mother would have her mobile home and Gwenn would have a suitably small apartment.

All the cast members had their lines memorized by Thursday night, even JoJo.

Gwenn sat onstage crocheting, listening to JoJo argue backstage with a woman about her wardrobe.

"You shouldn't be in charge of wardrobe!" JoJo said loudly. "You haven't any sense of color. Grey isn't for me. I need bright colors." JoJo flounced out onto the stage wearing a grey sweater and black skirt.

Gwenn whistled. "JoJo, you look stunning."

The actress ignored Gwenn's comment. "Randy? Randy?" JoJo called through the theater. "I need your expert advice."

Randal and Tank continued discussing set changes as they walked toward the stage.

"Randy! I can't possibly wear this in the play next week. It just isn't right for me. It's too drab."

"You look lovely, JoJo." Randal looked up briefly from his clipboard. "And if you'd check the back of your play book you'll find the scene calls for the grey sweater and black skirt."

"But this is all wrong!"

"Maybe it's not JoJo Adams's style, but it certainly is Natalie's. . . . You wear the outfit." Randal pointed to the stage. "Tank, you'll have to remember to have Edna's knitting basket outside the kitchen entrance when Act Two opens. The audience will think it's odd if during the second scene Gwenn is knitting thin air. . . . And also the magazine on the coffee table, Henry needs something more appropriate to read than *Playboy*. . . . I know it was Lyle's idea, but I'm the director."

The two men disappeared into the back room.

JoJo turned toward Gwenn. "What do you think, Mom?" she asked.

"Well, daughter, dear, anything you wear looks marvelous. Unlike your poor old ma, who has to slouch around in baggy housedresses."

"You're right, Gwenn. Next to you I'll be smashing."

Gwenn nodded and continued crocheting. The wardrobe mistress had a reprieve.

When Randal returned to the stage, Gwenn was alone. He examined her growing yarn project.

"This doesn't look like a scarf to me," he said.

"I couldn't remember how to make a scarf, so I'm making an afghan. And don't worry about the expense to the theater group. I bought the yarn myself."

"I hope its size doesn't make moving onstage awkward."

Gwenn pulled a miniature afghan from the basket at her feet. "If it's too big, I'll use this. Now let me be, I'm busy." She continued working on the afghan.

Act One rehearsal progressed for the first time without any prompting. Actors came onstage through the proper doors and exited in the same manner.

During the break between acts Randal beamed. "I think we just might pull it off. I had my doubts at the beginning, with the short rehearsal schedule, but you five have gotten it together. You're acting like a team, a professional team."

"I owe it all to my acting coach," said Charlie, lifting a vase off the mantel as if it were an award, "without whom none of this would be possible."

Gwenn changed housecoats during the break, as she would on opening night. Then she picked up her afghan offstage and continued working until Act Two began.

JoJo and Charlie were onstage arguing, or at least their characters were arguing, when Gwenn joined them. JoJo stalked off through the kitchen door after two lines.

Charlie turned to Gwenn, his face red with anger, about to say his next line. But before he could open his mouth, the entire stage shook.

Beyond the kitchen door a thunderous noise rattled Gwenn's painting on the back wall.

"An earthquake? In Wisconsin?" asked Charlie in surprise.

The kitchen door burst open as Tank raced out of the dark wing. Edna's knitting basket shot through the door after Tank, striking him between his shoulder blades when he reached center stage. The wood floor was showered with yarn and assorted hooks and needles.

JoJo limped through the door. She grabbed one pillow after another off the couch and hurled them at Tank. The barrage of pillows was followed by a flying magazine, a plastic bouquet of flowers and a chair cushion.

About the time JoJo was raising the floor lamp over her head, Randal reached her and bear-hugged her into submission.

"That fool! That idiot!" JoJo searched for the proper expletive. "That . . . that *man* left that stupid knitting garbage right outside the door where I tripped over it in the dark! I almost killed myself!"

"Natalie," Gwenn said in character, "you're too hard on the hired help. You know how impossible it is to keep a good man these days."

"Oh, shut up, Gwenn!" JoJo limped to the couch where she examined her bruised shin. "If you say another word, you might find a booby trap backstage, just for you."

Tank made a wide circle around JoJo as he returned backstage. "I'm sorry, JoJo. I didn't mean to hurt you," he said softly. "It was an accident."

"Fat chance." JoJo's words were almost spit out of her mouth. "You were trying to get even with me for dumping you."

"You dumped me?" Tank appeared confused. "Was that what happened when I stopped taking you out to those fancy overpriced restaurants you demanded to go to? You dumped me? *Huh.* And to think, all this time I've been under the impression *I* was the one who broke off whatever it was we had." He walked offstage shaking his head.

"You idiot! You fool! You . . . you . . ." JoJo looked for another missile to hurl at Tank but came up empty. "I dumped him," she said to the five people staring at her. "Well, I did!"

"We all know what a rotten person Tank Lormar is, JoJo," said Gwenn from a safe distance. "It's obvious you two would fit together like meat loaf and caviar."

"Actually, meat loaf and caviar aren't that bad together," said Randal.

Gwenn turned to Randal and wrinkled her nose. "I'm afraid I categorize caviar with escargots. Neither has passed these old lips." She leaned over and dragged herself across the stage in an impression of a very old Edna.

"A stagnant pond could never produce edible escargots and definitely couldn't begin to produce caviar. I'll have to take it upon myself to introduce you."

"How are you at force-feeding?" Gwenn asked.

"I have a technique of force-feeding you have never experienced," Randal said and winked.

Gwenn shuffled around the stage gathering her crocheting paraphernalia from the floor. "My mother told me never to pay any mind to a man who winks too much. . . . And . . . *and* she scolded me whenever I saw a younger gentleman caller." Gwenn sat in the armchair, drew the Afghan over her shoulders and looked at least eighty years old.

"Will poor Grandma Gwendolyn be able to drag her old bones up north Saturday?"

JoJo looked at Randal, forgetting her shin. "North? You and *Gwendolyn* are going north, for the weekend?"

"My name's *Gwenn,* JoJo Remember that if you care to finish this play alive. . . . And if it's any business of yours, Mr. Cochran and I are working up north, but not for the whole weekend. As it happens, we'll only be busy Saturday. In case you urgently need either one of us, we'll be available Sunday," Gwenn explained, growing younger as she spoke normally. "The appraisal's still on, then?"

"Can't think of a reason to cancel. My friend really needs some sound advice. I hope you don't let him down. . . . Let's pick up the scene at Charlie's line, right before JoJo bombarded Tank."

"He deserved it," JoJo said as she dramatically limped offstage.

Gwenn turned to Charlie as they resumed their places. "Do you think I should mention that I was the one who left the basket right outside the door?"

"Not too loud, Gwenn," Charlie whispered. "I don't think you could take the pounding the way Tank did. JoJo would probably kill you."

Gwenn smiled. She would express her appreciation to Tank later for not snitching.

CHAPTER 13

Randal arrived at ten Saturday morning wearing blue jeans and a brown plaid shirt under his suede jacket. He opened the car door for Gwenn, who was dressed in grey corduroy slacks and a lime turtleneck.

She carelessly tossed her lined trench coat in the back seat along with her briefcase. "I thought I'd be prepared in case the sun decided to duck behind rain clouds," she said.

"I hope those are good walking shoes you're wearing." Randal pointed to her feet. "The property has quite an area of woods. I thought you'd want to walk through the pines and maybe follow the lakeshore, to help you appraise the land, that is."

"This is the best I can do today," said Gwenn. "My boots are packed away in some unmarked box in the attic. I may not find them until March. But don't worry. These shoes are old and comfortable. They can handle a bit of walking."

As the car rolled northward out of town, Gwenn opened a black plastic box between the bucket seats. Inside she found cassette tapes: Strauss, Mozart, Tchaikovsky, Bach, Handel, Haydn, and Beethoven were intermingled with twentieth-century compositions.

Gwenn chose a tape and put in the car player. The sound of violins surrounded her in the small car. She had been nervous about riding alone for such a long distance with Randal. Since there was no turning back she forced herself to listen to the music, to enjoy the northwoods scenery, to relax.

Neither driver nor passenger spoke right away. Gwenn was glad Randal didn't expect to fill the drive with idle chatter. The last few weeks had tired her beyond measure.

The music soon relaxed her tight nerves. She leaned her head back against the high seat and sighed. "I hope you won't think I'm poor company if I happen to doze off," she said. "Long car rides have always made me sleepy ever since I was a child."

"Be my guest," said Randal. "If you reach in the back, you'll find a pillow."

Gwenn pulled a rectangular velvet pillow from under her coat and placed it behind her neck. She continued to struggle to keep her eyes open studying the countryside rolling past her window. But her eyelids refused to cooperate. Slowly they went down and hid the scenery from view. A yawn escaped her lips, then another. Soon Gwenn was asleep.

Images drifted through her mind; first vague impressions, then strong, vivid figures. Gwenn recognized Fred. She felt his arms around her shoulders, his hands gently stroking her back. He appeared as he had last year, before the car accident, before he walked out of her life forever, a man filled with important ideas and outrageous dreams.

The touch of his hands rekindled a warmth Gwenn had fought to discard after his disappearance. It felt comfortable to be in his arms again.

But Fred didn't stay in Gwenn's dream. Suddenly he pushed her away and vanished into a growing mist. Gwenn wanted to cry, but didn't. But her body shivered as if she had stepped barefoot into snow.

Again, out of the mist a man walked toward Gwenn. Not Fred, but Randal. He took Fred's place in Gwenn's dream. His strong arms went around her shoulders, his hands stroked her body; his lips caressed her neck, moved to her cheek, then her mouth. She felt whole and warm. But the warmth didn't last. Randal pulled away from Gwenn and turned his back on her. Soon the mist enveloped him, too.

"Gwenn. Darling. Gwenn, we're almost at the cabin."

Gwenn heard the words through a haze. Darling? No, she realized the word was part of her dream, a word her own mind had implanted in her ears. A chill crept up her spine. She brought her arms up and hugged herself.

"Gwenn? Are you awake?" Randal smiled at her as she opened her eyes. The music on the tape player had changed. It was Mozart.

She stretched awake, the way Westminster did when leaving his warm nest on her bed.

"I thought you would want to see the area surrounding the cabin," he said.

"Of course," Gwenn said as she shook her head and shoved her dreams into a cobwebbed corner of her mind. She yawned. "I'm sorry I wasn't much company. I'll be taking a long rest after the play is over. . . . Where are we?"

"We're just leaving the Nicolet National Forest."

Gwenn focused her eyes on the miles and miles of pine trees lining the highway. "How much further is it to your friend's cottage?"

"Maybe ten minutes. Did you have a good nap?" Randal asked.

"You shouldn't have let me sleep so long." Gwenn looked at the electronic clock on the dashboard. "It's been over two hours!"

"I was beginning to think I had taken Sleeping Beauty on this trip. Not that that thought was bad. If you hadn't stirred by the time we arrived, I was more than ready to kiss you awake."

"Really, Randal. I hardly look like a sleeping beauty." Gwenn pushed stray strands of hair off her cheek. "And you . . . well, you . . . ," Gwenn stammered. Knowing she was beginning to blush, she turned to the right and pretended to look at the landscape.

"Yeah, I know. I make a rotten Prince Charming."

Gwenn imagined waking and finding Randal's lips on hers. Her heart started to speed up and pound harder. The vision was too clear. "No. I mean, uh, oh, forget it," she said. "How much longer?"

"If you keep watching to the right, you'll soon be able to see the lake through the trees. It's not a very big lake, but my friend owns over half the shoreline. The three other residents on the lake are very private people, too. They've cooperated in banning noisy motorboats, except for two hours a day in midsummer for waterskiing."

"It sound ideal."

He nodded.

Gwenn strained to see the lake through the trees. Finally she caught a glimpse of blue, then more and more blue as the trees thinned.

Randal turned off the highway onto a private gravel road leading to the lake. There were several wooden "No Trespassing" signs on fence posts near the mouth of the road. "We have to go to the north side of the lake. This first place here is owned by a Chicago lawyer. He comes up about as often as I do."

On a bluff above the lake, in a well-trimmed pine grove, sat a two-story log cabin with a three-car garage, a built-in swimming pool and a clay tennis court.

A quarter of a mile along the winding road was a second set of buildings. The rustic A-frame house was nearly hidden by the trees, but the two smaller cottages were nearer the road, in a clearing.

"Theodore Layton owns this. He's a retired corporate executive. He likes to bring his family up for visits, even flies his grandchildren in from Texas. The two small cottages were built for his teenage relatives and their stereos. Theodore said building them was the only way he could preserve what hearing he has left."

Randal's car absorbed most of the bumps and holes that dotted the gravel surface. At times the winding road brought them within a hundred yards of the water; at other moments the lake was barely visible through the trees.

Randal stopped the car and rolled down his window when they reached a clearing near the shore of the five-hundred-acre lake. He pointed across the water. "If you look beyond that peninsula, you can see the cottage."

Gwenn squinted. Trying to filter out the sun's rays reflecting off the water, she followed Randal's outstretched finger north. Beyond the point of land she saw the far shore as it sloped upward toward a huge glass-fronted home. Gwenn gasped. "You call that a cottage?"

"I suppose it does make a statement of a sort."

"I should say so. Even from this distance it tells me that your friend isn't hurting for money. Is he rich?"

"By some people's standards, but I wouldn't say so."

Gwenn humphed. "By Randal Cochran's standards a person hasn't made it unless they own General Motors lock, stock and carburetor."

"I'd have to check GM's financial statement first, before agreeing with you. They've been known to have hard times now and then." He put the car in gear and continued around the lake.

"I don't know if I'm the right person to appraise this property," Gwenn said as she rummaged through her briefcase. "That's no cottage, at least not the kind I'm used to seeing. I will have to do some research, to check the records in this county, wherever we are, and find out how much similar properties have sold for recently. It may take some time."

"There's no hurry."

"Won't your friend mind? I thought he wanted to liquidate this property for a business investment."

"Nothing urgent. He's just considering his options."

Gwenn started jotting notes in a steno notebook. When she looked up from the paper they were turning into the drive at the rear of the house.

Twenty-foot pine trees lined the drive. The same large trees were scattered profusely around the well-kept grounds surrounding the building. Past the house the wild thicket grew under the pines.

Randal parked his car alongside a two-car garage jutting out of the back of the two-story building.

The house rose up in front of Gwenn. She stretched her neck close to the windshield to achieve a better view. She looked intently at the building, from the severely trimmed hedges skirting the base, to the top of the rectangular stone chimney high above the roof.

Timbers two feet across cut the rugged building into four tan quarters of masonry, giving it an old world flavor. Weathered wood shutters hung as sentinels outside each tall French window. Even the small window near the roof had its own set of shutters.

The car's passenger door was being opened before Gwenn realized Randal had left the car. "You'll have a better view if you get out of the car," he said as he offered her his hand.

"This place is beautiful!" Gwenn said. She didn't take her eyes off the building for a second as she exited the car. "It couldn't have been built by humans. It must have grown up with the trees, part of the forest." Her eyes were wide with excitement.

As Gwenn surveyed the building the carved oak door at the back of the house opened and a heavy red-faced woman stepped out, wiping her hands on her white apron.

"At last!" the woman exclaimed. Her mousy gray hair was in a tight bun at the back of her head. "I thought we'd have to leave before you arrived. I'm glad I waited until the last minute before setting your lunch back in the icebox. Now you and your friend can come right to the table and eat a hot meal." She waddled across the stone walk and gave Randal a bear hug.

"Flora," Randal said after the woman released him and he could breathe again. "Let me introduce my friend, Gwenn Nichols."

"Hello, hello," Flora said as she gave Gwenn one of her smothering hugs. "I'm sorry I won't be here to take care of you both this weekend. And to think we haven't had company for weeks. But Ebner and me are headin' to my daughter's in La Crosse. We're baptizing our first granddaughter tomorrow."

"How many grandchildren does that make, Flora, ten?"

"Where have you been? She's number fourteen. Can't imagine how our five girls could have had all those boys first. But I'll take my little doll any way I can get her. It sure is going to be a wing-ding of a party tomorrow."

"Don't let us keep you," said Randal. "Gwenn and I are capable of feeding ourselves."

"There's chicken, beans, scalloped potatoes and a fresh lettuce salad for you this afternoon." Flora beamed as she spoke to Randal. "Tonight you'll probably want to grill. I have two beautiful steaks in the icebox waitin' for you. I know how you men feel about your steaks."

"Thank you. But we won't be here long enough for those steaks," said Gwenn.

"You wouldn't dare let those steaks go to waste, would you, dear?" Flora looked up at Randal, her face redder than before.

"Don't worry about that meat, Flora," said Randal as he put his arm around the heavy woman's ample shoulders and started toward the house. "I'll take time to eat them, even if I have to make a raw steak sandwich and eat as we drive south."

"Oh, I almost forgot." Flora stopped in her tracks. "Ebner said you were to go down to his basement workroom as soon as you came. Said there's somethin' needin' your attention. He's there waitin' right now."

"I'll only take a minute, Gwenn," Randal said as they stepped through the back door. "Flora, see that Gwenn starts on that marvelous lunch I smell."

Randal took the stairs opposite the entrance as Flora tugged Gwenn by the elbow. "Better do as he says, dearie. Looks like you could use a good meal, put some flesh on your bones."

Gwenn allowed the woman to steer her into the kitchen. In the center of the room was an eighteenth-century table surrounded by four early Windsor chairs. Two stoneware place settings waited there for Randal and her.

The north wall had floor-to-ceiling cupboards with the same dark finish as the table, but of newer material, stained to look old. The countertop and backsplash around the sink and range were made with turn-of-the-century paving bricks. Wicker baskets and bunches of drying herbs hung from the heavy ceiling beams that were both support and decoration for the building.

"How long have you known Mr. Cochran?" asked Gwenn as she sat down at the table and touched a fork to the lettuce.

"I've known him for years and years. I used to cook for him and his Mama back East." As Flora talked she straightened the kitchen and poured Gwenn fresh coffee. "She always was a picky eater. But not my Randal. He ate everythin' I cooked for him. Helped him to grow up to be a fine man, I did. When Ebner said it was time we retire, he let us come up here to live like regular kings." The large woman took off her apron and folded it squarely before placing it on the towel rack.

Randal returned about the time Gwenn finished her first cup of coffee. He was followed into the kitchen by Ebner, an extremely tall, extremely thin bald man.

"Time to go, Flora," Ebner said to his wife as he nodded a silent greeting to Gwenn. "We're going to arrive late enough as it is."

The old couple each picked up a shopping bag overflowing with pink packages and backed out the door, Flora apologizing all the while for leaving.

As the door clicked shut Randal sighed. "Finally," he said and smiled broadly. "If that baby was another grandson, Flora would have insisted on staying. . . . Eb wants me to look at a tree by the shore; said it was struck by lightning last week."

"Randal," Gwenn said, her voice flat, without emotion. "Couldn't you be honest about the owner of this *cottage?* What was all that business about a friend needing an appraisal?"

"Honesty? Why in the world would you expect honesty, and from me of all people? If I told you outright that *I* wanted the appraisal, would you have come?"

"I . . . I would . . ."

"Answer *honestly,* Gwenn."

"Okay, so I probably wouldn't have come. You could get a fair appraisal from someone local. Haven't we been thrown together enough, what with the play and your designs on my house?"

"I wanted you. And if I had to tell a little white fib to get you here, well . . . Anyway, you're here now so you might as well eat lunch and enjoy yourself. It's too pretty a day to waste arguing."

"Who's arguing? I just don't care to be cast in the part of a fool. That's all. . . . I should have known. . . . I must be more tired than I thought."

"All I know is that I'd never be crazy enough to underestimate you, Gwenn. You're definitely not simpleminded, not by any standards. . . . Now eat your lunch so we can take our tour of the grounds."

Gwenn ate the succulent chicken in silence. Would she have actually joined Randal for the day in the northwoods if she had known who owned the property? Or had she suspected from the very beginning?

If Randal had indeed tricked her, she would have to be on her guard for his next trick. If subconsciously she had known, she would have to be wary even of herself. Either way, Gwenn felt like she would be walking through a mine field instead of a forest that afternoon.

Gwenn started to clear the table. "Leave the dishes in the dishwasher," Randal said as he picked up his place setting. "Flora would be upset if we washed them, especially since she wasn't here to mother us to death."

"Do they live here year-round?"

"You couldn't blast them out anymore."

"Then why are you planning to sell out from under them?"

"An appraisal doesn't mean I'm planning to sell this second. It means I want a realistic, unbiased look at the property I own. No matter what you may think, I'm no Simon Legree, tossing that old couple out for the wolves. Pick up your notebook and let's get moving."

The formal dining room had a long oak table suitable for a sit-down dinner for twenty. It was a small room compared to the living room.

A natural stone fireplace took up most of the west living room wall. Facing the glass-faced hearth was a brown sectional couch and an overabundance of pillows. A log fire crackled merrily behind the glass.

"Eb doesn't turn the furnace on until it snows," said Randal. "He's a very conservative person." He opened the glass door and poked the log with a brass poker, then took a second log from a nearby bin and tossed it on the fire.

On the couch was a red bow, tied around a notecard that had Gwenn's name printed on it. Both were attached to the tail end of a length of string. The rest of the white cotton string trailed out of the room.

"What's this?" asked Gwenn.

Randal shrugged and examined the string. "It doesn't feel heavy enough for a hanging, maybe you should follow it and find out."

"I think I've just about figured you out, Mr. Cochran. You're crazy," she said as she picked up the end of the string.

A six-inch section of a thick maple branch appeared in Randal's hand. He offered it to her. "This might help," he said. Gwenn began to wind the string onto the stick as she went.

First the string went around the legs of a press-backed chair and under a pine hutch, then inside a hutch drawer. There, tied to the string, was an expensive bottle of French perfume.

"For me?" she asked as she untied the string.

Randal winked. "It must be yours. I personally use a musk."

She sniffed the soft scent before pocketing the bottle and then continued following and winding the string.

As Gwenn moved around the room, carefully taking the string from around two oil paintings and a delicate china vase, she realized she was actually going to miss Randal's odd house negotiations: the gifts, the time together; yes, even the innuendoes. Never again would she meet a man like him.

Gwenn trailed the string to a maroon silk scarf. Randal gently tied the scarf around her neck before she followed the string into the glass-enclosed sunspace on the south side of the house.

There she came to the end of the trail. Tied high above her head in a ten-foot olive tree was a magnificent nylon kite, a rainbow of color arching across its sky-blue background. On the tail of the kite was what Gwenn knew would be Randal's last offer on her house. She went pale and sat down in a natural wicker chair when she picked up the long satin tail and the hand-printed card attached.

"For heaven's sake, Gwenn!" Randal looked at her white complexion. "I only thought it was time for another offer. You surely expected it, didn't you?"

"Yes, I expected it, kind of." She looked at the card for the amount but her eyes couldn't focus on the numbers. "Can we talk about this later? I'd like to get some fresh air."

Randal retrieved the ball of string from the floor where Gwenn had dropped it. "I was hoping we'd have a breeze so we could fly this kite."

"You wouldn't want that beautiful creation to fall out of the sky and into a mud puddle, or worse, get ripped to shreds in a tree. Would you?" The pink color started to return to her complexion.

"Aren't kites made for flying?" he asked.

"Not this kite, not yet, anyway. . . . Paper kites are for flying. Hand-sewn nylon kites are not."

"If this kite isn't going to fly in the sky, where it belongs, what will you do with it?"

"I'll hang it in my house, maybe in my bedroom."

"I consider that a waste. . . . Since you've taken the fun out of my kite-flying for today why don't we go for our walk while the sun is still high. You can leave your notebook here."

He led Gwenn through the greenery in the glass-enclosed sunspace and out the door onto a redwood patio.

The trees opened wide before the house, giving them a spectacular view of the lake.

A stone walk wound down the sloping ground to the shoreline where a boat dock and a sand beach waited empty after the summer's fun. The air was fresh, clean, free of city pollution. The only thing that marred the setting was the sight of the newly damaged tree, its life ended with one vicious blast.

"Lucky the lightning strike didn't start a fire," Randal said as he examined the charred remains. "Earlier in the year, during the drought, the whole area would have gone up in smoke."

"Nature doesn't play favorites." Gwenn thought about her mother's hurricane. Soon she would have to tell Randal about her decision.

They walked along a path paralleling the shore. Gwenn breathed in the aromas of fresh water and decaying pine needles. She forgot she was supposed to be working, appraising Randal's property. The day was too inviting.

"If you don't mind my asking?" Gwenn interrupted the silence. "Why all the games, Randal? Why waste your time on the kite, perfume and scarf?"

"I asked myself that same question. . . . I don't know. Maybe I just like watching your eyes light up."

"My eyes don't light up. . . . Do they?"

"Only about as bright as a Fourth of July fireworks display, that's all."

"But . . ."

Ahead, Gwenn caught a glimpse of movement in the underbrush.

Randal held his finger to his lips and ended her unspoken question. Silently they crept forward, until the form of a deer could be seen alongside the path. A crack of a twig under Randal's foot brought the deer's head up and in an instant it was gone.

"Those white-tails give me a lot of grief," said Randal.

"How could a lovely creature like that give you trouble?"

"I won't allow hunting here. Certain business associates I won't bother to name think they should be able to negotiate hunting rights into contracts. I've lost out on two or three deals because of those deer."

"For once I applaud your stubbornness. I never could understand how people could shoot such an animal, if it wasn't absolutely needed for food."

"Next week hunting season opens. And even though I don't allow hunters, some do slip onto my property. Just walking through these woods during that season could be hazardous if one doesn't wear blaze orange."

They became quiet again. Absentmindedly, Gwenn played with the carpet of needles and leaves on the path, moving them to the left and then to the right with her feet. She said little to Randal as she walked, but her thoughts were flying.

"Should I tell him now?" she asked herself. "It would get the pain over with. . . . It would have been better if I hadn't even come today, taken his last bid. But mother can use the extra money he just offered. Anyway Randal can afford it. It's only a game to him."

A tree root lay across the path, hidden in decaying leaves and needles. Gwenn moved her foot through the fallen debris and caught her toe and toppled forward. Randal was there. His arms were around her, saving her from the fall.

The abruptness of the moment brought Gwenn quickly out of her reverie. Randal's arms remained around her, strong and warm. She looked up into the eyes staring down into her flushed face. Slowly his face came toward hers, his mouth slightly open. She was ready.

Randal's lips were about to touch Gwenn when suddenly a scream from the lake pierced the stillness. Abruptly he set Gwenn on her feet as he turned toward the water. "What the . . ." Through the trees they could see a boy struggling with something on the shore.

With long powerful strides Randal crossed the scrub brush between the path and the lake. Gwenn followed more slowly, pushing the snagging brush out of her path as she went.

When Gwenn caught up to Randal, he was relieving the boy of his fishing rod and the catch attached to the nylon line. Flapping wildly on the gravel and mud shore was not a fish but a black and white gull.

"Don't get too close to that bird, lady. He bites," the boy said.

Gwenn looked and the youngster held up his red-streaked hand as evidence of the power of the struggling bird.

Randal didn't look at the boy. "If we cut the line," Randal said, "the bird will probably fly off, get tangled in some tree and starve to death."

Gwenn stepped between Randal and the bird. "If he bites you there will be blood. . . .

"I've already considered my problem, Gwenn." Randal pushed her aside. "I'm thinking."

"Mr. Cochran," said the boy, "my grandfather isn't going to be happy if I lose his favorite rod and reel. He hasn't let me use the boat since I dumped the motor in the lake. If that bird breaks the pole, Grandfather won't let me out on the lake at all."

"Don't worry. I've got an idea. Here, Gwenn. Hold this." Randal handed Gwenn the fishing rod and took off his suede jacket. "If I'm lucky, you'll get to keep your tackle and I'll get to keep my fingers. . . . Gwenn, try to keep the line taut until I get this over him."

The bird's constant frantic flapping made it almost impossible for Gwenn to keep the line taut. But she did the best she could.

Randal crept up to the gull, his jacket held out in front, a massive bird net. When the gull stopped to catch its breath, Randal dropped the jacket down over it and grabbed it.

"*Eeeeekk!*" the gull screeched, and pecked at Randal and at the material surrounding him.

"Get a knife! Get something to cut the line!" Randal sounded desperate.

The boy fumbled through his tackle box. "I hope I didn't lose my pocket knife. Grandfather wouldn't like it if . . ."

Gwenn reached into the box and brought the knife to Randal.

"Watch out for his beak!" yelled Randal. "Oh, God, this bird smells like it ate a boatload of dead fish. . . . The line's around its right wing and its legs, Gwenn. I'll try to hold it still while you cut the line off. And watch so you don't cut me instead. I wouldn't do this bird any good if I pass out on top of it."

Carefully Gwenn took the pocket knife and cut the nylon fishing line. The bird whipped its beak out of Randal's suede jacket and pinched her hand. Gwenn's thumb turned pink, but no blood flowed.

Two more cuts with the knife and the bird was free of the fishing line. "Stand back," said Randal. "I don't know what it's going to do when I let go."

After Gwenn took three paces back, Randal dropped his coat and the bird and trotted toward the trees. The bird shook free of the coat and flew out across the lake.

"Thanks, Mr. Cochran," the boy said. "I'm giving up fishing. I never caught nothin' anyhow. Maybe Grandfather will teach me to hunt." He gathered his belongings from the rocks and walked away along the shore.

Randal watched the boy. "I think I'll talk to Eb about posting "No Hunting" signs around my place. I don't think I'll feel safe if Theodore's grandson gets his hands on a loaded gun."

Gwenn picked Randal's filthy jacket off the shore with two fingers and walked toward the path with him. He was still breathing hard after his fight with the gull.

"Tell me, Gwenn. Is the life of one gull worth the price of suede?" Randal said as he took the jacket from her. "That fish smell will never come out. . . . Stupid bird shouldn't be this far inland anyway. They've been a plague all summer. I should have just wrung its bothersome neck."

Gwenn laughed. "Really, Randal, I was beginning to consider you a knight in shining armor and you go and ruin my fantasy by talking like the Randal Cochran I know and . . ."

"And? And what, Gwenn? And love?"

"You saved me from a marauding gull, not a dragon, Randal. Love doesn't enter into gull rescuing."

"Shucks. Maybe . . . maybe I'll be lucky on the walk back to the cottage and we'll run into a bear or something."

"I think it's time I get back to my appraisal. That's what you brought me up here for, wasn't it?"

"Was it?" Randal's eyes twinkled.

"Remember, I left word with Shirley to notify the authorities if I don't return tonight."

They walked back listening to the chatter of busy squirrels and twittering birds, and thinking their own thoughts.

CHAPTER 14

Dusk was slowly enveloping the land when Gwenn entered the final room of Randal's cottage, the master bedroom.

A strong feeling of doom and dread overcame Gwenn as she walked into the spacious room, a feeling that she was about to do something . . . well, something stupid.

She could almost feel Randal's hot breath on her neck as he followed close behind. How many women had he escorted into the room before? Gwenn found herself staring at the bed, as if she would find notches in the cannonball bedposts numbering his exploits.

"Why don't you go downstairs, Randal? You could get a head start on those steaks Flora left, while I finish here," she suggested. "Charcoal takes so long to burn just right."

"No charcoal here, the grill's gas," he said as he walked past her and stretched out on the king-sized bed. "I prefer waiting."

Gwenn took a deep breath before going past the bed toward a drafting table beyond. A blueprint lay opened on the table. "You're interested in architecture?" she asked.

"I dabble, when I have time, which isn't often. Passive solar energy interests me. . . . Flora should have opened those drapes this morning. This room would have warmed nicely today."

Taking the suggestion to heart, Gwenn tugged the drapery pull and exposed glass terrace doors that opened to a balcony in the upper story of the sunspace. In fact, her colorful kite hung in a tree just beyond the balcony railing.

She slid the doors apart and felt a rush of warm air enter the bedroom as she stepped into the sunspace. Far to the west Gwenn saw the sun setting, red, orange and purple above the trees.

"If this was my house," sighed Gwenn, "I'd never leave it. And I'm positive I wouldn't even consider selling it."

"I can only cope with so much serenity. After a week of quiet I have to rush back for a fix of chaos. Besides, it's not easy conducting business from this distance."

"I wouldn't mind trying."

"You wouldn't last a month. You're a people person, too. Eb and Flora are different. They love talking to each other; or not talking to each other. Anyway, I don't think it's healthy to get attached to any one person, place or thing. I look for the unexpected. There's always someone ready to throw a monkey wrench into the best plans." He watched her intently from his place on his bed. "Why close the door if something better might come along?"

"The unexpected." Gwenn turned away from the sunset and returned to the bedroom. Randal had been an unexpected development in her life as was her mother's hurricane. She had not planned for either. "I'm ready for that steak now," she said as she quickly walked out of his master bedroom.

Randal stirred the hot coals in the fireplace. This time he didn't close the glass doors but let a log crackle openly before his eyes.

"You shouldn't put any more wood on the fire," said Gwenn from her seat amongst the throw pillows on the floor. "I don't want to leave late."

"If I'm not worried about the lateness of our drive, why should you be? Remember, you had a nap." He sat on the floor, very close to Gwenn, a glass of red wine in his hand.

Gwenn set her empty wineglass on the floor. It was her fourth glass that evening, far beyond her usual one. She cleared her throat and prepared to say the words that would relinquish her house to Randal, but stopped before they had a chance to escape.

For a moment Gwenn stared into the fire as the flames licked upward and began to devour the newest log. Her courage was slow to gather.

"It's only an old house," she repeated to herself. "So what if Mother was born in it. So what if Grandmother loved it. Family history could be remembered without owning that big old barn. And Mother needs the money. . . ."

Deep in her own thoughts, Gwenn didn't realize Randal had moved even closer. She didn't feel his presence until his hand moved her hair off her shoulder and his lips touched her neck.

"We could stay, Gwenn, you and I, here by the fire the rest of the night." His whispered words burned her ear. "The drive could be put off until tomorrow, or Monday, or next week for that matter. We could experiment, see if you would flourish in this peaceful atmosphere."

His lips traveled up her neck to her cheek, and stopped on her mouth.

At first, Gwenn didn't move. Her body became rigid. When their lips met she melted into his arms and returned his kiss, releasing a passion held dormant since Fred's disappearance.

A strong hand held her head. Randal's fingers intertwined with her lush dark hair. His other hand eased around her waist and stopped at the small of her back, gently pulling her towards him.

Then slowly, passionately, he used his weight to lay her back on the pillows. Gwenn eagerly anticipated the touch of his hands on her flesh.

"I'll wire Flora and Eb that they're on vacation." Randal's breath was hot and sweet on her skin. "We can stay here until Christmas."

The mention of Christmas jarred Gwenn back to reality. He was not ready for a commitment and she definitely was not ready for a short affair. She took a deep breath and spoke softly into his ear. "You can have my house."

"What?" He continued to nibble on her ear.

"I said, you can have my house. Or at least you can buy my house. I'm accepting your kite offer."

He sat straight up, pushing away from Gwenn as if her skin scalded him. "What do you mean, I can have your house?"

"I mean, I'm going to take your money and run for the hills like a bandit." Gwenn's skin felt cold. Randal's body wasn't close to warm her.

"We had an agreement. I would bargain until Christmas. It's not even Thanksgiving!"

Gwenn knew the date. The fact that it wasn't Christmas made her heart ache all the more. "I knew I should have written the rules down in black and white." She forced out bitter words. "Since my memory's better than yours and since I set the limits in the first place, I'll refresh your memory. Everything was scheduled to end at Christmas or on the day I agreed to sell, whichever came first. And I'm selling today, or as soon as our lawyers can draw up the papers. Considering the circumstances, I prefer using a lawyer instead of personally handling the transaction. Unless, that is, you've changed your mind or don't have the money."

"You're babbling. Of course I have the money. But I had plans for us: tickets to the ballet, seats for the Milwaukee Symphony . . ."

Gwenn wanted to end everything with Randal with one swift blow. There was no use hanging on to false dreams. He wanted her for the moment, not a lifetime. "Oh, if that's all that's bothering you," she said. "I'm sure JoJo would kill to go with you or, if JoJo's booked, which she probably is if I know JoJo, you can give me the tickets and I'll cash them in. My car does need snow tires."

"Money?" Randal stood up, went to the fireplace and looked down at Gwenn. "Is that what you want? The money?"

"So what if it is? Didn't I tell you from the beginning I was going to take from you? Well, I'm taking. You are now the proud owner of one broken-down old house. I hope the two of you will be very happy."

"You should have waited a few more weeks. I was prepared to go ten thousand higher."

Gwenn's mouth was so dry she could barely talk. She lifted her empty wineglass and looked for the bottle. "So we're both fools," she said. "I need the money now and you're paying twice what the house is worth." She found the half-full bottle on the end table and poured the red liquid to the top of her glass. Quickly, she gulped the wine and refilled the glass. Her courage was slipping away. Gwenn had to fight to hold onto what remained.

"Would it have hurt to wait until Christmas?"

Gwenn nodded. "More than you know. . . . All you have to remember is it's kinder to your pocketbook this way. You can take that extra ten thou and invest it." Her speech slurred. "Earn a bundle and make the IRS happy. You like doing that, don't you, Randy? You love making money more than anything else in the world."

"It seems I'm not the only one here that's interested in money." He set his unfinished glass of wine on the mantel. "I think it's time we were leaving."

Gwenn failed in her first attempt to stand. As she sank back on the pillows she said, "Don't forget my kite. I have to give it to my lawyer as evidence of your bid. He'll think you're crazy, of course, offering so much for my house. And I'll have to tell him that you are and I'm taking advantage of your insanity."

"You're drunk."

On her second try to stand Gwenn succeeded, though she swayed on wobbly legs. "By golly, so I am," she said. "How nice of you to notice. It's a good thing you're not the kind of man that takes advantage of a poor helpless woman."

"Gwenn, what's come over you?"

"Nothing. Now you know the truth. This is the real me. I'm a money-hungry, drunken witch. And if you know what's good for Randal Cochran, you'll stay far away from me from now on."

"That's fine with me."

"Then take me home." Gwenn turned to walk around the sofa but her left foot caught the fringe of a large brown pillow. She was catapulted toward the end table.

A shrill cry escaped Gwenn's lips as she fell. Her hands went forward, trying to stop the momentum. The wineglass she held struck the wood table first; it splintered, a shard becoming embedded deep in her hand.

Gwenn continued to tumble forward over the table, somersaulting, finally landing in a heap behind the sofa.

Randal called her name as he raced across the room. "Gwenn! Gwenn!"

"Stay away from me!" she shouted as she cradled her bleeding hand against her green sweater. "What good are you? There's blood. What are you going to do, run over here and faint in my lap? I'll still bleed to death." She picked the glass out of her palm and released a rush of blood.

Waves of nausea surged through her body. The pain, the blood, and the wine were going to make her sick. She took a deep breath, then another, trying to gain control.

Randal had disappeared from sight. Gwenn felt alone. Her blood was flowing freely, turning the green of her sweater red. "Don't leave me, Randal," she whispered.

The room became distorted, moving in waves as if the walls were affected by rising summer heat. Gwenn's thoughts circled through time. There were papers on her desk in Woodston. Shirley wouldn't be happy if she didn't return to finish those transactions. And what about the play? Her funeral would cause the play to be canceled, or maybe only postponed if a replacement could be found.

Reality turned into a hazy dream world. Gwenn felt herself being lifted off the floor. She watched from a far-off distance as her hand was bandaged and her green sweater vanished to be replaced by an oversized blue plaid.

Her stomach lurched. A cool hand held her head as she emptied the contents of her stomach in a bathroom.

Who did that hand belong to? Distorted thoughts reasoned that it was Gwenn's mother.

When Gwenn was able to fully open both eyes the first object she could focus on was the digital clock in Randal's car. It was 2 A.M.

"Oh," she groaned.

"If you need to throw up again, let me know, I'll pull over." Randal's face appeared odd, lit only from the dashboard lights.

Gwenn concentrated on the queer signals her stomach was sending to her brain. Her whole body felt ill and confused, but not ready to empty itself again. She shook her head. "I'm all right."

"Don't be afraid to say so. I can be off the road in seconds."

Gwenn started to push her hair back from her face, but stopped when she noticed the neat gauze bandage that crossed her palm and circled her hand. She fingered the white material with her left hand.

"Is the bandage too tight? I wasn't sure."

"It's fine. You did this?" She marveled at the bandage on her hand.

"Odd, isn't it." He nodded. "May be I'm cured. Or maybe it was the fact it was an emergency."

"Thank you."

"Forget it. I just pretended you were that gull. It was easy after I threw a blanket over your head."

A smile crossed Gwenn's lips. "Sorry, the wine went to my head."

"I hope you're not going to use that excuse to back out on the sale."

The smile faded. "No, I was sober enough when I agreed to the sale. The house is yours."

"Good," he said with finality.

"Good," she said too.

Gwenn didn't escape into sleep during the remainder of the drive, but stared out at the darkness. Absentmindedly she counted the dawn-to-dusk lights dotting the countryside. The last hour of the drive they rode in silence.

The next words spoken came as Gwenn stepped out of Randal's car onto her driveway. He reached into the back seat and brought out the brightly colored kite. "Don't forget this," he said. "My offer is still attached to the tail."

She gathered it into her arms with her coat and briefcase.

"See you tomorrow night at rehearsal. You should be sober by then."

The car moved away as soon as the door closed. Gwenn stood alone in the darkness. She had done her job well. Randal had enough of Gwenn Nichols, enough to last his lifetime. He would never annoy her again with his suggestive wink or smile.

Gwenn needed to talk to someone, but Shirley wouldn't like receiving a call at three in the morning. She would have to wait. Surviving the last week of the play with director Randal Cochran was going to hurt. She would have to weigh every word she said to him, acting both on and off the stage.

Shirley wasn't the supportive friend Gwenn needed Monday afternoon.

As she peeled and sliced carrots she gave Gwenn her views. "So, you'd only have an affair until Christmas," Shirley said. "I've had shorter. Remember that vacation I took to Paris? Jean and I couldn't become an item, but I'm glad I didn't pass up the chance to be with him."

Gwenn stirred the cup of cold coffee she had stirred at Shirley's kitchen table for the past half hour. "You know that's not for me, Shirl, though I have to admit, I did consider it. I thought I had everything with Fred. It almost killed me when he left."

"He almost killed you in that car crash, or don't you remember?"

"I remember every time I part my hair." She touched her bandaged palm to the hair that covered the scar. "He didn't have to leave. It was an accident. I didn't blame him."

"Face it, Gwenn, Fred was a rat. He didn't want to be hooked up with a cripple. When he thought you wouldn't recover fully, he skipped."

Tears filled Gwenn's eyes. "He didn't even say good-bye."

"Blast that man!" Shirley picked up a carrot stick, stuck it between her lips and tried to puff on it. Quickly, she attempted to cover up the slip by eating the vegetable.

"Maybe I should take up smoking," said Gwenn as she picked up a piece of carrot and munched along with Shirley.

"You'll end up like me, craving nicotine while hopelessly in love with some health freak."

"Is loving a health freak any worse than caring about a *businessman?*" The last word Gwenn spoke sounded like a swear word. "Oh, God, how am I going to get through this week?" Gwenn buried her face in her hands.

"You'll be too busy moving into the apartment I found for you." Shirley had to wipe her hand on a towel before patting Gwenn's shoulder. "By next year," she said, "you won't even remember Randal Cochran."

Gwenn tilted her head and peeked at Shirley from between her fingers.

Shirley shrugged. "So, what else was I supposed to say? The man will take forever to wash out of your system? I'm working on being a mother figure today." Shirley patted Gwenn's shoulder again. "You're better off without him. He's no good for you. Loving him will only ruin your life. . . . Know any other clichés?"

A smile touched Gwenn's lips and she hugged Shirley. They held on to each other for a moment, supporting, caring, loving as only two women can.

Carol's tap on the back door ended the hug. "Mae's on the telephone, Gwenn."

Shirley looked Gwenn straight in her eyes. "Why don't you tell that old woman to stuff it. You don't need her problems, too."

"Listening to Mae and her stories helps me forget my own problems. She's a *great* old lady. If you gave her half a chance I'm sure you'd like her."

"I'm not soft-hearted, or soft-headed. You were endowed with all the heart in this partnership."

"You're right, sir." Gwenn saluted. "Should I tell Tank you don't have a heart, but were born with a calculator? . . . Better yet. Since you're all business, you should pair up with Randal Cochran."

"I'm not that crazy. . . . Mae's waiting, Gwenn."

"Can I come see you, Gwenn," asked Mae.

"You want to visit?"

"No, I mean can I come see you in the play? Phyllis was just reading me the newspaper. It said the play was this week."

"I told you that, Mae."

"I'm old, I forget. . . . Anyway, Phyllis said she couldn't take me to see you. She's busy all week. I know she's just tired of taking care of me. . . ."

"If Phyllis said she was busy, believe her, Mae. And yes, I can pick you up. What night do you want to go?"

"Wednesday."

"But that's only dress rehearsal. There won't be anyone in the audience."

"I don't need all those people to watch my Gwenn. . . . Won't they let me come Wednesday? I'll sit up close to the stage, but I won't bother anyone."

Gwenn agreed to bring Mae to the play Wednesday. "I'll have to pick you up early. I need time to put on my makeup.

Monday night's rehearsal was terrible. Randal wouldn't even look at Gwenn when she first arrived. Then when she tripped over her lines, he came down hard.

"I thought everyone in the cast knew their lines last week. Did you have a memory lapse, Gwenn?"

Gwenn looked at her clasped hands as she sat at the end of the stage. "Stage fright, I guess."

Lyle leaned against the stage and patted Gwenn's foot. "We're all nervous, Cochran. No need to pick on Gwenn. What about me or JoJo, we all stumbled all over the stage tonight."

"Randal's right," said Gwenn. "I muffed it. I even lost my character when I forgot my lines. It won't happen again."

The director made a note on his clipboard. "It better not."

"Let's get the heck out of here," said JoJo. "I think we've been spending too much time in this spooky old theater. We all need to get out and have some fun. Bennie's, anyone?"

Randal looked up, and for the first time that night, looked Gwenn in the eyes. He questioned her without opening his mouth.

Gwenn shook her head. "Sorry, not me. I'd better go straight home like a good little girl and go over my lines again."

"Oh, don't let Randal bully you, Gwenn," said Lyle. "We all know you know your lines. It's nerves, that's all. It happens with every play. The last rehearsals, even dress rehearsals are always rotten. That's a good sign. The play's bound to be a success."

"I hope you're right, Lyle," said Gwenn. "But I'm still going straight home."

Gwenn telephoned her mother late Monday night. She was going to tell her about the house and about Randal.

"Hi, Mom. . . . It won't be long and you'll be in your own place again. I'll wire the money to you next week. . . . You should be happy you're down in Florida even if you are still sharing a bed. The weather's turning cold already. We might have snow by the weekend. . . . I wish you could be here for the play, too. I'll tell you what. The next time I see you I'll act out part of the play for you. You'll hate it. It's about a mother and daughter that can't get along. . . . I know we get along just fine. You just remember to add me to your prayers, so I don't forget my lines like I did tonight at rehearsal. . . . I'm eating right, Mom. How about you? Taking your pills? . . . I love you too. . . . No, I don't think I'll be able to come for Thanksgiving. Maybe I'll be able to fly down after Christmas. There won't be anything for me here this coming January. . . . No, there wasn't anything else I wanted to talk about. I just wanted to hear your voice. . . . No, Mom, I still don't want to move to Florida and share your mobile home. It doesn't matter how much room you'll have. . . . No, I'm not busy with the house. I finished remodeling. There's nothing left for me to do. . . . Take care, Mom."

Gwenn wanted to open up to her mother. But what could the woman do for her in Florida, except to worry and feel sad. Gwenn figured she could do enough of that for the both of them. She was going to make it through the holidays all by herself. She had to. She had no other choice.

CHAPTER 15

Wednesday morning the sun shone brightly, but didn't warm the Wisconsin countryside. A cold wind blowing out of Canada saw to that. By afternoon dark clouds were rushing in from the north, heavy grey forerunners of weather to come.

By the time Gwenn was driving out to pick up Mae a bone-chilling rain was falling. "Are you sure you want to come to dress rehearsal, Mae?" Gwenn asked. "Tomorrow the weather bureau's predicting clear skies."

"I'm all set to watch you tonight," said Mae. "You wouldn't want me to miss out, would you? I'd feel so bad."

"There are other performances. You wouldn't miss a thing, Mae. I could bring you into town another night. In fact, if you came to a regular performance you might run into some old friends at the theater."

"I want to go to dress rehearsal so I don't run into any old friends. If they really were my friends, they would come out and visit old Mae once in awhile. But if *you* don't want to be bothered with me tonight, I'd understand. I'll just stay home alone and sit in the dark." She began to unbutton her heavy wool coat.

"Mae! Don't be silly. I'll take you. I didn't think you'd care to go out in the cold rain, that's all."

Gwenn turned her car heater on high as she drove Mae into town for dress rehearsal. The warm air couldn't take the chill out of Gwenn's bones. She shivered uncontrollably.

"Gwenn," said Mae, "you have to learn to dress for this weather. That coat you're wearing isn't worth the material it's made out of. What you need is something like this coat of mine. I've had it for years. Wool wears like iron."

"I'm afraid wool and I don't get along, Mae. I get these big welts on my skin if I touch it too long."

Mae wiggled as far away from Gwenn as her seat belt would allow.

"You should have told me. I wouldn't have worn this old rag. I would have stayed at home. . . ."

"Don't get excited. I can tolerate your wool coat as long as you don't force me to sleep with it naked."

"Don't be silly, Gwenn. Why in the world would I force you to sleep naked with my coat?"

"I was joking, Mae. Can't you take a joke tonight?"

"You shouldn't go and make fun of my coat. It's the best one I have."

"I wasn't, really. . . . Do you think it will snow tonight? I'm tired of seeing the dreary bare countryside. A fresh coat of white snow would brighten the scenery. Don't you think?"

"I would sleep naked with my coat, if it was the only thing I had to cover me. . . ."

Mae forgot about Gwenn's problem with her wool coat by the time she was being escorted to a front row seat by the director.

"This is as close as I can get you without adding you to the cast, Mae," said Randal.

"If I'm in your way, you just let me know. I promised my Gwenn I wouldn't be a bother. She's busy putting on makeup, you know."

"Yes, I think I recall someone mentioning putting on makeup before the play started. . . . It will be about forty-five minutes before curtain, Mae. Are you sure you want to sit here, alone?"

"I said I wasn't going to be a bother to anyone tonight. I know how busy every one of you are. . . . But I wouldn't be one to turn down a cup of tea, if you were to offer one to me."

Randal laughed and kissed Mae's cheek. "One cup of tea for madame, coming up," he said, bowed deeply and backed away from the queen of the evening.

Backstage Gwenn was sitting with her eyes closed while her theatrical makeup was being applied. Anne was an expert with the heavy makeup. When Anne was finished Gwenn looked like Edna. Later, onstage, it would be Gwenn's job to become Edna.

Gwenn felt extremely calm. JoJo obviously wasn't.

She sat across the room at a second mirror with a second volunteer makeup person, Carl. "You've got it all wrong!" JoJo said as she took the stick of color out of his hand and pointed to her reflection in the mirror. "Gwenn's playing the mother, Carl. She's supposed to look old. I'm playing her beautiful daughter!"

Taking the dark eyebrow pencil, Carl tried again to mask the scowl on JoJo's face and regain her beauty.

"Ouch!" JoJo yelled as soon as the pencil touched her skin. "What are you trying to do? Poke a hole in my head? Get away from me! I'll do this myself!" She grabbed the pencil out of his hand and pushed him away.

"Carl, I need your opinion." Anne waved to her makeup cohort. "Do you think Edna looks her age?"

When Carl joined Anne at Gwenn's side, they whispered a few choice comments about JoJo.

"I must not be man enough for this job, Anne, at least that's JoJo's opinion," said Carl.

"I know what your problem is," said Anne. "You're happily married. If you were single or had a divorce on the horizon, JoJo would treat you like . . ." Anne stopped talking as Randal came into the room and walked over to JoJo. As the actress started bubbling all over the director, Anne quietly finished her sentence, "treat you like our director."

Carl shook his head. "I prefer it this way, thank you. Better yet, next time I'll bring my wife backstage. She can protect me from JoJo."

Gwenn was properly chastised by Anne when she giggled. "Don't wiggle or you'll have eyeliner all the way to your ear."

"Sorry, Anne." Gwenn's face became sober again. "Anne, how would you survive if you didn't have any female friends?"

Anne pursed her lips as she thought. "No women friends?" She shook her head. "Impossible. Who would I talk to, my kids?"

"I know how you feel," said Gwenn. "I don't think I could cope with life if I didn't have any women to share my feelings and my fears with."

Anne, Gwenn and Carl turned to look at the woman across the room. Gwenn shook her head. "Women need female friends," said Gwenn.

"If you don't shut up and close your eyes again, Gwenn, you'll find yourself shy one female friend," Anne said as she went back to work. "Gwenn, have you been sick?"

"No. Why?"

"I know I've never done makeup for you before," Anne said as she stepped back to view her creation better. "It's just that I never noticed you with dark circles under your eyes before and I know the flu has been going around. All our kids have it."

"Sleep's my problem. A little extra sleep and I'll be fine. I suppose I'm excited about the play—nerves, you know. I'm also working full-time and packing furiously, trying to move into my new apartment this weekend."

"Are you crazy? Why didn't you wait until the play was over before you moved?"

Gwenn shrugged. She wasn't close enough to Anne to explain why she felt the urgent need to be out of her grandmother's house. Shirley was the friend who knew all the intimate details of her trials and tribulations with Randal Cochran. She was the only confidante Gwenn needed at the moment.

Dress rehearsal was awful. Lights came on when they were supposed to be off, and off when they were supposed to be on.

Lyle started out the evening by tripping over the cord for the floor lamp again, but managed to save it from crashing over Gwenn's head. Throughout the evening he tripped over every second line.

JoJo didn't need any prompting to shoot him looks of hatred.

Things ended especially badly when the front doorknob came loose. Instead of JoJo storming out of the house during the final scene she had to stop and reinsert the contraption.

Mae clapped and clapped and clapped when it came time for curtain calls. The actors and actresses took their bows, but didn't even try to smile as they would have to on Thursday night.

When the curtain finally closed, Randal walked down the aisle shaking his head. The cast reappeared and sat on the edge of the stage, JoJo on one end of the group and Lyle as far away from her as possible. As he sat there, he bowed his head so low it nearly touched his belt buckle.

The director looked at Lyle and shook his head.

"Don't say anything, Randal," said Gwenn. "You don't have to tell us how terrible we were. I can assure you, we know."

"Speak for yourself, Gwenn," said JoJo. "I was marvelous. It was the little people . . ."

"It won't happen again," Lyle said without looking up.

"It better not, you clumsy old man!" JoJo leaned forward so that Lyle could catch every word she shot at him. "If you step on my lines tomorrow I'll personally scalp the rest of the hair from your head."

Gwenn reached out and touched Lyle's hand. "Don't worry," she said. "We all know that a bad dress rehearsal means a great play. You used up all your mistakes tonight."

"No one needs comments from Miss Goody Two Shoes," snapped JoJo. "I say if Lyle bombs out again, he dies."

"Don't get so excited, JoJo. This was only dress rehearsal." Randal stood cross-armed in front of the cast. "I can't say that I liked what happened onstage, but I will say we won't string anyone up from the rafters. We're in this thing together, so instead of squabbling over who did what to whom, let's go over to my place and forget the whole affair over a couple bottles of wine."

"I'll be out of this makeup in five minutes." JoJo leaped to her feet. The three male cast members followed her.

Still in her front row seat, Mae finally spoke. "I loved the whole thing! You were wonderful, Gwenn. You too, Randal."

"But I wasn't onstage," Randal said and smiled at the old woman. "I hope we have at least a hundred people like you in the audience tomorrow night, Mae. A good audience can help a play."

Gwenn slid off the stage and stood in front of Mae, side-by-side with Randal. "I'll be cleaned up in a few minutes, Mae," she said. "Then I'll drive you home."

"Don't worry about me. I'm having the best time I've had in years. I'm not one bit tired. You just go as slow as you want to, unless you're in a hurry to join all these young people at Randal's."

"No . . ." Gwenn tried to avoid looking at the man next to her. "I'm too tired for a party tonight."

Randal finally looked directly at Gwenn, something he hadn't done very often since Saturday. "If you feel the need to unwind, to talk, by all means join us. I have soft drinks, too."

"Go, Gwenn," said Mae. "You youngsters need to have some fun. It's us old dinosaurs that have to go to bed early."

Gwenn wondered, could she cope? Would Randal say something later that would make her hurt more than she did that very minute? The closeness of his body, the scent of his aftershave, the sound of his voice, everything about the man bothered her. But of course, JoJo would occupy him that evening. Gwenn wouldn't have to worry.

"I suppose I could stop by, after I take Mae home, for one glass of *wine*," she finally answered.

"We'll expect you then." Randal gave Gwenn his address. "Be careful out on the streets. It's been sleeting the last half hour and the roads are glass."

The city streets were slick. The country road Mae lived on was coated with a thick layer of ice. Gwenn didn't say a word about the driving conditions to Mae. She figured that since Mae couldn't see the ice the news would only upset the woman.

Idle conversation for Gwenn during the tense drive back was almost as difficult as the driving. She let Mae do most of the talking.

"Your mother would have loved to see you tonight. Too bad she's so far away. . . . My niece wouldn't have thought much of the play though, I'm sorry to say. If it's not from *Hollywood,* it's nothing, according to her highness. . . . I think she's glad you're taking care of me, even if I haven't sold the house. That was the smartest thing she ever did in her whole entire life, signing with your firm. . . ."

Mae chatted on as Gwenn held tight to the steering wheel. It was a relief when the old woman was safe in her home. Gwenn made sure Mae was settled into her easy chair, sipping a hot cup of tea, before she headed her car out onto the ice again.

"I should go straight home," she thought as she turned out of Mae's driveway. "No one would miss me, especially Randal and JoJo."

The wind had picked up speed, blowing the thick, ice-filled rain at a ninety-degree angle. Gwenn strained to see. It was almost impossible to make out the outline of the dark road in front of the car.

She maneuvered the vehicle around the sharp curve on Briar Road. Suddenly, from out of nowhere a white-tail deer bounded out of the brush-covered ditch and sailed in front of Gwenn's car. She automatically hit the brakes.

The rear of the station wagon spun to the right, out of control on the ice. The deer leaped across the road, untouched, and disappeared into the underbrush.

The car continued to slide toward the deep ditch. A flurry of information went through Gwenn's mind as she tried to remember the proper driving procedure. "Turn away from the skid? No, turn into the skid." By the time she remembered and had the steering wheel in the correct direction, the car was sliding over the lip of the ditch.

A feeling of helplessness came over Gwenn as she hung on to the wheel. For a brief moment she relived the accident with Fred. Their car was rolling toward a head-on collision with a camper. Fred continued to smile as he had throughout the evening. He made no move to turn out of the camper's path. She wrenched the wheel from him and forced the car out of the other vehicle's lane. The last thing she remembered was the speeding approach of an elm tree. After that the world stopped abruptly.

There was no elm tree in the ditch Gwenn's car stopped in tonight. It was only full of scrub brush and muddy water.

Gwenn rested her head on the steering wheel for a moment, catching her breath. She was unhurt. The accident was a minor inconvenience, she told herself, nothing to get upset over.

She switched off the engine and switched on the overhead light. Water was seeping in under the back door. Gwenn literally hung in the driver's seat, suspended by her seat belt.

"What does a person do in a situation like this?" she asked herself. The car lurched deeper into the ditch. "She leaves!"

It was incredibly hard to get out of the car, hanging off the roadway as it was. Gwenn had to climb out while holding the heavy door up out of the way.

The driving rain stung her face when she turned to look for the nearest source of help. Darkness and the blowing rain obliterated any signs of the nearby farmhouses.

Gwenn walked around to the front of the car. The headlights lit the ditch and the upper half of the woods across the gravel road. Her car wasn't going anywhere, except maybe further down.

She started to walk toward Mae's house. The rain had already drenched her coat and was presently soaking through her clothing. Gwenn wrapped her arms around herself and marched on.

About a hundred yards down the road, she stopped walking. What would happen if she surprised Mae looking like a drowned cat? Could the old woman handle it?

Gwenn returned to the car. "Anyway, I have to turn off the headlights," was how she rationalized the idea of getting back in the car. "At least it's not raining in here. I'll go for help after the rain stops."

It was even more difficult to climb back in the car than it had been to get out. The door kept blowing shut, once pinching the fingers on her right hand. "God, I could use a little help down here," Gwenn yelled skyward as she cradled her smashed fingers.

Finally, she was back in the car. Everthing seemed stable enough. But it was uncomfortable trying to sit behind the wheel. Gwenn kept sliding down the seat. After struggling to sit upright she swung her feet across the seat, propped them against the far door and lay down, shivering and exhausted.

"Mae was right, God. I should have gone for warmth and taken my shabby old winter coat. . . . You will send help, won't you?" Gwenn didn't think rescue would come her way until morning. No one would be traveling down that dead end road that night. "I wonder what hypothermia feels like?" Gwenn asked the darkness when she couldn't control the shivering rattling her teeth.

"God, if I'm a good person and don't complain much about living in an apartment, will you send help? . . . I'll even move to Florida, if that's what it takes to get rescued. . . . And I'll really, honestly try to be civil to JoJo, too."

It seemed like hours passed as Gwenn lay listening to the noisy pelts of rain bombarding her car. Many times she had listened to rain before, when its sound on the roof made soothing noises. This rain was different. It was cold and it was dangerous.

Gwenn finally closed her eyes and dreamed.

There was a hot bath waiting for Gwenn in her dream. She hurried to undress and lower herself into its warm depths. The perfumed water and bubbles felt like heaven as they covered her cold skin. She closed her eyes and rested her head against a satin pillow that appeared out of nowhere, and decided she would remain in the warmth forever.

Suddenly the water turned to ice. Gwenn was no longer alone in her dream. Randal had entered. He was putting buckets of ice in the tub and laughing.

Gwenn woke, shaking uncontrollably. Wind and rain were again hitting her face, coming through the open car door above her head.

"Gwenn!" Randal called above the sound of the wind.

Startled, Gwenn looked up, but didn't move. "What are you doing here?" she asked.

"Don't tell me I needed an invitation to come looking for you? Are you hurt?"

When Gwenn realized she had a real rescuer she climbed out of the car and into Randal's arms. "The party over already?"

"What party? Shut up and get in the car! I'm taking you to the hospital."

"That's not necessary. I'm fine. No cuts, bruises or abrasions, see." She spun around in front of his car's headlights. "I'm just cold. Take me home, please."

"I knew you were going to have trouble driving Mae home tonight. . . . Why in the world you let that old woman talk you into driving her in such lousy weather is beyond me. . . ."

"You didn't have to rescue me. I was just waiting for the rain to die down before going for help." She had to yell to be heard above the storm. But Randal would have yelled no matter what the weather.

"For God's sake! Next thing I know you'll be sending me away. . . . Get in my car!"

Gwenn took a step toward her station wagon. "Let me get my purse first."

"Get in my car! I'll get your purse." He mumbled a few obscenities into the wind as he turned toward the lopsided vehicle.

As Randal reached for the black handbag that was dangling from one of the radio knobs, he lost his footing and went down under the car. The door slammed shut, narrowly missing his fingers.

From inside the warm sports car, Gwenn heard him cry out as he fell. The flurry of obscenities that followed was distorted by the wind.

"Randal! Randal?" Gwenn called out the window.

Randal pulled himself up from the underbelly of the station wagon. He was wet and muddy, and walked with a limp.

He flung Gwenn's purse into his car before sliding into the driver's seat. Without saying a word he drove her home.

Gwenn noticed that every time Randal used his foot on the clutch he winced with pain. But the set of his jaw told her not to inquire about his injury. She sat quietly shivering, soaking up as much of the warmth from the car heater as she could.

Before leaving Gwenn at her back door, Randal finally spoke.

"You sure you're all right?"

Gwenn nodded.

"The play goes on tomorrow as planned. See that you're there on time."

"Don't worry about me. You take care of your . . ."

Randal didn't wait for Gwenn to finish speaking. He pulled the door closed and sped away.

Gwenn angrily threw her rain-soaked clothing onto the bathroom floor as she undressed. She was furious with Mae for forcing her to travel out of her way that night, furious with herself for needing rescuing, and furious with Randal for being her rescuer.

"Stay away from me, Randal Cochran! I'll finish your stupid play, you can count on that. Then I'll be out of your life forever."

The steaming bath Gwenn soaked in didn't warm her as she had dreamed. In bed, no matter how many covers she pulled over herself she continued to shiver. "The warm body of a man would come in handy tonight, Westminster," she said to the purring cat by her head. "Except for body heat, who needs a man? They're only trouble. . . ," she confided through her chattering teeth.

Shirley sent Gwenn home after her young partner showed up at the office the following morning. "You look like death warmed over. . . . And you should consider that a compliment. . . . Get your fancy little butt home and put it between the sheets, girl, where it belongs. I don't need another sick kid around here. Robin's enough of a baby for me to mother." Shirley touched Gwenn's flushed cheek. "Maybe you should stop off at the doctor's office before going to bed."

Gwenn shook her head. "It's only the sniffles," she protested.

Shirley wouldn't listen. "You're not going to infect me with whatever bug's biting you. Tank and I have a special weekend planned after the play is over, a reward for my quitting smoking. And you're not going to ruin it for me. Now get."

Gwenn knew Shirley's gruff orders were for her own good; but as weak as Gwenn felt, the sharpness of her partner's tongue felt more stinging than it ordinarily would. She wanted someone to hold, to hug, not the commands of a well-meaning drill sergeant.

Her mother would have treated her like a child, wrapped her in a warm blanket and spoon-fed Gwenn her own brand of medicine, a steaming cup of chicken soup. Gwenn knew that if she wanted home-made soup today she would either have to cook it herself or to buy something resembling chicken soup at the deli. Neither would be as appetizing as her mother's.

Fred had once attempted to nurse Gwenn last year when she was down with laryngitis. His homemade chicken soup came from a can. When Fred brought a bowl to his patient it ended up dumped all over Gwenn and her bed. Lucky for her Fred had forgotten to heat the soup.

This cold Gwenn fought alone.

She remained in bed as Shirley had ordered and slept most of the day away. Westminster even deserted his pillow on her bed for a seat on the sofa.

When Gwenn awoke it was time to get ready for opening night. She still didn't feel any warmer than the previous night. But before leaving home Gwenn made a solemn pact with herself that no one, especially Randal Cochran, would know how ill she felt. When the play was over she would see her doctor, and not before. If it was more than a cold, she didn't want to know.

CHAPTER 16

"Don't you go telling me all you need is a little sleep," Anne said as she smeared the base makeup on Gwenn's flushed cheeks. "I've been a mother too many years. I know sick when I see it."

"I can't be sick until the play's over, Anne," Gwenn whispered her secret. "I'm not going to give in. And don't you go blabbing to everyone that I am."

"All right," said Anne. "JoJo would probably blame you for catching pneumonia and ruining the play on purpose, anyway."

"It's only a cold. I caught a chill, that's all."

"How high a fever do you have?" Anne asked.

"I don't even want to know, putting a number on it would make me feel worse than I already do. And if I feel any worse I might as well roll over and die."

"And you're telling me not to let anyone know you're almost ready for the coroner's office?"

Gwenn nodded. "I'm a fantastic actress, don't you know? I'm going to get through this play, if it kills me. For two hours a night, for the next four nights, I'm going to give the best acting performance this town has ever seen . . . *and no one,* except for the two of us, is ever going to know about it."

"If that's a threat, Gwenn, I get your message. . . . But what about Shirley?"

"My life's filled with mothers! . . . Don't say anything to Shirley. She'd try one of her quick cold cures on me, one concoction has castor oil or something in it. . . . I'm already sick enough, thank you."

"So, how's the real estate biz?" Anne changed the subject when Randal limped into the dressing room supported by a hand-carved cane. "My brother-in-law said it's going to hit rock-bottom next year."

"Oh, he's in real estate?" Gwenn asked half heartedly.

"No, he's a truck driver, but he thinks he knows absolutely everything."

Randal nodded to Anne as he passed through the room.

"I don't think our director's too happy about that sprained ankle of his," said Anne. "He won't even tell a soul how it happened. . . . Silly how some men get so embarrassed about a weakness."

Gwenn didn't need to hear the story from Randal. She knew exactly how he had hurt his ankle and she wasn't ready to talk either.

The bright stage lights helped emphasize the fever that raged inside Gwenn's body. The heavy grey wig felt tighter and tighter with each passing line.

As she went from scene to scene Gwenn thought, "Don't sweat, Gwenn. If you break out in a cold sweat, everyone will know what a fool you are, so don't sweat."

The command didn't stop beads of perspiration from forming on her forehead under the grey curls.

Anne met Gwenn each time she exited the stage and dabbed at the sweat. She shook her head as she added more makeup between the acts. "You're crazy," she mumbled.

"You're not telling me any great news, Anne," said Gwenn. "But there's only one act left. And this crazy woman is going to make it, then she can crawl home to bed."

"You shouldn't have even left home tonight. . . . This isn't Broadway, Gwenn."

"No, it's worse than Broadway. It's a small town, where I have to live and work. . . . I'm not sick, Anne. I'm not sick. I'M NOT!" Gwenn struggled as hard to convince herself of her good health as she did to convince Anne.

To Gwenn's utter amazement she successfully finished the play that evening. After the applause of the curtain call died she wanted to disappear into a black hole, but couldn't. Half the town had been in the audience and was backstage ready with hearty congratulations.

The energy she needed to continue with her performance another half hour was ebbing from her body.

With fingers crossed Gwenn spoke to the banker, to the high school principal and to her next-door neighbor. It was a relief that no one commented on her health, good or otherwise; that was one benefit of wearing the theatrical makeup.

JoJo had rushed offstage, refusing to talk to a living soul until she had fixed her face to its normal sheen.

"We're all going to my house tonight," said Lyle. "Everything's arranged: cheese, crackers, veggies, a fancy cake and enough booze to knock an elephant off his feet."

Gwenn didn't acknowledge the invitation as she walked out the dressing room door. There would be no party for her tonight. She had hardly enough strength left to remove her own makeup. Her only wish was for sleep. She had to go to bed before she fell over.

A second full day of rest did not improve Gwenn's health as she had hoped. A hacking cough added to her growing list of symptoms. The strongest cough drop could control her constant hacking cough for only a few minutes at a time.

Gwenn held her head as she coughed. "God, did I really deserve this?"

Before the Friday night performance Anne used makeup more to cover the flush of Gwenn's fever than to age her. "I don't know why I'm keeping my mouth shut. I must be as crazy as you are," said Anne. "If you die because I didn't say anything, I'll never forgive myself."

"I'm not going to die, Anne. No one dies because of a simple cold." Gwenn's words couldn't stop the terrible aching that traveled through every muscle in her body. At that moment a quick painless death, if there was such a thing, seemed a suitable alternative to the pain. But Gwenn couldn't even choose death, not yet. She would finish the play first.

Gwenn struggled through the second performance, coughing only four times onstage. Backstage Anne helped her repress the coughing by anesthetizing her throat with a bad-tasting anesthetic antiseptic spray.

Afterwards, when well-wishers came backstage, Gwenn was nowhere to be found. She had slipped out of Edna's housedress and into her jeans and blouse before leaving by the side exit thirty seconds after the final curtain.

Though Gwenn's body longed for more rest when she was home Friday night, sudden bursts of coughing refused to allow her the comfort of sleep.

Gwenn was forced to roam the house. She wrapped a warm blanket around her shoulders, over her flannel pajamas and robe, then walked through all the empty rooms of her grandmother's house.

Downstairs the nearly completed rooms were warm. Gwenn stood in the middle of the living room and pictured the tall decorated spruce tree that would have stood in front of the window, with its silver stars, calico bows and popcorn strings. She would not have room for such a large tree in her new apartment.

In the kitchen Gwenn brewed a pot of mint tea, but forgot about it when memories of Randal's unpredicted kiss entered her thoughts.

"God, why can't I pick a man who wants marriage and children, who would be satisfied with me, the way I am? . . . Maybe there's no one like that for me."

The dark enclosed stairway was drafty. Gwenn needed to walk through the rooms on the second floor. Tonight she paced them like a ghost, going from one room to the next, tracing the cracks in the plaster with her fingers, walking the hardwood floors in her bare feet.

Once there were children laughing and playing in the rooms Gwenn walked in. She wondered when the sounds of happy young voices would fill the house again.

Images of angelic little faces looked at her from every dark corner: the faces of her children. That had been Gwenn's dream for the big house.

She stopped for one last look out her grandmother's bedroom window. It would be her final good-bye.

The bay window was the focal point of the room. A spinning wheel had once spun wool into yarn in front of that window.

As a child Gwenn had looked up at the "tower" window from the yard and thought it was a witch's tower, where spells were cast and bitter drinks brewed. Later she learned it was the room where babies had been born and where adults had died.

This room, her grandmother's room, was to have been Gwenn's next big remodeling project. Tonight she laid that dream to rest along with thoughts of her own children.

"Grandma, remember me after I leave here," Gwenn said to the silver moonlight coming in through the uncurtained window. "If Randal Cochran changes this room, you have my permission to haunt him. . . . He better not . . ." Gwenn turned away from the night sky as she started to cough again.

It wasn't until a half hour before the last performance that anyone other than Anne noticed Gwenn's deteriorated health.

"If I didn't know better, Gwenn," said Charlie. "I'd swear you have the same hangover I had after drinking Lyle's cheap booze the other night. You look absolutely rotten."

"Thanks, Charlie," said Gwenn. "I've been fighting a virus, or something. I would appreciate it if you didn't spread the news. . . ."

Charlie wasn't listening to Gwenn, but waving Randal over to their corner of the dressing room. "Take a look at this, Randal. Want to bet she doesn't make it through the first act?"

Gwenn was trapped. She had no makeup on to disguise her illness. She watched as the director tapped across the wood floor with his cane.

Randal touched her forehead with the back of his hand. "Can you make it through the performance?"

"Of course."

"I'll take you to the hospital after." His comment was short, but definitely a command. Gwenn knew he would not change his mind about taking her for medical help.

She felt relieved. Everything would end tonight: the play, the illness, and her tenuous relationship with Randal Cochran. Gwenn wondered which of the three gave her the most pain. She easily concluded that it was the last.

Sunday night it was Gwenn's turn to trip over the floor lamp's cord during the performance. Her feet felt lead heavy as she moved from stage right to stage left, but she continued to move and to act.

The other cast members looked distorted to Gwenn. But from some hidden reserve, Gwenn's mind retrieved memorized lines and forced them out through her mouth.

Backstage she allowed Anne to take over, even to the point of letting Anne help her out of a chair when she was cued back onstage.

"How am I doing, Anne?" Gwenn asked between coughing bouts. "I can't tell. . . . Am I still acting? . . . Have I ruined the play?" A cup of hot lemon tea soothed the raw feeling in Gwenn's throat and washed away the bad taste of the throat spray.

"You're doing fine." Anne massaged Gwenn's shoulders and neck, trying to relieve the built-up tension. "No one in the audience will ever know you were sick. . . . Are you sure you're going to make it? . . . I knew the theater group should arrange for understudies."

"I'm almost done," said Gwenn in between coughs. "And we're not big enough for understudies. . . . I swear when the lights fade tonight this will be the last play Shirley will be able to goad me into."

Intermission was over all too soon and it was time for Gwenn to return to the stage. In this act she amazed herself. All signs of her cough were left backstage.

The cast and crew, except for the prima donna playing Natalie, picked up on Gwenn's weakened condition and did everything they could to make her work easier. She didn't need to grope for props in the darkness. Tank personally handed them to her.

Once when Tank handed Gwenn Edna's knitting basket, she nearly dropped it. Gwenn gasped. "What did you put in here, Tank? Bricks? It weighs a ton."

Tank didn't have time to answer before Gwenn walked out onstage. While sitting in the armchair Gwenn searched for the added weight. All she found inside the basket was yarn, the small afghan square, and a plastic crocheting hook. It was definitely time to see a doctor.

Lyle hugged Gwenn longer than necessary during Act Two. He even held her arm and eased her down into the armchair while, to their right, the characters played by JoJo and Charlie and Floyd argued.

"Edna," Lyle whispered in her ear as he held her. "Why don't you give your *lovely* daughter over there, a great big kiss good-bye tonight. A few shared germs would be a fitting parting gift, I think."

Gwenn didn't giggle. She didn't even smile, because she didn't care anymore. In ten minutes the play would be over and she could joyfully quit acting and collapse.

When the curtain came down, Gwenn sagged to the floor next to the knitting basket. Lyle was right by her side. "Forget the curtain call, Gwenn," he said. "It's not important."

"All I need is your arm, Lyle," she said as she allowed him to help her to her feet. "And Charlie's arm." Gwenn looped an arm through Charlie's. As the cast moved forward for their bows Gwenn saw Randal in the wing. She would have liked to see him wink at her, but there was no humor in his cold eyes tonight.

There were people standing, applauding wildly. The cast smiled and bowed together; all arms were linked, except JoJo's.

After the curtain went down, Randal walked out to join the cast. He still sported a limp, but had discarded his cane. "I don't know how you five managed it, but tonight was superb. Thank you all for all your time and trouble. It has been a pleasure working with each and every one of you. Good night," he said as he took Charlie's place by Gwenn's arm.

The applause continued to sound through the curtain.

"Hey!" said JoJo, "don't I get *my* curtain call?"

Randal's face was cold as ice. "This play is over," he said. "If you want more adulation, the tryout schedule for the next production is posted on the dressing room bulletin board."

JoJo pouted and backed away from the curtain as the applause died and the house lights were turned on. "I don't know why the rest of us have to suffer, just because Gwenn doesn't know how to take care of her health. . . ."

Gwenn didn't argue with her escorts as they helped her offstage. Her leg muscles had turned to mashed potatoes. She could no longer slide her feet across the floor without benefit of her male assistants.

"Listen, Randal," said Gwenn. "Shirley's in the audience. She can drive me home. Your director's job is over. We're all on our own again."

"Ms. Nichols, you are *not* going home. Before I hang up my clipboard for good, I'm seeing to it that you have proper medical attention. I have a feeling a slapped-on bandage won't help you this time."

Lyle and Randal waited outside the screened changing area while Anne and Shirley helped Gwenn out of her housedress, wig and makeup. This was the only night visitors were barred from the backstage area.

"Maybe we should post a quarantine sign on the front door," said Gwenn with a Mona Lisa smile. "Shirley, please don't hate me if business is rotten for a while. The whole town's bound to think I have cholera or maybe the black plague, when all I have is a col—" A series of coughs ended Gwenn's vain attempt at humor.

The male sentinels assumed their positions at Gwenn's side when she stood to leave, and escorted her to Randal's car.

"This play was on the way to being perfect," said Lyle. "If not for Gwenn getting sick tonight and JoJo's sharp tongue . . . I'm going to miss kissing you, Gwenn. Even if they were only pretend, I enjoyed every one."

Gwenn held Lyle's hand longer than necessary. He bent close and she kissed her leading man on the cheek. "Now I know funeral directors have big hearts."

"Lyle," said Randal, "I'd appreciate it if you would help Tank close the theater tonight. There's nothing much to do. Volunteers are due in later in the week to do a thorough cleaning job."

Tank came running out of the theater just then. "Randal, one of your warehouses is on fire! We just got a call from the police!"

Gwenn started to get out of the car. "Shirley can drive me."

"Stay where you are!" Randal's jaw was set. He wouldn't take any arguments.

"Are you nuts? You're wasting time worrying about me. Tank said your warehouse is burning! I'll keep. Your oak bar might be in flames this very minute."

"I have more than one warehouse. But since you seem to be more worried about my antique than I am, Gwenn, we might as well watch it burn together."

Randal revved up the car's powerful engine and raced away from the theater.

A red glow reflected back to earth from low-hanging clouds. The night beacon from across town pointed the way to the warehouse.

As they approached the industrial section of the city, smoke could be seen billowing out of the doors and windows of the long warehouse that housed Randal's prized bar. An odd kind of smoke worked its way out of the far end of the warehouse. It was different than any other Gwenn had ever seen. It was heavy and marbled, both black and yellow-green.

The volunteer fire fighters rightly measured their distance from the odd-scented blaze.

Randal swore out loud when he saw the fire. "I told them they couldn't store chemicals in my warehouse!"

He skidded to a stop next to the road blockade and shouted to the police officer standing guard. "Have someone call Millin Industries. That's their chemicals burning! Let the place go! Keep everyone back! I don't know what's in there!"

He left the car, limped through the crowd of fire watchers and sought out the fire chief. In a few minutes, the police were backing the onlookers farther away from the blaze.

A TV news crew showed up in time to capture the collapse of the warehouse roof.

Gwenn watched the unfolding drama from the safety of Randal's car. Mixed emotions bombarded her as she saw the flames shoot twenty feet above the roof line.

The bar from the brothel was gone. She was delighted that it wouldn't be placed in her grandmother's house.

But the bar was gone. And that meant Randal wouldn't *need* to purchase her house. Her mother wouldn't be receiving the check that Gwenn had promised.

Yes, the bar was gone, burned to ashes, and a part of history gone with it. Randal would be disappointed.

A depression crept over Gwenn as the flames disappeared and only grey smoke drifted into the night sky. She didn't want to watch any longer and closed her eyes.

How could one ridiculous antique cause her so many mixed emotions? It had been beautiful. And Randal's eyes had always sparkled when he spoke about it. The bar had been an expensive toy that made him happy.

But at certain times didn't Randal's eyes sparkle even brighter when he looked into her eyes? No, then they were different. Then he looked at her as a challenge he had to conquer.

Gwenn had enjoyed Randal's company, away from his structured business world. In fact, she loved him, when he smiled at her and she could tell he saw only her and nothing more.

Her body had tingled when she found him gazing at her, when he winked, when his hand touched hers.

She would miss him terribly. But she would survive.

Yes, Gwenn knew she would survive after Randal was out of her life forever. Didn't she go on living after Fred left?

She had conquered a broken heart before. She could again.

But Randal wasn't Fred. His humor and warmth had touched her even deeper, sharper, like the cutting edge of a chef's knife.

The second shattered heart was going to take more time to mend. Thoughts of Randal wouldn't leave her easily. But she would deal with that pain tomorrow.

Gwenn's thoughts were interrupted by Randal's return.

His limping was more pronounced. Ashes covered his jacket and dirtied his face. The smell of smoke was so strong on his clothing that it made Gwenn's stomach lurch.

Suddenly Gwenn started coughing uncontrollably again as the throbbing in her head grew and grew.

It took a couple of coughs of his own before Randal could clear the smoke from his lungs and speak. "If you'd like to say 'I told you so,' I'll accept it with bowed head. You were right. I should have let Shirley take you to the hospital this evening."

Gwenn didn't say one word. She chose instead to work on erasing the memory of Randal from her thoughts.

She wouldn't listen ever again for his teasing laughter or wait to see his taunting wink. Gwenn tried to wash away the memory of the scent of his aftershave and the image of him scribbling on his clipboard.

Randal was out of her life forever.

When the car stopped at the hospital emergency entrance and Gwenn opened her eyes, he was beside her, in full life.

It would be like climbing Mount Everest, forgetting Randal Cochran. Gwenn was too weak for the battle at that moment.

CHAPTER 17

"For goodness sake, Mom, if I had called you from the hospital all you could do from Florida was get upset," Gwenn said into the telephone while petting Westminster. "I'm fine. It was a viral infection. . . . So, Shirley said it was pneumonia. A lot she knows. She's not a doctor, no matter how many medical television shows she's watched. The antibiotics are doing their job. I feel a lot better today."

Gwenn listened as her mother instructed her in proper health care. Many of the orders her mother gave Gwenn from Florida were identical to her doctor's.

"Don't you want to hear about the play, Mom? I was fantastic. . . . I'm glad you moved in with that other woman. Now maybe with your own room, you'll be able to get some sleep."

Her mother didn't care about the play or about her own shared living quarters; she was too upset about Gwenn's three-day hospital stay. "Really, Mom. I'm fine. . . . I promise to follow my doctor's instructions, Mom. I have to go. There's someone at the door. I'll call you back tomorrow. 'Bye."

The ruse to get her mother off the phone turned out to be true. The back door opened and Randal Cochran walked into Gwenn's life again.

"What do you want? The play's over and I'm on vacation from the real estate business for the time being."

Randal held out a white business envelope. "I thought you might want this check."

He handed Gwenn a check for the full price of her house.

She sagged down onto a kitchen chair. "But . . . but . . . your warehouse burned . . . your antique bar's gone."

"We made a bargain and I never go back on a bargain, you can ask any of my business associates."

Gwenn could barely force the words to form in her mouth. "I thought that after the fire you wouldn't want my house."

"I made you an offer. You accepted it. The fire had nothing to do with it. I don't remember the qualifier in our agreement: I'll buy this house only if my warehouse isn't turned to ashes. . . . My God, you look terrible." He looked intently at Gwenn's pale face.

"I'm always in the mood for a compliment, thank you. . . . And I was feeling pretty good . . . until you came in. . . . Randal, I don't think I want to sell any more. Mother's sharing a little house with another retired woman. Her room's furnished and she's happy. I don't need to sell." She handed the check back, but he refused to take it.

"It's no good, Gwenn. I negotiated in good faith. I have plans for this house."

Tears filled Gwenn's eyes. "You always have plans. Who do you think you are, a god or something? . . . How could you be so callous, Randal? I just got out of the hospital."

"I know. Those days away from you gave me time to think."

"How nice. I hope you had a nice time, thinking how you would take my home away while I was lying on my sickbed. Did you and Sean take another tour of the house?"

"Gwenn, listen to me. Some time ago I quit wanting to force you out of this house." He knelt in front of Gwenn and turned her head so she had to look at him.

"Sure, that's why the necklace offer . . . and the kite offer."

"Let me finish. . . . Brief encounters have been a way of life. The women have always been willing. But you were different. . . ."

"Yeah, I wouldn't jump into bed with you, so you thought you'd make me suffer for turning down your advances."

"I didn't mean to hurt you, Gwenn."

"Funny, I was beginning to think you were making a career out of it."

"It wasn't that bad all the time between us, was it? You made me laugh and . . ."

"And faint, you mustn't forget your fainting episode. . . . Did that laughter you mentioned come when we kissed? How flattering."

"My God, Gwenn, if you're going to be my wife, I'm going to have to get a word in now and again."

"Wife? What's this wife stuff? Aren't you angry with me? Isn't that why you stayed away from the hospital?"

"No, I was angry with myself. A little over a month ago I could analyze a failing company's profit/loss statement and know if the touch of Randal Cochran could turn the business into a money maker. I can't any longer."

"Oh, what happened?"

"You happened. Since you came into my life . . ."

"Correction. You came into my life."

"Okay, have it your way. Heck, since I came into your life, I haven't been able to even analyze my own bank statement. I can't concentrate. *You* made me angry."

"I apologize for getting under your skin. I didn't plan to," Gwenn said sarcastically.

"I'm trying to explain . . ."

"That you had to take your anger out on me."

"Gwenn, you were vulnerable, an easy target. What made matters worse, I began to enjoy picking on you."

"I'm glad I made your day."

"You didn't. You tore it apart. God, how you tore it apart."

"So you think your life will be better if we live together?"

"Not live together, get married. There's a difference."

"I know there is. I didn't think you did."

"When I first met you, I didn't want more than a casual affair. Now I couldn't live in this big house alone, if someone paid me a million dollars."

"How about two million?"

"Stop it, Gwenn. I'm trying to be serious."

"Exactly what are you asking, Randal?"

"All I know is that when I'm not with you I'm thinking about you, Gwenn. I was at a meeting the other day, desperately trying to concentrate on a cash flow problem, but then I would close my eyes and there you were. . . . If I don't marry you soon all my business interests will go down the toilet."

"Do you hear what you're saying? Marrying me would be good for business. . . . I don't know if I like the sound of that. I envision parties of the first part, whereases and contracts instead of wedding vows."

"Gwenn, what do you want? Violins and roses?"

"That would do, for a start."

"If I supply the flowers and music do you think you could bring yourself to live in the same house, this house, with a *businessman?*"

"I don't know. . . . I'll have to give your question a great deal of thought."

"Gwenn, are you going to make me suffer before giving me your answer?"

"You better believe I am. And I'm going to enjoy every minute of making your life miserable, Mr. Cochran, Mr. Businessman." She returned his check to his jacket pocket. "If you're looking for me, I'll be right here in *my* home, enjoying your torment."

The four roving minstrels arrived at Gwenn Nichols's doorstep at three that same afternoon.

Roses by the gross arrived a half hour later.

Gwenn managed to hold off giving Randal her answer for a whole five minutes after he knocked on her back door with a diamond ring at four.

"Mae, if Shirley didn't want you to join us at her house for Christmas dinner she would never have asked you," Gwenn said as she put pink sponge curlers in Mae's grey hair.

The old woman was sitting in front of Gwenn's dressing table while Westminster batted at the loosened belt of Mae's robe.

"I hope she doesn't make me eat herring," said Mae. "I'll burp for three days if I eat pickled fish."

"No one's going to force you to eat anything today, Mae," said Gwenn. "Your niece isn't here, remember."

"What did Miss Fancy Pants say when you told her I was moving in with you for the winter?"

Gwenn picked up another pink curler and glanced at the brightly colored kite hanging across the room. "What could she say? You are a grown woman, aren't you, Mae?"

Mae's eye's twinkled. "Not on Christmas I'm not."

Robin skipped into Gwenn's bedroom and grabbed Westminster around his big round belly.

"You two little girls let my cat alone. Remember he just finished eating a stockingful of kitty goodies," Gwenn said to Robin and Mae.

"Oh, Aunt Gwenn, you're supposed to go in the kitchen," said Robin as she tickled Westminster's belly.

"What's the problem? I'm busy."

Robin shrugged. "I can't tell you. *He* said it was a surprise."

"Oh, he did, did he?" Gwenn turned the last roller in place on Mae's head before walking out of the bedroom.

Right outside the door, in the middle of the hall, Gwenn found a neatly wrapped package with a kite string attached.

She opened the box, pulled out a string of pearls and read the note inside.

My Love,
    I don't know how can I give you more than my heart, but I'm
willing to spend the rest of my life trying.

                                                        Randal

Gwenn followed the string as she had at Randal's cottage. It led her
first into the bathroom where she found a large box tied with a red
ribbon. Inside the box were three dozen assorted scented candles, a
bottle of white wine, strawberry-scented bubble bath and a Mozart tape.
    The kite string continued out of the bathroom and into the living
room where it was wrapped around an antique dry sink standing next to
the eight-foot-tall Christmas tree. A large package waited under the tree
with Randal's name on it. It was the afghan she had made.
    Gwenn found a second note attached to the dry sink.

Darling,
    I thought and I thought what to give my very special lady for
Christmas. How am I doing so far?

                                                        Randal

"You're doing just fine," Gwenn said as she picked the string up
between her fingers and followed it to the kitchen.
    On the table it wound around a bottle of champagne and a jar of
Russian caviar, black.
    Gwenn grabbed her jacket from a hook by the back door because the
kite string continued outside.
    It ended high up on the back end of a flatbed truck. Randal stood in
the bed of the truck, his hand resting on a large tarp.
    "Is this all for me?" Gwenn asked.
    "No one else."
    "Do I have to guess what's under the tarp?"
    He nodded.
    "New snow tires for my car? The plasterboard for the upstairs bed-
room? Oh, I don't know, slippers?"
    Randal threw back the tarp.
    Gwenn collapsed in the newly fallen snow, laughing hysterically.
    "Don't get excited, honey," said Randal as he rubbed the oak bar
with his sleeve. "This one came out of a saloon, I swear. I had the
dealer trace its history before I agreed to buy it."
    She looked up at the carved wood, with its swirling decorative vines
and scrolls. "What, no nudes?"

"If this bar doesn't suit you, I located another I could get but it's in California. . . ."

Gwenn continued laughing. "I'll be satisfied with this Christmas present. I'm stuck with it, the same way I'm stuck with you, Randal Cochran. I'll learn to love it, in time. I learned to love you, remember?"

Randal leaped off the truck bed and wrapped his arms around Gwenn. There they stood alone in the snow, two very satisfied business partners.